ON THE MAD RIVER

ON THE MAD RIVER

Lucrecia Guerrero

MOUTHFEEL PRESS

ON THE MAD RIVER

Copyright © by Lucrecia Guerrero, 2024

This book is a work of fiction. Names, characters, places, and incidents are the product of the author's imagination or are used fictitiously. Any resemblance to actual events, locales, or persons, living or dead, is coincidental.

All rights reserved. No part of this book may be reproduced in print, digital, or recorded without written permission from the publisher or author.

Mouthfeel Press is an indie press publishing works in English and established poets and writers. We publish poetry, fiction, and non-fiction.

Cover Design: Cloud Cardona, cloudelfina.online
Interior Design: shadypeakstudios.com

Contact Information:
mouthfeelbooks.com
info.mouthfeelbooks@gmail.com

ISBN: 978-1-957840-26-0
Library of Congress Control Number: 2024931285

Published in the United States, 2024

First Printing in English
$18

MOUTHFEEL PRESS

ON THE MAD RIVER

For my children, Alejandra, Esperanza, and Peter

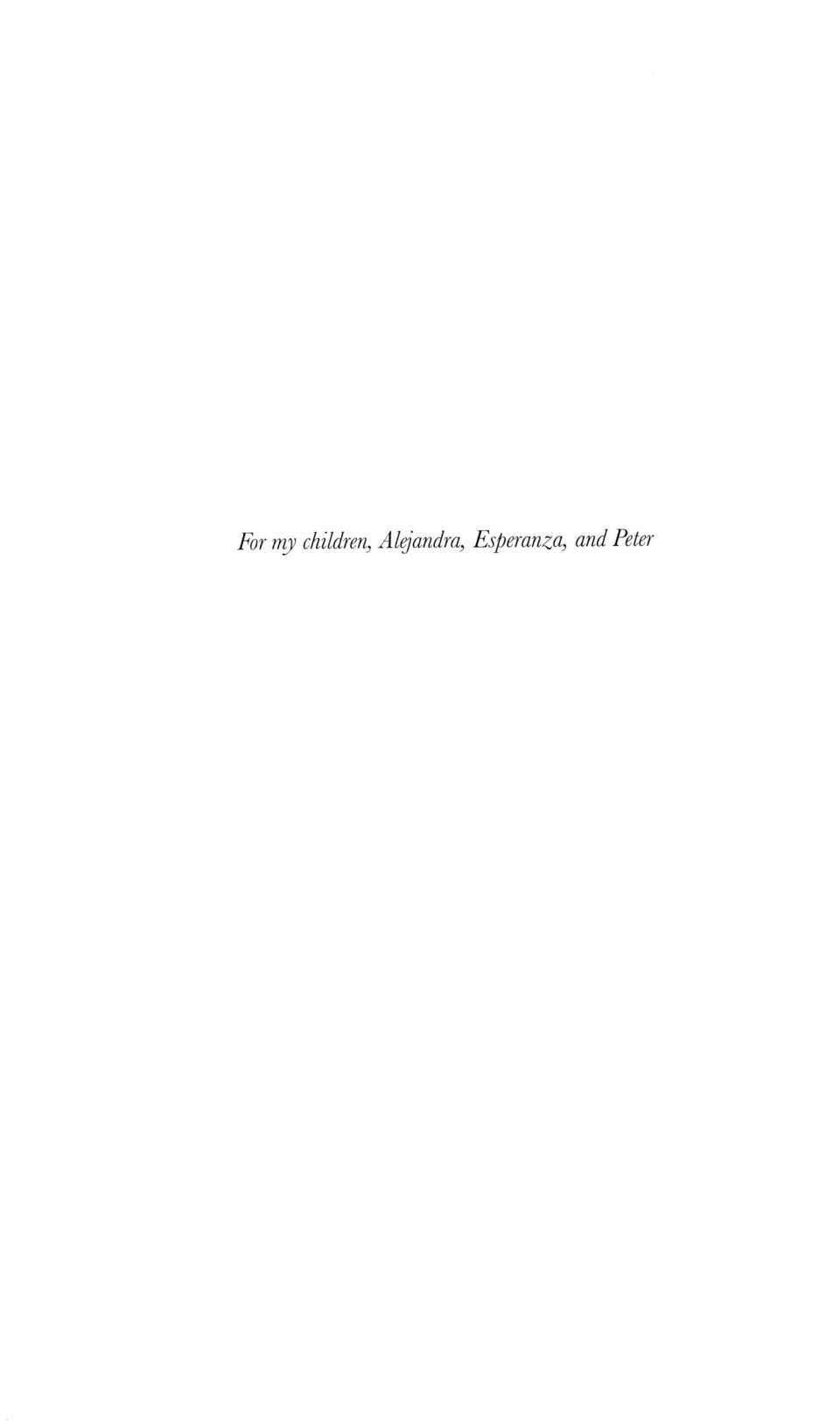

CHAPTER ONE

Mad River, Ohio

"Mornin', pretty girl," the man said, his voice soft yet intrusive. "You holding onto that valise like you think it's gonna run off." He chuckled, leaned back from the counter stool as if to block Rosa Linda's way. "I seen you pert near drop it when you sashayed across from the Greyhound."

Rosa Linda followed his gaze to the window that ran the expanse of the Buckeye Family Restaurant but couldn't see into the predawn gloom beyond. Ghostly reflections from inside the restaurant wavered, grease-distorted, on the glass.

"See us two? Like lookin' back at yourself, ain't it?" he murmured.

Meaning what? she thought. Something in his eyes made her intestines squirm. She pried off the wad of gum she'd stuck on the edge of her suitcase. Crack-pop, crack-pop. Speaking to the back of the waitress clearing a booth table, she said, "When you're finished, I'm going to sit there."

She wished there had been a booth up front by the two nurses or even the group of construction workers who had given her the usual approving eye before returning to their early morning coffees.

"Need some help with that?" The stranger pointed to the suitcase.

"No," she said, her voice flat and loud enough to make the waitress look up. "I'm OK by myself." She brought the suitcase in front of her, held onto the handle with both hands.

"Don't need nobody, I reckon," he said. "My, my."

A faint crease between his eyebrows made him look old, maybe in his late thirties. His gray eyes were of a shade so pale she thought they would turn to ashes if exposed to sunlight. For some reason, she was reminded of the spirits that chilled the night breezes on the Sonoran Desert.

She shivered and stepped inches past him but felt his gaze at her back, a pull so strong that she glanced over her shoulder. He had turned away, his attention now on the front page of a newspaper.

Careful not to snag her jeans on the taped slash running the edge of the vinyl seat, she slid into the booth. She extended her legs under the table and pushed off her flats. If anyone commented on the Frito smell, she'd play innocent. (Let them travel three days on a Greyhound with cheap shoes and no shower.) She would wrinkle her nose, look around along with the accuser, searching out the owner of the smell.

Giggling, she pulled out her cosmetic bag, was relining her eyes in black when the waitress — Hi! I'm Ruby, her name tag announced — appeared next to her in a faded odor-cloud of Tabu cologne and hamburger grease. With the tip of her tongue, Ruby wet the pencil's lead before tapping on her order pad.

After Rosa Linda asked for a cherry Coke, Ruby gestured with the worn-eraser end of the pencil, toward a sign on the wall: "Booths Reserved for Two or More." "But now," Ruby said, "you order some food with that soda pop, the boss won't say nothing. Sorry, kid, that's the way it works. It's not the likes of me and you that makes the rules."

Rosa Linda wanted to tell her to go to hell, that now she was on her own and made her own rules. Nobody — nobody — could tell her what to do anymore. She noticed the soft bags — skin thin and crinkled — beneath Ruby's tired-as-time eyes and only nodded. She had change for a Coke in her jeans pocket but not enough for fries, too.

"I was just about to ask the young lady if I might could share her booth," the stranger said. "I been on the road a good while. Could use a little more stretching room myself."

Rosa Linda dug in her purse, fingers raking the bottom for loose coins that she might have dropped in, all the while blocking, with her forearm, Ruby's view of the switchblade she'd carried with her since leaving Nopal, Arizona — Cisco's old switchblade that he'd kept at the back of his sock drawer. The knife had slipped out of the rolled-up copy of *People Magazine* in her purse. She flipped the pages of the magazine for an errant coin. Nada, nothing. If she wanted to keep her comfy booth, she would have to take her suitcase to the bathroom, fish out one of the ten fifty-dollar bills tucked deep beneath the cardboard lining.

"What's it going to be, hon?" Ruby said to Rosa Linda.

"Come on now," the stranger said. "I can see you got a good heart even if you tryin' not to show it. You don't need to be scared of me." He sipped his coffee, gazed beyond the rim of the cup, and a tiny glint of flame shimmered like a challenge deep inside his steel-colored eyes.

"Nobody scares me," Rosa Linda said, and shrugged her permission. There was nothing to fear from men. Chicanos, Mexicanos, gringos of every shade: They were all the same, and she was the chica who knew how to handle them. She had repeated this thought like a mantra every day she'd been on the Greyhound, and she silently repeated it again today. The important thing was to make him believe it.

"See now," he said, after settling in across from her, "we're all brothers and sisters, one big happy family."

Before Rosa Linda could respond, he turned to Ruby, instructed her to give them a few minutes. "Now that we got them rules covered," he added.

He offered his hand across the table to Rosa Linda. "Excuse my manners," he said. "I ain't even introduced myself.

I been called lots of things, but you can call me Enon." He chuckled at his own joke. "And you. Who might you be?"

"I might be lots of people," she said, ignoring the offered hand, "depending on my mood."

He smiled — a sad, lonely movement — and for a second, he looked almost sweet.

"I'm sorry," she said, "that was rude. I'm just really tired."

"Don't matter none," he said. He waved as if shooing away any hard feelings. "So . . . you don't want folks to know your name."

"Just being funny," she said, "like you," and rolled her eyes.

"Ah, well see, I ain't so smart like some."

"Ophelia," she blurted. The name had been the first word to pop into her mind. Maybe because she'd recently viewed *Frida Still Life*, a movie starring Ofelia Medina as Kahlo. Or maybe for the Ophelia she'd played in a high school drama not so long ago.

"Right pretty," Enon said, "only I was thinking it might be María, or some such." When she said nothing, he added, "And your last name?"

"Just Ophelia."

"Just Ophelia," he repeated, and paused as if savoring the sound. "We-ell," he said, drawing out the word, "all's I can say, if you was my little girl, I'd never let you get away."

"I'm nobody's little girl, so—" she began, when he cut her off, and called out to Ruby that he was ready to order. "Number three," he told the waitress. "How's about you, Just Ophelia, care for a bite?"

"I'm not hungry." She inched her crossed arms lower and pressed her stomach to muffle the grumbling gases. She was too tired to eat, but she was thirsty. Maybe once she got rid of this guy, the waitress could suggest a nearby hotel that fit her budget while she made plans for her future in Mad River. Sleep was what she needed. A woman at the back of the bus had boarded on the second day of the trip, and her colicky baby had fussed and cried off and on the entire time. No babies for Rosa Linda. She was nobody's wife and nobody's mother. Her wings were just now budding, preparing to take her far and wide. She wasn't clear on why here or why there or for how long. But freedom was like a lick of honey on her tongue. She wanted more.

"Suit yourself," he said, then added to the waitress, "put a rush on that order, will you, darlin'? I'm in a hurry to hit the road. Got a lot of miles to cover." He nodded to Rosa Linda, opened his newspaper with a little snap. He rattled the paper, asked, "You want a piece?"

"Too depressing," she said.

"Yeah," he said, "all that boring stuff about earthquakes, hijackings, AIDS, Reagan's second term. But then maybe you're not old enough to vote."

"I'm plenty old enough to do what I want," she said. "Anyway, I didn't say *boring*. There's nothing I can do about the world's problems. I have my own."

"You got that straight," he said. "Still, I reckon it don't hurt none to know what's going on around you." He held her gaze a second too long, and she felt her face flush.

Her stomach complained again. She pushed hard against the emptiness.

When Ruby placed Enon's breakfast on the table, Rosa Linda stared at the full plate, imagined herself poking at the edges of egg yolk with a corner of toast. Pride wouldn't allow her to say she'd changed her mind, so she was grateful when he seemed to read her thoughts.

"Bring an extra plate so's we can share," Enon said to Ruby.

The bacon smelled of home. Rosa Linda prepared to stick her chewing gum on the plate Ruby brought to her. She would need every cent she had, so why not let Enon spend his money since he seemed to like her company so much?

She ate, but his untouched food went limp with grease while he talked. Each word distinct, separate, but strangely melodic — a song, broken. The words didn't take root, but the tune soothed her. She yearned to lay her head on the table and doze for a few minutes.

"You getting off here or just passing through?" Enon said,

his voice loud. She assumed that her mind had drifted off, and he was having to repeat himself. "I can see," he said, "you don't belong to these parts. Even so, there's something mighty familiar about you, like maybe I know you — or should."

"Where *you* heading?" she said.

"Chicago. Got me a brother there I ain't seen for going on ten years now."

"Chicago," Rosa Linda repeated, pronouncing the word carefully.

"Uh-huh," Enon said. "You ever been?"

Rosa Linda shifted her gaze to the window, the unseen beyond, and thought of her father's sister Bea, who lived in Chicago. Rosa Linda's dad had taken her there once for a visit, then taken off — by himself — after one day, leaving her with a sour-faced aunt. Sidewalks there pulsed with the heartbeat of the city, tall buildings reached for the moon and the stars. Of course, Rosa Linda had eventually messed up and was sent on to her next temporary stop.

All her life Rosa Linda had been tossed from one relative or friend to another. She and her brother had been separated and turned into orphans of a sort by their parents' dreams. Mami and Papi had taken off for Hollywood, determined to turn Mami Roxana, a mestiza beauty, into a movie star, another Rita Hayworth. When one relative grew tired of Rosa Linda — she was conceited, didn't do as she was told, stole, ate more than she was worth, etcetera, etcetera — there was no discussion; she simply was told to pack and move on to the next home willing to take her in.

Eventually she began to feel as though she were looking forward and running away in equal measure. Away from what or toward what she couldn't say. But when things got tough, her instinct was to get the hell out of Dodge. Fate had brought her to Mad River, but now what? She had no plan, didn't know anyone. She didn't even want to think about it. Enon was offering her a way to keep moving forward. Run, Rosa Linda, run.

"What a coincidence," she said, "that's where I'm headed."

The moment she spoke the words she knew it was the truth. After all, it had been one of the cities she'd considered.

But when she'd found the bus ticket for Mad River, Ohio, in the bathroom stall, she'd been certain Mad River was her destiny. Then again, maybe she'd only been brought here to meet this man, be offered this ride. To a city that she *had* considered. Her head ached with the confusion. In all the homes she'd been in, decisions had been made for her. Now it was easier to spin the wheel and go with fate.

"Well, there ain't nothing I like better than a coincidence," Enon said. "They's plenty room in my ol' Buick. I welcome the company — if it's the right kind."

He leaned forward, his voice as whispery and gentle as a mother's lullaby.

"Lookie here," he said, "you don't want to ride with me, that's cool. Young ladies can't be too careful nowadays. I get it. Only thing I'm saying, it'd be fine having somebody to shoot the breeze with, and you, why you get yourself a free lift that's going to land you in the big city all the quicker."

He sat back. "Fact is, it don't make me no never mind what you do."

Her thoughts were fogged by lack of sleep. Stay or go? Go or stay? She spun the wheel of fortune. "Sure," she said finally. "Why not?" She'd accepted rides from strange men before. Even her relationship with Cisco had started that way. She knew what to do if a pendejo tried anything.

"Why not?" he repeated. "That's the spirit." He fidgeted with a packet of grape jelly on the table, tap-tap, tap-tap, like an insistent salesman at the door. "So," he said, studying her, "then you *was* heading to Chicago all along. Thing is, you give me the impression of a gal at her final stop. But now I could be wrong."

"Whatever. You giving me a ride or not?"

He grinned, swiped his keys up from the table. "Let's get this here show on the road, girlie."

As they walked to the front to pay the bill, she caught a glimpse of Ruby standing at the counter. Rosa Linda had been drawn to the diner when she left the bus depot and spotted the oasis of light across the street, pink neon glowing. Inside, the bright artificial light, like the flash of a camera, had captured the room in a tableau: booths, tables, stools, and the waitress, who she now knew to be the weary Ruby. Leaning back against the stainless-steel counter, Ruby seemed to be beckoning to her. Now she understood Ruby, lost in her thoughts, was staring as if hypnotized at her own reflection on the glass.

*   *   *

Rosa Linda pushed at the glass door, stepped out into the still-gray light. A gust of wind blew from across the street, whipping strands of her ponytail into her face, and she pulled the loose hairs from her mouth. Bus fumes and grit whirled over the pavement. She coughed until she caught her breath.

"You'll be fine, just fine," Enon whispered. "I'm right there, the old Buick."

"You're not from Ohio, either," Rosa Linda said. She pointed to the Florida plates. "You from there?"

"There, here," he said, "nowheres." He paused. "I expect you know all about that."

He opened the car door for her, made a sweeping motion. "Welcome to my coach."

From blocks away church bells rang. Rosa Linda paused, remembered early masses with her grandmother, her beloved nana, long ago — the comforting hum of prayers, the sweet smell of incense curling up. She glanced back at the diner, but there were no windows from this view, nothing to see but a brick wall and a dumpster, a plump rat scampering over the side. As for her grandmothers, they were both dead now. Granny del Río died shortly after her husband years ago when Rosa Linda was a baby. But Nana, she'd known well; Rosa Linda would only ever visit her again in memory.

"Whyn't you put that valise in the back seat right behind you where's you can keep an eye on it?" Enon said, winking.

When Rosa Linda hunched against the door on her side,

he said, "Better lock that door, Just Ophelia. Don't want to lose you before we even get started."

"You worry about driving, and I'll worry about me," she said. Her purse lay in her lap, and she held it tight with one hand, felt the comfort of Cisco's switchblade inside. One of her cousins had once grabbed at her breast when she was peeling potatoes, and she had sliced his hand open without a moment's hesitation. Rosa Linda had laughed at the shocked look on her primo's face. Her aunt and uncle promptly kicked their crazy niece back to her grandmother's house. But it had been worth it. She would laugh now if she weren't so tired.

"My, my," Enon said, and grunted.

She turned her head, not enough to let him out of her peripheral vision but enough to watch the streets pass by through her dirty side window. The city buildings in downtown Mad River were too close together; overhead, trolley lines ran in a web-like maze. She tried to take a deep breath, but the humidity wrapped around her like a wooly blanket.

The engine revved and hummed as Enon braked at red lights, shifted through the green. Once they were on the overhead highway, Rosa Linda gazed down at a neighborhood near downtown Mad River. The playground, a large square of bare earth and patchy grass, hunkered, isolated and lonely amid old buildings, a mix of businesses and houses. The sun peeked over the horizon, and the back and forth of a swing caught her eye, a lone little boy with auburn hair swinging high, a plane preparing for takeoff. Something caught in her throat. She swallowed and shifted her eyes far to one side, to the watery serpent gliding through the green.

"What's that river?" she asked.

"Mad River, like the town."

"What big river does it connect with?"

"Ohio. No, Miami. Maybe. Hell, don't matter none. Sooner or later, they all end up in the same place," he said, and shrugged.

Rosa Linda imagined herself a white rose floating down a river. Had she seen that image in one of those Mexican graphic novels, thick paperbacks in tones of sepia? She was free-falling into sleep and imagined the rose being carried by the current, sharp rocks jutting out, catching at the petals, tearing them, the whiteness sucked beneath the shimmering surface.

"That's right," he crooned, "you sleep, darlin'. Ol' Enon's gonna look out for you."

"I'm not a bit sleepy," she said, and whispered, "Stay awake, chica, stay awake."

The ringing of the church bells faded into memory.

CHAPTER TWO

In Mad River's east end, the bells of St. Francis called to the faithful, the hopeful, and the lost for 5:00 a.m. prayers. The bells had announced sanctuary and redemption for fifty years, but most of those within hearing range had grown weary of promises broken, hope deferred. Jeering outsiders had dubbed the neighborhood Hillbilly Heaven, but the inhabitants tweaked the name to Hillbilly Holler, a banner of defiant pride. Mostly from the hills and hollows of Kentucky and Tennessee, they had traveled to Mad River for once plentiful factory jobs that had slowly bled from the area with the companies' never-ending search for cheaper labor. Now, the people of the Holler batted away the mournful chimes as they would a pesky fly.

Two blocks away the morning air breathed, warm and heavy, through the dusty screen of Donnie Ray Camper's open window, and the bells of St Francis tolled through the deep waters of his nightmare. In the twists and turns of his fitful sleep, he had trapped himself inside sweat-damp sheets. He strained against the cocoon of cotton, swallowed his screams, growled deep in his throat.

"Uhhh," he groaned, and broke one arm free from the tangle. "No," he yelled, voice hoarse. He thrashed at the darkness that threatened to swallow him. "No-ooo." The word stretched out, broke into bits of sound that bounced inside his head like a stuttering echo.

Shadows swirled in murky waters of greenish-brown and submerged tree roots twisted around his legs, sucking him down into the bottom muck of a river while overhead swift currents tugged him upward. He would be ripped apart, quartered.

Why fight it? an inner voice whispered, a soft caress that promised sleep, deep and peaceful. Break free, another shouted, break free. He gritted his teeth, pulled with all his strength.

"Fuck, no," he shouted.

"Donnie Ray," a voice outside him called. He clawed the air, tried to reach the voice. Shayne, was it Shayne?

"Donnie Ray."

Light flashed white on Donnie Ray's closed eyelids. With one last burst of energy, he shot up into the guiding ray, broke through the surface of the river. Fists drawn, he bolted into a sitting position. His heart pounded; his pulse thrummed in his ears.

"It's just me, Donnie Ray." Tara Fugate stood next to his side. She wore only her panties, and the reading lamp shone on her goose-bumped, shivering thighs. Arms crossed at waist, she hugged her middle.

In the distance, the bell-song ended with a reverberating ring.

He startled and pulled back a fist, and she took two steps back. "Hold on now," she said.

She held up one hand as if to stop him. "You were having a nightmare, babe."

He unclenched his hand and shielded his eyes from the harsh light of the lamp. Tara stood so close, he could have reached out and touched her. What was she doing in his apartment?

"I tried to wake you up," she said, "but when I pushed at you — just a little poke, really — why, I thought sure you'd haul back and slug me good."

"What're you doing here?" The previous night was a haze. He'd gone to the Bottoms Up Bar. Too much whiskey. And then?

"I drove you home last night. Remember about James Lee?"

"God," he thought, now what had he done? He glanced at the back of his hands, the bruised and scraped knuckles. And his toes ached, the way they did when he'd been kicking something. Spots of clarity broke through his mental haze. Something about his mother and sister coming into the bar, crying about how only a few weeks would mark the day, wanting him to help plan a memorial.

Hell, Shayne's funeral had almost killed him. On that day, his mom and sister had leaned on him, wet his shirt with tears and snot, but he'd never cried. He'd swallowed his grief, let it sit like a lump in his heart. He was the man they expected him to be, the man his parents had taught him to be. Now, his mom and sister wanted to relive the letting go. He understood they needed to ease their conscience. Hell, maybe he did, too. But while they needed the sympathy of others, he needed to be alone with his thoughts, and the lump that grew and hardened.

"What about James Lee?" he asked, although his memory of the night before was slowly slipping out of the shadows. He didn't really want to hear, but it was his punishment. He forced himself to listen.

"Poor thing asked, could he buy you a drink cause you looked so pissed off about something, and well, he did pull on your arm," Tara said, her voice humming like a buzz saw, "and you just cold cocked him." She shook her head slowly, still not understanding.

"I kicked him?"

"Kicked him? Nah, just that one punch and that man was down. Arlie and the boys got ahold of you." She placed a hand on her jaw. "You did kick at that big pole in the middle of the dance floor. Can't you remember none of it? Arlie said you was the one who usually broke up fights, not started them. Now then, he did say he would overlook things on account of he knows what you're going through."

"I'm getting pretty damn sick of people telling me to remember shit. Let me wake up before you start bitching at me." He regretted his words as soon as he heard them. Tara was good people with a kind heart. He almost trusted her. But his head pounded like a wild animal was clawing inside desperate to escape. He needed to be alone. He needed silence.

"My goodness, you're so touchy these days," she said.

He leveled her with a look, and she fell silent, even though he knew she'd have more to say later on. He liked that about Tara — she understood when he'd had enough, and she didn't push his buttons. She gave him space, and he did the same for her.

Gray light poured through the window next to his bed. Within its frame the branches of the old maple resembled the gnarled roots of his nightmare. A breeze billowed the old screen and fluted the gauzy curtains. A shadow shifted across the wall that faced him, over the chest of drawers, and rested on the bike rack that hung on brackets there. That bike had been on his wall for nearly a year now. It kept his hatred fresh, jolted him with an angry energy like live electrical lines snapping through his veins.

"Shayne." He didn't realize he'd spoken out loud until Tara repeated the name.

"Shayne?" she said. "Your little brother. Is that what you was dreaming about?"

When he didn't answer, she added, "Why're you staring like that, Donnie Ray?" She turned her head to follow his gaze. "There ain't nothing there. Oh, that? Since when do you ride a bike? What's wrong? You're freaking me out, babe."

Fully awake now, he reached for his pack of Kools from the end table. He'd been seeing Tara for almost three months, since she'd moved from Portsmouth to the Holler to work at her mother's new business, Ladybug's Beauty Parlor. She was starting to get ideas about their future together — all those comments about cute babies. Even though he'd told her right from the start that he was not the marrying kind. Her thinking she could change his mind could be partly his fault. He was comfortable with her — she fit in the Holler through and through. And she had her own interests and didn't expect him to give her life meaning. He never brought women back to his apartment, avoiding them getting ideas about staying over. Now he'd gone and brought her back to his sanctuary.

"Donnie Ray . . . " she said, letting the second name drift, as if searching for words.

He flipped the Zippo, lit his cigarette. "Well, go ahead," he said.

"We — well, me, I . . . you were a little scary last night. Every little thing was making you so mad. OK, OK, don't look at me like that, I'll stop. But if Arlie and the guys hadn't pulled you off, I wonder—"

"James Lee's still alive and kicking, right?" Had he really hurt his friend? Donnie Ray remembered how after a few too many whiskeys last night, he'd looked around, waiting for someone to say something, anything to give him an excuse to beat them until his anger seeped out. If he hadn't had so much to drink, he never would've focused on James Lee.

"Nah, he's good," she said, "mostly his feelings was hurt, bless him."

He inhaled deeply of his cigarette.

"Hey, you know what?" Tara said, and tilted her chin at him. "Did you know Tammy Wynette's licensed to do hair? Says she ain't never giving it up on account you just never know. Can you believe it?"

He grinned at the unexpected remark and at her attempt to change the conversation. "And?" he said.

"And just goes to show, don't it? Anyways, I'd love to do your hair."

He asked Tara if he looked like the kind of man who went to hair salons. "I go to the same barber's that's been doing my hair since I was a kid."

A metallic sound, shriek, shriek, cut in through the window on a gust of wind. "Listen," she said, tilting her head toward the window. "I'll bet that's those old rusty swings from the playground. Ain't that something? Kids playing at this hour."

"Kids, hell," he said, "more likely some dope dealer, waiting for his client."

"Maybe. But I heard it earlier, too." Her delicate Scotch-Irish features grew animated. "Know what I heard down to the beauty parlor? The city's wanting to wipe the playground right off the face of the earth. Says it's an eyesore."

"You saying it's not?" The wind billowed the window screen. Dry thunder rolled in the distance.

She eased down onto the side of the bed. All this time he'd avoided bringing her to his home, always going to her place for sex. He wanted companionship and understanding, not a happily ever after. It wasn't fair to lead her to think otherwise.

"We can't let them do it," she said. She crossed her arms and sat up straighter. "We got to save the playground for our kids. We can't let them." She waved her arm to indicate the beyond. "We can't let them take that away from us." Her small hands curled into fists, and she pounded softly on her thighs.

Tara's family had moved away from the neighborhood when she was a toddler, and when she returned, she'd been shocked by all the gentrification that Swiss-cheesed the Holler. She and her mother tried to convince people to stay put, show everybody they couldn't be pushed around.

"Nobody around here's got time to save playgrounds," he said. "People down here got families and jobs to worry about."

"But it's for the kids. Why, it would lift spirits, kind of a way of showing the city it can't do every which thing they want to us, and—"

Donnie Ray threw off the bed covers with a snap. He told himself that what irritated him most about Tara was her eternal optimism; her sunny view could almost blind a person to reality, create hope when nothing but disappointment lay ahead. When he was being honest with himself, he could silently admit that he liked Tara's childlike faith. He didn't want to see her get hurt.

His hand shook when he stuck a fresh Kool between his lips. He'd been clutching the Zippo until it was slick with sweat. He clicked, but it didn't take. He tried again. This time a small flame jumped up.

"You still got a live one." Tara pointed to the cigarette in the ashtray.

He stubbed out both cigarettes then slid his legs over the side of the bed. The cool linoleum soothed the soles of his feet.

"Calm down, babe." Tara spoke softly, her voice soothing. "I just want to help. I love you."

"Christ," Donnie Ray muttered. Couldn't she see that was the problem? He didn't want the burden of love. Although he admitted to himself that he cared about her, he was not in love with her. If he'd ever thought he was in danger of that, he would have dropped her in a heartbeat. Loving too much led to heartache.

Anyway, why did Tara care so much about what he thought? He would never understand why women tried so hard to please men. Even when the man wasn't good enough to shine the woman's shoes. His sister Dee would have done anything for Fred Dunlap. Fred was twenty years older, married, with no intention of divorcing his wife, yet the man felt free to hook up with a young, single woman who was nothing to him but a piece of rough. Dee had gone on about him like he was some prize. Look what that got her.

At least he knew Tara was independent, involved with her career, and consumed by a need to help the community. When she and he were finished, she would cry but her tears would not drown her. She would find someone much more deserving of her.

"Donnie Ray," Tara said.

"Time for you to go home," he said. "I got shit to do."

"But I ain't driving," Tara said. "Remember? I left my car down to the Bottoms Up? You going to ride me over there?"

Minutes later, when he heard the spray of the shower, he turned to the stack of books arranged with the largest at the bottom moving progressively up to the smallest. He carefully slid the hardback from the bottom of the stack, *Buffalo Soldiers*, to take to work with him. He bought his books at Brownie's Used Books, a business that had been in the Holler since he could remember. Once he read the books, he traded them back to Brownie. A person could get too attached to possessions, and the next thing you knew you had a houseful of memories.

His reading preferences leaned toward the usual classic westerns — Brand, L'Amour, Grey — and crime paperbacks, standards such as Chandler, Hammett, Spillane, but also Robert Parker, Lawrence Block, and Elmore Leonard's westerns and crime novels. James Ellroy, and the author's obsession with his mother's unsolved murder, had recently held appeal until he discovered the murdering bastard had never been identified. Those were his favorites, but he left himself open to throwing in any book that appealed to him. He didn't need anybody telling him what he should or should not read. Once, a slim book of poetry by some guy named Omar with a last name he couldn't pronounce had somehow made it into his bag. He figured he'd picked it up by mistake with his stack. He skimmed through it, but it was too sentimental for his taste.

Sometimes he allowed himself to daydream of the Southwest from his western paperbacks, imagined himself as a desperado, living life free and on his own terms. And as he flipped through *Buffalo Soldiers*, he was initially surprised to find he identified with the black warriors. Hell, they were outsiders, same as him, enduring, standing like a man, having to prove themselves time and again to a society that reviled them.

* * *

When Tara finished in the bathroom, Donnie Ray turned on the shower water, already gone cool, full force. Increasingly colder needles of water pricked the bunched muscles at the base of his skull. He dressed in his usual: jeans, creases sharply ironed; short-sleeved T-shirt beneath a long-sleeved shirt, cuffs folded precisely to three-quarter length below his elbows; white socks; and motorcycle boots, polished to a high shine. His appearance mirrored that of his apartment: neat with no nod to fashion or fad.

When he entered the living room, Tara lounged on the

arm of the couch he'd bought from the Goodwill down the street. She gestured with the steaming mug in her hand to a matching mug on the coffee table.

"Coffee's ready," she said, her gaze over the rim of the mug, scanning the living room. "Know what? Your apartment's kindly small, but it could be just as cute. Add a few more things here, get rid of one or two there."

"Yeah?" On the side of his mug, he tapped his fingers to the beat of the monster hangover banging against the inside walls of his skull.

"There's hardly no room in that bed of yours for a body to stretch. I'm thinking you need a nice big bed — king-size — with one of them pretty bed sets, everything matching, spread and pillow shams, you know? They got real pretty colors and designs these days. Or you know what?" Her voice raised with excitement. "I bet you my mimaw would make a special quilt. When she came up here and met you, why she just loved you to death. She thought you was the handsomest thing she'd ever seen. And you were so good to her." Her eyes shone luminous with possibilities.

"You're full of ideas today for changing things: the park, my apartment, what's next?" he said, and grinned. One of the reasons he'd chosen his apartment was for its compactness: one-bedroom, small bath, tiny kitchen opening into the living room. He swept and dusted regularly, found a place for everything, and kept it there. No room for extras, no room for change.

"Let's go," he said, and snatched his car keys from the dish on a small table near the door. He stepped out, and the humidity enveloped him, not allowing any of the chaos ricocheting inside him to escape. He wished for torrents of cleansing rain.

It took two tries to fire up the ignition, and he cursed beneath his breath. The car was twenty years old, and his friend Loren, who repaired cars in the garage of his house, had told him he could get him a good deal on a newer used car. Donnie Ray had only to give Loren the word. But he wasn't ready to let go of the Chevy. New used car, new problems. Anyway, change didn't necessarily mean better.

Five minutes later, he pulled to the curb in front of the Bottoms Up and behind Tara's parked car. He glanced at her, the car engine idling, but rather than get out, she turned toward him.

"Follow me over to my place, why don't you?" Tara said. "I'll make you a big ol' country breakfast, eggs, hash browns, biscuits and—"

He shook his head. "Hangover," he said.

"You need somebody to look after you, babe. Why don't you let me help you?"

"I been taking care of myself for as long as I can remember," he said.

"OK, OK," she said, and reached for the door handle.

A car turned the corner onto Logan Avenue, screeched to a burned-rubber stop. The woman driver stuck her head out the window and yelled in their direction: "Keep your dog out of the street." She gunned her engine, a dark cloud of muffler exhaust trailing behind her.

"Oh, my goodness," Tara said, and squealed.

The puppy stood on trembling legs in the middle of the street, afraid to move. Small with a shaggy brown coat and a fountain of beige fur springing from the top of its head, covering its floppy ears, it could have been mistaken for a stuffed animal. Donnie Ray jumped out of the car. He scooped up the puppy with one hand and stroked its knobby head with his other hand. "I got you, buddy, nobody's going to hurt you now."

Tara reached for the dog and wrapped it in her jean jacket. "Did you see?" she said.

Donnie Ray clenched his jaws so tightly he thought he heard a molar crack. Yes, he'd seen the bull's-eye painted on the puppy's side. "If I get my hands on the son of a bitch who did it, I'll break his fucking neck." He smacked the steering wheel with both hands.

"Shush now, little sweetie," Tara whispered tenderly to

the puppy. "Good grief, Donnie Ray, you're scaring the pee out of him." She turned the jacket to show him the spreading wet spot.

Donnie Ray took a breath. "You got yourself a dog," he said.

"You bet," she said. "Donnie Ray, meet Spike, Spike meet Donnie Ray."

"Name suits him." Donnie Ray touched a finger to the furry spray on the puppy's head. He took one trembling paw between his thumb and finger and shook it. The puppy licked his finger, and he chuckled. He told her that he'd pay for the initial check-up visit to the vet. He had done this before for strays, and then found them a home. No pets for him. Although he did think that one day he might find time for an iguana.

After Tara drove off in her own car, Donnie Ray pulled to the curb in front of the kiddie park. He lit a Kool and leaned back. He had played there as a kid and later he would bring Shayne when he was just a little boy, skinny and clumsy.

In the twilight of early morning, the wind lifted pieces of paper and fast-food cups thrown on the playground, caught them in tiny tornados that spun-skittered across the grounds. The swings had rusted away, the broken twirl-go-round lifted to the ground on one side, and the gazebo stunk of urine.

Moms once gathered here and, while their kids played, caught up on the neighborhood gossip. Families met beneath the line of trees — cut down years ago after being rotted by disease — for a cookout and picnic. The playground had been the heart of the neighborhood. Now the broken and rotting heart was a reminder of what had been.

Donnie Ray's skin itched as if blisters popped and ran, bubbling hot beneath. Tara and her plans. A regular Little Miss Optimism. The muckity-mucks weren't going to listen to her. They had their own plans for the Holler.

A bent figure shuffled from around the corner of Bottoms Up and onto the sidewalk. The old man ducked his massive head to peer into the windshield as he continued toward the car. He scratched his thatch of still-thick white hair. "That you,

Donnie Ray Camper?" the raspy voice demanded. "What you hiding from, boy?"

The worn face, deformed by scar tissue around his eyes and a nose broken so often that it resembled a plug of putty, leaned down to better see into the open window. Donnie Ray held his breath against the stink of underarm sweat and a halitosis that smelled of dirty dentures, booze, and coffee. No one knew much about Boom Boom's past. But by the looks of his face and his punch-drunk actions, he'd been hit once too often in the ring. He'd moved to the neighborhood when Donnie was a teenager, had been old and beat up then. Chuck Ritter, who managed the gym, let him hang out; some of the guys swearing that when Boom Boom knew where he was and what was going on, he gave good ring advice.

"What did I tell you about roaming the streets when there's nobody out and about?" Donnie Ray said. "Remember what happened to Crazy Joe?" Joe, once a neighborhood fixture, slow in the head but fast on his feet, had been proud of never accepting a ride. Crazy Joe could walk anywhere others could drive. A month back, he'd been beaten so badly by a carload of thrill-seeking teenagers that he had to be hospitalized. When he came out of the coma, his family had him institutionalized for fear he'd be killed the next time a carload of teens wanted to have some fun.

"Aw, get off it," Boom Boom said, "I ain't no pussy. I can take care of myself."

"Not everybody in the Holler knows you these days. Things aren't like they used to be."

Boom Boom scratched his gray whiskers and scrunched his features into the center of his face. "Ain't it your turn to buy us breakfast?"

"Yeah, you got the last one." Donnie Ray always paid when he and the old man went for coffee or a meal, but Boom Boom liked this game of pretending that they took turns picking up the bill. Or maybe he actually believed that was how it went.

"Over to Willa's Country Kitchen?" Boom Boom asked.

He ran a thumb across his lips, as if already imagining the plate before him.

Donnie Ray's headache had dulled, but now a sudden flash of white pulsed in his temples. Every-fucking-body wanted to rub his face in the upcoming anniversary of his brother's death. But that was bullshit. He didn't have to look into Boom Boom's watery, bloodshot eyes to know the old man simply had a craving for good home cooking.

Donnie Ray and Shayne had been regulars at Willa's. Since Shayne's death, Donnie Ray had chanced two tries at Willa's Country Kitchen. As soon as he had stepped through the door, a faint roaring began in his ears. That first time he sat in his car, sweating and fighting the plumes of blackness inking around him. The second time, he'd made it to the counter, but when Sheila came over to take his order, her eyes were moist with a pity he could not bear. He'd jumped off the stool and waved a "forget it."

"What're we waiting for?" Boom Boom slid into the passenger seat, bringing with him the odor of unwashed flesh and cabbage.

"What the hell, why not?" Donnie Ray said finally.

As Donnie Ray pulled away from the curb, a gust of wind rattled the rusty chains of the park swings. Air whistled through the crisscrossed metal of the old gazebo's walls, an eerie keening sound. If he didn't know better, he could've sworn it ended on a sigh that whispered, "Shayne."

CHAPTER THREE

"You got a clue who you're with or where you are?"

Rosa Linda cracked her heavy eyelids in the direction of the voice. A tourist, she thought, by the sound of his accent, but then reality slowly returned. She wasn't in the Southwest anymore, she was far from home, in a stranger's car. Mierda, she'd fallen asleep.

"Well?" There was a sharpness to his words now—authority beginning to hone the edges.

"Enon. From the restaurant," she said, and sat up, reached for her purse, but it was no longer on her lap. They were on a dirt road, the car moving but barely creeping forward. She looked out the windshield, twisted around to see out the rear window. The road stretched out in front and back, winding, disappearing.

In front of her, in back, a vacant country road wound into nowhere, nothing. Nada. How long had she been asleep? The sun had risen and now shone high in a true-blue sky with scattered islands of floating clouds.

"That's right," he said, and chuckled. "It's nobody here but me and you." Enon eased the car onto the grassy shoulder and turned off the engine.

"Why aren't we on the highway?" Rosa Linda said. "Something's wrong with the car?"

"Worried about the engine, are you, Just Ophelia?" he said. His voice pressed on her, as stifling as the trapped air.

It took her a second to remember why he'd called her Ophelia. She glanced down at the floor by her feet, checking for her purse, but it wasn't there, either.

"I want out. Now." She tried the door handle. Locked. A shock prickled her spine. She reached to release the lock.

His hand darted out in front of her. "Leave it," he said, and something in his tone made her freeze.

"Think you're too good for the likes of me?"

"The window," she said. "Open it. I can't breathe."

"You ain't giving the orders," he said. He leaned back against his door, one leg bent and resting on the seat, the other stretching into her floor space. "The humidity's getting at you, that's all. You can't take it, maybe you shoulda stayed home, baby doll."

A wayward breeze whispered through the cracked-open window on his side, and she sucked in the air, wanted to fill herself with oxygen and light. He kept his eyes on her parted lips, as if he were breathing in each breath she released.

"No use trying to act all goody-goody. We both know why you got in my car, you little bitch." He snorted. "Yeah, bitch in heat."

His mouth was working, but he had so many words inside him he couldn't get them out. She waited.

"So all-fired sure of yourself," he said, "jumping into a stranger's car with nary a second thought."

"I just wanted a ride to get to Chicago sooner." She spotted her purse near his feet.

"Then why'd you get off the bus at Mad River? Maybe you figure you're so damn special you can just snooze off, not pay me no never mind. I ain't a man to reckon with, not to your way of thinking."

"No, no. I think you're a nice man."

He barked a phony laugh. "Don't treat me like some retard, you stuck-up harlot. You think your shit don't stink?"

An image of two turds appeared in her thoughts, and she swallowed the nervous giggle that almost slipped out. "I'm not that kind of person," she said. Her words echoed from far away. She wasn't certain that she'd actually voiced them until he answered.

"I seen you back in that greasy spoon, stretching out, dangling that shoe, posing. A regular prick teaser. Oh, I got your number. But you ain't so hot like you think. I've had better. That's a fact."

A wave of cold started at the base of her neck, spread down her spine and through her limbs. She tried to form a plan as he spoke.

"What you keep lookin' for? This?" He plopped her purse on the seat between them. "It fell off your lap. I tucked it away for safe keepin'. You scared I stole the money you ain't got to buy even a plate of fries? Anyways, I been too busy driving to take nary a peek inside that pocketbook of yours."

The drawstring opening was turned toward her, and she willed her fear-stiff fingers to inch into the purse. Cisco's switchblade. He'd told her that years ago he carried the knife on him when he'd gone on interstate hauls in the semi. *Por si acaso*, he told her — just in case.

"I'm not accustomed to men talking to me this way," she said, hoping to distract him. Her lips stuck to her teeth. How could her body feel so clammy and her mouth so dry? "Where I come from, men are gentlemen."

He laughed. She swallowed bile, sour and warm. "I been most everywheres," he said, "and one thing you can count on, people's the same wherever you go." He gazed in the distance beyond her as he spoke. "But I gotta say, me and you, there's something going on, like we was meant to be."

Her hand squirmed into the purse, searching. Would she have enough time to pop the knife open and plunge it right through one of those gray eyes of his and into his brain? Her heart pounded, do it, do it.

With a movement as quick as a scorpion's tail, his hand whooshed down, closed around hers, squeezing until her knuckles crunched.

"Ay. Stop," she cried out.

"Ay, ay, ay, Quicks Draw." He imitated the accent of the cartoon horse.

"I only wanted to get out my compact," she said.

He clamped her wrists with one large hand. His fingers were thick, powerful, his palms calloused with hard work. With his free hand, he reached beneath the seat, drew out her switchblade. "And here poor ol' stupid me thought you was looking for this." He pressed the knife's button. The pearlized handle jerked, the blade sliced through the air, locked open with a click.

A small cry escaped her. His eyes glinted, and she understood — her fear had excited him.

She remembered barrio bullies sniffing the air for the scent of fear.

Still holding onto her wrists with one hand, Enon studied the Spanish inscription on the knife blade. "What's this here mean in English?"

"Souvenir of the beautiful valley of Mexico."

"Well, sir, that's just rude." He laughed, then broke off suddenly, and sucked his teeth. "Fact is, you're a liar. They's no ticket to Chicago in that pocketbook." He nodded toward the purse. "But now I did find a stub says you was going from Nopal, Arizona, to Mad River, Ohio. Nary a mention of Chicago. And I'll tell you something else ain't there — no ID. Why might that be, Just Ophelia?"

She almost sighed with relief. He hadn't checked inside her suitcase, where she'd tucked her driver's license with the cash she'd taken — borrowed, really — from beneath Cisco's mattress. That had been her lucky day. All that money, then when she'd made it to the Greyhound she'd gone into the bathroom, and there tucked behind the toilet tank peeked the corner of a dirty envelope. As she peed, she'd discovered tucked inside a folded sheet of paper. In block letters, it said, "YOUR LUCKY DAY FREE I DON'T NEED IT NO MORE." It was a one-way ticket to Mad River, Ohio. When she'd left Cisco's, she had several destinations in mind. The found ticket changed all that. Fate. So incredible, so lucky. But luck was abandoning her.

"Somebody on the bus stole it when I fell asleep," she said. "I didn't realize until I was looking for money back at the diner."

"There ain't nobody waiting for me in Chicago, and there ain't nobody waiting for you. Me and you's just a couple a nobodies." He released her wrists. "Only difference, I done figured that out long time ago. You, you still thinking you somebody. But now, if we was to merge, run together, like a couple of dark rivers meeting up . . . ."

In one movement, she slid to her door, flipped up the lock with one hand, the other pushing down on the door handle.

Her head snapped back. He'd grabbed her ponytail, twisted it around his hand, and yanked so hard she felt roots at her hairline being ripped. He whipped her around to face him, wrapped his other arm, with the hand holding the knife, around her neck. He pressed his chest against hers, hard. The window crank dug into her back. Her clawed fingers flew to his face.

He brought the flat of the blade to her throat. "Scratch me, bitch, and I will cut your goddam head off."

Her arms fell. She heard herself panting, not wanting to, seeing how her fear, her recognition of his strength was exciting him. Calm, she had to stay calm. Find another way. She couldn't let him win. She willed herself to breathe deeply. When her parents dropped her off for "a little visit" with yet another friend or relative, she'd always figured out what her hosts wanted her to be and, chameleon-like, she tried her best to become that person. Sooner or later her real self would pop out, like with the touchy feely primo. But for a while her acting could fool them.

Enon pulled back a few inches, but his faint odor of Old Spice remained. Did she, too, smell of him now?

He probed inside the front of her blouse, tugged at the cord that hung around her neck. "Don't fuckin' move," he said, when she startled. "What the hell?" He tapped the shellacked vine bean threaded on the loop.

"Ojo de venado," she said, "eye of buck. It's a seed."

"What's with the pictures?"

"One side the Sacred Heart," she said, "the other the Virgin of Guadalupe. To protect me from the evil eye, keep me safe. My grandmother gave it to me when I left Arizona." In fact, Cisco's mother had given it to him, and he'd given it to her. Only a little lie, to let Enon know that she had people thinking about her, waiting for her. She had value. She wasn't a throwaway teen no one would miss.

"Some might say that seed ain't done its job." He cackled, tugged the cord, breaking it away from Rosa Linda's neck, and stuffed it into his pants' pocket.

He clapped his hand over her mouth even though she hadn't spoken. "Why'd you get in my car, why can't you answer that? Ain't no use trying to fool me, girl. I know you better than you know yourself."

"Know how?" She shook her head.

"When we first looked into one another's eyes, back there in the diner, the window. Remember? Yeah, you seen it, too. Hell, it was like looking back in front of myself. You said as much yourself. Two sides of the same coin. One not complete without the other. You're same as me, leastways you on the path, just ain't ready to fess up to it yet."

Enon leaned forward, rubbed his cheek against hers — light stubble scratching, poking into her pores. "Getting into a car with a perfect stranger, like some truck-stop prostitute. I reckon it's me's been sent to change your whoring ways."

She didn't realize she hadn't stopped shaking her head from side to side until he yelled for her to stop. She wasn't like him, never would be.

"Look over yon," he said. "Them woods. That's where they'll find you. Some hiker or some kids out playing where they shouldn't ought to. Ever smell a rotting body? Hey, I'm talking to you."

She moved her lips, but no sound came out. She remembered the carcass of the small dog in some alley in Texas — or was it Oklahoma? — long ago when she was a child. She imagined herself going stiff, bloating, bursting, maggots spilling out of her. No, no. She couldn't let Enon win.

"When it comes to dying," Enon said, "we're all alone, don't matter who you are."

Enon mashed her breasts with his chest. "Listen." He held up one finger. "It's like our hearts was one."

His tone was flippant, but had she detected some hint of hope beneath the brittleness?

Together they listened to her pulse — wild, racing, tripping over the hypnotic throb of his. Slowly, matching his.

She concentrated on the scene outside, the colors so suddenly vivid that it seemed more like a Technicolor scene from a movie than reality. On the trees, each distant leaf shone a brighter green than she had ever seen, and each shape stood out as distinctly as if outlined in black ink. The treetops swayed with a light breeze, plume-like, but too distant for her to hear. Majestic. Was there nothing beyond this world, or would she exist again but in some form that she, with her limited knowledge, could not imagine?

A car engine hummed in the distance.

Enon shoved away from her so quickly that she flinched. He tossed the knife beneath his seat, sat up, eyes darting from her to the distance. The large car rattled toward them—possible escape riding in a cloud of dirt.

Different scenarios shot through her brain: If she unlocked the door, jumped out, ran toward the road, would Enon try to pull her back with the other driver watching? Would the other car stop, or would the driver, afraid to get involved, speed away?

The car slowed as it approached. An old man drove, his gray head and neck jutted forward — a turtle out of its shell. At his side, an old woman, a floral scarf tied beneath her chin, peered around him. Rosa Linda tried to make eye contact, but the woman ducked back into the scarf. The man sank down into his shoulders and gunned the engine as he passed. She'd been right about them. She'd learned long ago she needed to depend on her own smarts to save herself.

Rosa Linda said nothing. The break had given her time to think, come up with a plan. Physically fighting him while trapped inside a small space wasn't going to work. The muscles in the side of his face twitched. As if in slow motion, Rosa Linda and Enon turned to face one another. Only the rasp of their unified breath moved the heavy air inside the car.

The cold spread into her brain, leaving crystalline thoughts. Slowly she reached up, forced her stiff fingers to open the clip and release her ponytail. She tugged her fingers through the thickness, arranged sections around her shoulders.

"What're you doing?" he said. His voice shook slightly.

"It gives me such a headache when it's not free." She angled a glance at him, lowered her lids to emphasize her long eyelashes, showed him he was a man worth flirting with. Hadn't he been letting her know all along that he wanted her to like him? All that talk about them being two sides of one coin, and the rest of the shit he was spewing. "It's almost lunchtime, I bet," she said.

"And?" He searched her face.

"Maybe you like having me here with you?" she asked. "Me and you together."

Something had switched inside of him when she'd ignored the other car; she could sense it. She had to strike quickly while his delusion lasted. "Maybe it's like you say." She paused, afraid of moving too fast. "We were destined to meet."

His breathing became more shallow, more rapid. Turned on, or angry?

"Uh-huh," he said, "all of a sudden you got the hots for me." He waited. Hoping to be convinced?

"You woke me up earlier. Everything happened so fast, I just didn't know what to think." She grazed his hand with her fingertips. He stiffened, maybe angered by a too-obviously aggressive woman, and she pulled away.

"Don't play me for a sucker," he said. He rubbed his palms on his thighs. "You know," he said, "You don't look so stuck up with your hair all loose." He smiled, the lonely smile that she remembered from earlier in the restaurant and, for the first time, she noticed that in a sad, angry way he wasn't so bad looking.

"I'm hungry," she said.

"Man is born hungry."

"Well, can't we go someplace for food?" she asked, and pouted. She had learned that all people, not just men, believed what they needed to believe.

"Oh, sure, right. One minute you a-telling me you're my heart and soul, next thing I know you fixin' to take off."

She pretended not to notice the anger that sharpened his words. She struggled to keep her tone playful.

"Hey," she said, "I didn't try to get away earlier, did I? I didn't do a damn thing."

"Watch your language," he said. Sweat beaded on his upper lip. "Ladies ought not cuss."

"Think about it, I didn't even try to signal those people. Anyway, I don't think I can get my shoes back on." She lifted one swollen foot.

"Could be some trick," he said, "you a wily one."

"It's like you said, fate brought us together." Although she was mimicking his earlier words, she wondered if it might not be true.

He nodded slowly, and she rushed on. "I don't even want to go in," she said. "I'm a mess after three days on a bus. You go, get us some takeout."

"Well . . . I might could . . . We passed a little diner a ways back. But don't go trying to leave the car, you hear? I'll catch you if you do. Let's put it this way — that switchblade? I'm a damn good whittler."

For a moment, she thought she would wet herself. She tightened her muscles and her resolve. "I want a cheeseburger," she said, "with mustard and onion. And fries, lots of them."

"Think you're pretty cute, don't you?" he said, but not in an angry way.

When he wheeled back onto the road, she rolled the window down without asking permission. The wind whipped through her hair, offering her the illusion of freedom. "Do you mind if I sit a little closer?" she said. "I want the air, but the wind, full blast, is messing my hair."

She lifted her purse from between them and plopped it in

her lap, wanted to believe that the power was shifting. So he wouldn't become suspicious, she fished inside for two sticks of Trident gum. She unwrapped a stick and held it to his mouth.

He chewed for a moment. "I was married once," he said.

"Yes?" Rosa Linda turned to study his expression, but it revealed nothing, so she held off any further comment until certain of how he felt about this marriage.

"She looked just like Ann-Margret. Ever hear of her?" She answered that she thought so, and he said that his wife was even prettier. "A trapeze artist in the circus, she was. Flew through the air as beautiful as any bird."

Enon squinted at the road as if looking into the past. "Only woman could ever get me off," he said. He scratched the stubble on his chin. "Shoot off into the darkness of a woman's body, and you know you're still alive."

Rosa Linda braked her feet against the floor as if to stop his ugly words from entering her. Enon and Cisco were so different, yet both thought they could possess her. They would not. Back in Nopal, Cisco's insistence on marriage had begun to feel like chains around her ankles. That day when they'd first met, she'd told him that she had no plans to marry and definitely was not going to be staying in Nopal. But he was one who chose to believe what he needed to believe. That last day after she heard his pickup tires spit gravel, she'd packed her clothes along with Cisco's hidden savings, and ran, hot and sweaty. She'd broken free then, and she would break free now.

* * *

A lone building, "EATS" painted across the picture window, squatted at the far end of a graveled parking lot. Enon parked as close to the highway as he could. Three vehicles were parked near the building: a battered van to the side, and in front, two pickups.

She swiped at the sweat at the back of her neck. "God, it's so hot." She twisted her hair in a knot, then quickly released it so that it cascaded down her back. Remember," she said, "mustard and onion. And make it well done. Oh, some of those ketchup packets for the fries."

"You stay put." He hesitated, then swung the door open. "I'm taking your word, darlin."

"Maybe we can find a cool spot for a picnic," she said.

He glanced back twice as he walked to the diner; the second time she waved. Her heart banged against her chest so hard it felt bruised. The diner door closed behind him, and she clenched her hands in her lap to keep from grabbing for the door handle too soon. Give him enough time to turn in the order but not long enough for the food to be done. She grabbed her suitcase from the back floor space.

Her mom had bought the case at Goodwill and given it to her when she was four, the first time her parents had dropped her off for a little visit. Since then whenever the time came to leave, Rosa Linda took only what fit in the suitcase. Travel often and travel light.

Once outside, her legs wobbled with excitement. As the diner grew nearer, the building rippled like the heat waves in the Southwest. She wished she still wore her ojo de venado so she could touch it, say a little prayer.

The glass door stood inches from her; the interior of the diner hidden by a venetian blind on the inside. She entered the small room.

Enon stood at the end of the counter with his back to her, but he jerked his head toward her. She lifted her eyebrows and nodded in greeting. "Hi," she said to him, then included the grill man with a glance.

"Hey," the grill man said, and told her to take a seat, he'd be with her in a sec.

Enon turned away. The grill man, a squat fire hydrant of a man with brown hair curling out of the neck of his T-shirt, and one hand on his hip, the other hand holding a spatula, flipped four hamburger patties.

"Menu's on the counter," the grill man said. An old man in overalls sat at the counter, hunched over a cup of coffee. He glanced sideways at her before returning to his catalog.

Three empty tables sat in the center of the room, and in a back corner, a small family sat at a lone table: a young mother with a ketchup-smeared toddler on her lap, and a man, probably the husband, across from her. He stared at Rosa Linda. He was in his twenties with muscular arms and torso, a man who could take care of himself.

"How about my burgers?" Enon said to the cook.

"You said well done, Mac." The cook's eyes traveled from Enon to Rosa Linda.

Enon shifted his weight from one foot to another. Rings of sweat spread on his shirt beneath his arms. "Them burgers look good to me," he said. "I got miles to cover."

"Suit yourself," the cook muttered, and slapped the meat onto the buns, wrapped them in waxed paper, and dumped them into boxes along with fries.

"Napkins," Enon muttered, and stepped closer to Rosa Linda. He reached across the counter toward the napkin holder. "Excuse me," he said, loud enough for all to hear, and to her, whispered, "We done found who we was looking for."

"Hey, Mac," the cook called out, "you got change comin'." The door wheezed shut behind Enon.

Rosa Linda perched at the edge of a counter stool. The adrenalin surge still raged inside her, wobbled her legs. Since she'd been on her own, she liked running full force toward the edge of forever, only to yank back at the precise moment before she tumbled into the abyss. The rush afterwards was like no other. Like now, after having escaped who knows what at the hands of Enon. She was relieved, excited, wanted to scream, cheer, cry, laugh. And, finally, she felt as though this time she'd felt the fingers of the abyss brushing against her ankles. If she laughed now, she suspected hysteria would take over.

She turned sideways, pulled a paper napkin from the dispenser on the counter, and dabbed at the moisture on her forehead. She asked for a glass of water. Her hand shook when she lifted it for a sip. Her voice uneven, she asked the grill man if there were any buses or taxis running this way. She'd had enough hitchhiking for today.

He shook his head *no*, and the old man at the counter, without looking at her said, to the grill man, "The Meyers has got a piece to travel. If she's going their way."

The grill man studied Rosa Linda, his black eyes searching for bad intentions. He nodded slightly. "What do you say Ben, Kathy? This young lady's wanting to be dropped off at the nearest bus depot."

"Closest one in our direction's Mad River," said the young man at the table. "We're going right by there."

Rosa Linda laughed, and the baby gurgled along with her, helping her to keep the sound normal. "What luck," she said. "Mad River *is* my destiny."

Rosa Linda saw irritation on the wife's face, and smiled at her as she walked toward them.

"*Destination*," said the wife, "not *destiny*."

"That's a cute baby," Rosa Linda said. She made eye contact with the woman and held it as she'd done with the grill man. She gave the woman a chance to get a read on her as much as she read the woman.

The young man removed a diaper bag from the seat, hung it on the back of his chair, patted the now-empty seat next to him. Rosa Linda sat, her attention turned to the mother. The man had a flirty twinkle to his eyes, and she wanted the wife to be certain she had no interest in her husband.

An engine started up outside, but the blinds blocked her view. Enon could be gone or simply hiding in the grove of trees across the road, waiting for her to leave.

"Something wrong?" the man said.

"Maybe you need to call the police," the wife said.

"No, no," Rosa Linda said. She didn't think Cisco would report her to the cops, but she couldn't be certain. Better not risk walking right into their hands if they wanted to haul her in.

The little boy held out his ketchup hand to Rosa Linda and garbled some words. She patted his head. "I just love babies, don't you?" she said to the woman.

"I'd be in trouble if I didn't." The woman stared pointedly at her husband. "We got to get going. Jude's needing his nap."

"Uh-huh," he said. "So, you hitching?"

"Not really," Rosa Linda said. "I had a ride with some friends, a nice couple, but their car broke down some miles back. They're getting towed to a garage in some little town. Can't remember the town. Anyway, I wanted to keep moving."

"We might be able to help you out there. I'm Ben Meyers and this here's Kathy, and that's my boy, Jude. I own that new pickup out front."

"Rosa Linda," she said.

"Nice," he said. "Pretty girl like you, thumbing's kind of dangerous."

"Dangerous for people who pick up hitchhikers, too," Kathy said. "Friend of mine told me about a kid who picked up two brothers. One of the brothers gets in the front seat with the driver and the other sits behind him. The one in the back shot that poor kid's brain out."

"That's why," Ben said, "we're going to give Rosie a lift. A good Christian woman like you, you wouldn't want to pick up the paper tomorrow and read about Rosie getting her head blown off — or worse, if you know what I mean."

"Don't you have somebody in Mad River you could call?" Kathy said. "There's a pay phone right over there on the wall. I got the quarter if you don't."

Rosa Linda wished she could turn down Ben's offer and walk out. But if Enon was out there, waiting, she didn't think she could find the strength to get away from him again. He'd be really angry now, and if he was able to force her inside that death trap again, well, who knew.

"I visited Mad River once years ago — just for a few days — when I was just a kid," Rosa Linda said, "and I promised myself to return some day. The people were so kind and helpful. I thought maybe it would be the perfect place for a fresh start."

"It's settled," Ben said, "you're coming with us." Kathy tried to speak, but his words tumbled out. "You looking for a job?" he asked, and without waiting for an answer, said to Kathy, "I was thinking about that McDonald's over by the house, they're always needing help."

"She *cannot* stay with us," Kathy said, her scowl as determined as her words. "Don't try pulling that live-in babysitter business again either, Ben Meyers."

"Oh, definitely not," Rosa Linda said quickly. "I would never impose on someone else's marriage. Really." She hoped Kathy believed her. She would never betray another woman by taking her man. There were too many single men available.

Ben snapped his fingers. "How you feel about old people?"

"OK, I guess." Rosa Linda told them how she'd lived with her grandparents before they died, and after high school she'd had a job at a nursing home, serving food. "Old people like me," she said.

"Karma," Ben said. "I think I got the solution to your situation. A job and a place to stay, all rolled into one." He glanced at Kathy. "You're thinking what I'm thinking, right? Melva's?"

"No, Melva Kopp did not even cross my mind." Kathy's scowl lines deepened.

* * *

Outside, Rosa Linda scanned the parking lot and, across the road, the thick underbrush and trees beyond. She couldn't see Enon, but the flesh on her arms had gone goose-bumpy. The tree branches swayed just as they had when she'd studied them from inside Enon's car. Atop one tree, a big crow perched.

Rosa Linda shaded her eyes with her hand and pointed. "He's watching us." She thought of the raven in Poe's poem that she and her tenth grade English class had liked so much. "What do you think it means?" she said.

"Who? God?" Kathy said.

Rosa Linda smiled. "The crow."

"Who even cares?" Kathy said, frowning.

"Once they all were in the cab, Rosa Linda adjusted the side mirror to get a better view behind the pickup.

"You expecting somebody?" Kathy said. "That crow maybe?"

Rosa Linda pretended to be nodding off to put Kathy at ease, but she was wide awake. Through her lashes, she kept her gaze on the side mirror. A car seemed to be following them. From such a distance she couldn't be certain it was Enon. Eventually the car turned off onto a side road. She could not see him, but she somehow felt his presence, like electricity in the air before a storm.

CHAPTER FOUR

The Chevy's tires crunched onto the Country Kitchen parking lot. At Donnie Ray's side, Boom Boom jabbered on, lost in a played-out memory of a boxing match from another time. Donnie Ray turned off the ignition and lit a Kool, every movement slow, easy. He was in control. A drop of sweat slid over his eyebrow into his eye, and he swiped at it with the back of his hand. He glanced at his wristwatch, told himself that maybe he didn't have time for breakfast and bullshit. The beer order was being delivered to Powers Pool Hall today; he needed to be there early. It was only a temporary job, but he believed in giving his employers an honest day's work. Arlie, his friend and boss at his regular job at Bottoms Up Bar, had asked him to spot Arlie's friend Kelly at the pool hall until his broken leg mended. Donnie Ray couldn't say no. When Shayne died, the family had only scraped together half the cost of Shayne's funeral. Arlie lent them the money, without interest. Donnie Ray repaid loyalty with loyalty.

Another reason to turn around and leave — he couldn't force food this early on his queasy stomach. If he got hungry later, he'd run into the restaurant next door to the pool hall, Melva's. Melva's made killer chili, and though he didn't have a sweet tooth, he liked a slice of their homemade apple pie now and then, with a slice of cheese when he thought of it. Why bother with Willa's?

"You want a to-go order?" he asked Boom Boom. He had to ask twice before the old man realized they'd arrived at the restaurant.

"Hell, no," Boom Boom said, his hand already pushing down on the door handle. "I gots to have me some elbow room."

Donnie Ray entered the room and paused, leaned his shoulder against the wall. He felt lightheaded, but he pretended he was looking around for someone he knew. A few customers glanced his way but, not sensing an outsider, most just went about their business. Sprinkled among the Holler residents, he noticed a few white, brown, and black faces from the housing project a few blocks from the Holler. Poor people who appreciated honest country cooking. When they'd first started coming in, some of the Holler regulars tensed for a territorial battle. Big Eric, the new owner — and himself Black — made it clear that as long as nobody caused a problem, everything was cool. Donnie Ray tensed his muscles and commanded them to move forward.

Sheila met them at the counter with two mugs of coffee. And with the intuition of a career waitress, she understood and remembered what she'd done wrong months ago. "Hi, boys," she said, her voice neutrally happy, her eyes cleared of pity. "Y'all want your usuals?" When Donnie Ray said he'd stick with coffee only, she winked at him, said, "Big night last night, huh?" and sailed off to the kitchen with Boom Boom's order.

Big Eric, perched at the opposite end of the line of stools with a newspaper opened in front of him, turned and glanced up over his readers. He nodded, behaving as if Donnie Ray had been coming in regularly just as he used to.

Donnie Ray felt Shayne's presence so strongly that he glanced at the empty space to his right, almost expecting to see his brother. Not that he was the kind to believe in ghosts. Shayne was gone forever. A low humming began in Donnie Ray's ears. Maybe, he thought, the reason no one was mentioning his brother was because they'd forgotten him. They didn't give a fuck.

Shayne was history — hell, the Holler would soon be history. The city had all those plans for that Washington District with expensive shops and restaurants. Nobody in the Holler could afford to even breathe the air in such places. But that was the plan, wasn't it? Fancy businesses attracted fancy people, buying up the houses around the area, renovating. Did they think Holler folks wouldn't like to fix up their shitholes if their jobs paid them enough to do it? And it seemed the more area the Washington District gobbled, the hungrier it got. They, whoever they were, were probably the same ones who wanted the playground. He wondered what they had in mind for that space. And Tara thinking she was going to do something about it. Those suits would squash her like an ant at a picnic. But nobody could convince Miss Sunshine of that.

Sheila placed a plate of steak, eggs over easy, hash browns, biscuits, and a side plate of two pancakes before Boom Boom. The special came with either biscuits or pancakes, but Sheila had brought him both. He sliced into his steak and one of the eggs and crammed a forkful into his mouth. "Where's yours?" he asked.

"Later," Donnie Ray said, but Boom Boom had already lowered his head to his plate. He made smacking noises with his loose lips and sopped the yellow of the other egg with a biscuit.

The scent of Willa's fresh-baked, buttermilk biscuits always filled the morning air, pulling in hungry customers. Ever since Donnie Ray had moved out of his mother's home at eighteen, he'd stopped by Willa's for breakfast at least twice a week, alone or with Shayne.

Five years ago, Willa sat at the counter with Donnie Ray and said, "Well, I done sold the place. Gonna take off to Florida. My old bones can't take one more winter. But I tell you what, it's like losing kin. What's more, I sold the place to a colored man. What do you think of that?"

"You leaving him the recipe for your biscuits?" he'd asked, and Willa had slapped him on the back and winked. "Everything but the secret ingredient," she said and hooted.

"Do I know that boy?" Boom Boom asked, as he soaked his pancakes in syrup.

Donnie Ray glanced to where Boom Boom was now pointing with a forkful of pancake. The coffee in Donnie Ray's stomach churned.

"You done?" he asked Boom Boom. "I got stuff do."

"He's coming our way," Boom Boom said.

Rafael Torres, 6'3" and 200 pounds, put men on guard, and his dimples, long eyelashes, and caramel skin attracted the girls. Shayne had been amazed when Rafi had chosen him to hang out with. Dressed in the white shirt and pants of the kitchen worker, Rafi pulled the white paper hat off his head as he approached.

"Hey, Boom Boom," Rafi said.

"Hay is for horses," Boom Boom said, and waited for Rafi to grin. Then, Boom Boom squinched his face in thought and leaned toward Rafi. "Do I know you?" When Rafi only laughed, Boom Boom said, "I mean it — do I know you?"

Rafi said his name, and when Boom Boom stared at him blankly, added, "From the gym. Boxing practice? You used to be there a lot."

Donnie Ray picked up the check, fished into his back pocket for his wallet. Rafi reached out a hand. "Wait, Donnie Ray."

"Oh, yeah, yeah," Boom Boom said. He scratched his whiskers. "You and some skinny white boy. What's his name?"

Donnie Ray had thought Rafi didn't work at Willa's anymore. When he drove by, he'd often see Rafi's beat-up old gray Ford, a mismatched red door on the front driver's side, parked out back in the employee spaces. Then maybe a month back, Rafi's tin can disappeared. Donnie Ray assumed that he'd moved on to another job.

Rafi was a year or so older than Shayne. Unlike Shayne, he was a born athlete, playing on the school's baseball and football teams. Back when Boom Boom was still hanging onto what was left of his thought process, the old man had worked closely with Rafi at the gym, telling anyone who would listen that the kid was a natural. But Rafi didn't take boxing seriously, told Shayne that he didn't like beating other guys for sport or money. The two had met at the gym, and Rafi became Shayne's teacher and protector when the other boys laughed at Shayne's flailing arms and spaghetti legs.

The muscle men magazine incident had happened a month or so before Rafi and Shayne met. For a while Donnie Ray observed the new friends closely, searching for a sign of a shared glance or a hidden touch. But their interest was centered around boxing practice, playing video games — *Tron* and *Donkey Kong* — and trading action hero comic books with an occasional *Daffy Duck* thrown in. Shayne would bend over laughing just telling Donnie Ray about Rafi's impression of the smart-mouthed duck.

When Sheila arrived with a coffee carafe, Donne Ray laid his hand over the cup. He slid the bill and money toward her.

"It's been too long, Donnie Ray," Rafi said. "I saw you the other day, you were driving past the gym when I was coming out, but you didn't see me."

"Yeah?" Donnie Ray said. Rafi was alive. Shayne was dead. And if Rafi hadn't filled Shayne with all that false confidence about his new strength and boxing ability, maybe Shayne wouldn't have thought he could take on a grown man. The ends of his nerves heated up, pinged beneath his skin. He clenched a fist. Unclenched. A twinge of shame pulled back the anger. He had to get hold of himself.

"I'm late," Donnie Ray said, and stood to leave.

Boom Boom rubbed the end of his nose. "Uh-huh, Puerto Rican, ain't you? And that white boy, he's got flat feet, can't box worth a lick. Where's he at?" Boom Boom gawked his neck, searching. His gaze lingered on Donnie Ray, sensing an answer lay there.

"I been hoping you would come in," Rafi said to Donnie Ray, "but you . . . Hey, I only work part-time here now. Washing dishes, like that. I still got my other job over in Middletown, but I'm looking for something downtown." He spoke rapidly, as if trying to stop Boom Boom from speaking. Donnie Ray eyed the door.

"I take the bus," Rafi said, his words coming faster now. "My engine blew up. That car was like thirty years old, you know? But what I wanted to ask about is I heard about a memorial?"

Donnie clamped his jaw. He snatched his keys off the counter. "Don't know anything about it. Talk to my sister." He turned away, batting his hand behind him when Rafi started to speak. "Later," Donnie Ray said.

Outside, Boom Boom stared into the distance. "I got a hurt inside. Something bad's about to happen, ain't it?" he said.

"You ate too much, that's all," Donnie Ray said.

*   *   *

Donnie Ray's bedroom had been off-limits to everyone since he'd hung the bike. In this room, he could be alone with his thoughts, his memories, without the outside chaos infringing. His room gave him the illusion of order. On the few occasions when his mother and sister came over, he closed the door to his bedroom, told them to stay out. He'd long ago learned that subtlety didn't work with them. Now he'd let Tara in.

The room still smelled of sex and Tara's Charlie perfume. He stripped the bed and set the sheets to washing in the small washer in the kitchen. The rest of the bedroom looked in order — neat book stack, emptied and washed ashtray. A light dusting would keep things tidy.

He left the bicycle for last, passed the cloth first over the bike bracket, then more tenderly over the bike. He kept it as pristine as if Shayne were taking care of it himself. The day he gave the green (Shayne's favorite color) BMX to Shayne, his little brother asked him to paint "The Hulk" on the side.

Even as a little boy, Shayne had loved speed, riding his Big Wheel on the sidewalk, bending his head into the wind, pumping the pedals as fast as his short legs could go. Maybe he imagined himself escaping his tormentors, the kids who already sensed his difference.

Donnie Ray brought clean sheets to his bed, folding corners

precisely. As he slid his hands beneath the mattress to tuck in the corners, he thought of the muscle men magazine and how innocently Shayne had thought he could hide his secret under his mattress.

When Shayne was about fourteen, their mother had called Donnie Ray, her voice shrill with hysteria, and vodka. "Oh lord, oh lord, my baby boy's queer," she'd wailed. She'd begged Donnie Ray to come over to the house she shared with Shayne and Dee to talk some sense into the boy. "It's your fault," she yelled. "I can't be mom and dad. And you don't have time for anybody but yourself."

Donnie Ray told her she was jumping to conclusions, that skinny Shayne was slow developing; the magazines' pics and success stories provided him inspiration, motivation. "Hell, lots of boys read those magazines," he said.

"You never did." She blew her nose and paused to consider his comment. "You think?" she asked.

If the magazines had been found under any other guy's mattress, Donnie Ray wouldn't have cared. He didn't have time to worry about other people's sex lives or fantasies. But Shayne was his little brother, and Donnie Ray had witnessed the torment that others could heap on gays. The ostracizing, name-calling, beatings, rapes.

Charlotte insisted Shayne sign up for boxing classes at the neighborhood gym. She said that it was hard for a boy living in a house with two women. And since Donnie Ray wouldn't move back home, what else could she do to make a man out of Shayne?

Donnie Ray thought, but didn't say, that if the kid was attracted to muscular men, the gym might not be the best place to cure him of what offended her so much. But he did agree that the exercise would do him good, help build the strength he was going to need.

A couple of years later, and after many boxing sessions with Rafi, Shayne was convinced of his invincibility. "Just let some asshole mess with me or my family now," he crowed to Donnie Ray only days before he was killed.

Outside the window, the maple creaked. He welcomed

the pleasant memory that the sound brought. When he was a kid, he had carved his initials into the trunk and had helped little Shayne mark his own beneath. "They'll be there forever, right, Donnie Ray?"

"Yep," he answered, "just like we'll be brothers forever."

He passed his hand over his eyes. In the living room, he pulled his sketch pad and pencils from the small drawer in the coffee table. Inspiration didn't bloom, so he closed the pad and laid his head on the sofa back.

*　　*　　*

He awoke with a crick in his neck and an ache in his jaws from grinding his teeth. He was thankful it was time for work. Arlie had cut back on Donnie Ray's hours at the Bottoms Up while he worked the long hours at Powers, keeping him on at the bar only on weekends and busy weeknights. Donnie Ray hadn't wanted his hours cut; work punched back the memories.

He drove down Logan Avenue, slipping his mind into cruise control — no thoughts, no anger, keeping his mind at a steady pace as he left the Holler. He passed the Washington District without even a glance toward the cancer that had taken hold of his neighborhood. He'd once liked driving down the side streets, appreciating the old and varied architecture. He had to admit those houses did look a hell of a lot happier with their new face lifts, defying the clutches of the grim reaper for a bit longer. Bright red graffiti on one of the corner houses caught his eye: "GET OUT FAGS," blood-red letters crudely painted on the side of a Victorian lady, dressed in pale yellow and lavender.

Once, one of the renovated houses was burned to the ground. Arson, the inspectors said. We're making things better for you, the city kept telling the Holler residents, not understanding the residents didn't want to be told what they needed. They wanted jobs that paid. They wanted to be left alone to live their lives as they chose, just as they had in the hollows of Tennessee and Kentucky.

The sweet smell of the Lovely Soap Factory rolled into his car like a nauseous fog, and Donnie Ray cranked up his window. Before the factory cut back its work and workers by over half, the smell had wafted through the length and breadth of the Holler. Over twenty years ago, his father had been among those who moved his family to Mad River, felt lucky to have secured a position at Lovely's, where he'd been a loyal employee for twenty years. Earl Camper hadn't allowed another brand of soap in his house. Then Lovely's laid him off with a month's wages and their heartfelt apologies.

One Thanksgiving Day, Dee and Donnie Ray sat on the sofa watching TV and having their pumpkin pie, baked fresh at Kroger's deli, with extra dollops of Cool Whip. Suddenly their father held up his water glass half-filled with Jim Beam and toasted: "Here's to the bright lights and what could be."

Charlotte, in the kitchen, yanked the bottle of vodka from the freezer and poured herself a glassful. "Don't start, Earl Camper. You are not stepping a foot out of this house."

Donnie Ray and his sister Dee stared hard at a rerun of *The Brady Bunch*, wondered what must it be like to be Greg and Marcia Brady? After a barrage of curses and broken glasses, Earl stormed out, yelling that there was a whole other life out there and, by God, he was having some of it. Charlotte clawed at his shirt, ripped it off his back.

With Earl's bag and Fender acoustic already packed, he and his Chevy careened away from the sidewalk and the Holler. He headed toward his yearnings and never looked back. Odd how Shayne would be the one to share Earl's wanderlust, when he was the kid who wasn't related to him, born long after Earl was gone.

*   *   *

The soapy scent had been left behind with the Holler, and Donnie Ray opened the window. He was out of his neighborhood but still in the east end, working class but with aspirations of moving up. Here lived those who had attained office jobs, secretarial or low-level management, or employment in the unionized factories, although the once-powerful unions were losing their grip and many of those jobs were but a memory.

Beyond the modest houses with yards fenced to announce ownership, stretched a small commercial strip. Peeping Tom's Show Bar boasted pole dancers, offering a few minutes of companionship to any man — or woman — willing to spring for a bottle of Cold Duck. A block down from Peeping Tom's and next door to Powers, separated by a narrow alley, Melva's Bar and Restaurant specialized in simple food with daily specials for both workers and neighborhood families. Across the street from Powers, Shipwreck Tavern was popular with neighborhood regulars and lured in music lovers or the brokenhearted with its outside speakers blasting jukebox tunes, rock and country. The small, box-shaped building had a back door opening to the interstate for easy getaways.

"What the hell?" Donnie Ray pushed on his brakes. Did the Buick in front of him mistake the driving lane for parking? The driver was stopped in front of Melva's, leaning sideways and ducking his head to see out the passenger window.

Donnie Ray tapped the car horn. He shielded his eyes and checked the license plates. Florida, an out-of-towner. With the sun in his eyes, Donnie Ray could only see the back of Mr. Florida's head in silhouette. It swiveled slightly as he looked up and down the line of cars parked in front of the two businesses, then he stretched his neck for a view of Melva's side parking.

Donnie could easily pull around him and park in the empty slot in front of Powers, but the guy was challenging him. He pressed his palm on the horn and held it a full five seconds. Let the S.O.B. say something.

The guy straightened behind the steering wheel and angled his head toward the rearview mirror. Donnie Ray couldn't see his eyes, but he felt them. He switched off the ignition and pushed open the door. The Buick still didn't move. Donnie Ray stepped onto the asphalt and shut the door behind him.

Bald tires spun and gained traction, and the Buick blasted away.

*   *   *

The bell over Melva's door ting-tinged Donnie Ray's arrival. Melva, sitting at the table at the back with a *Reserved* sign, lifted her head from her newspaper. Her thick glasses caught the light streaming in from the picture windows on either side of the door. The mirrored round lenses shone bright, and Donnie Ray blinked.

"Hey, good lookin'," he said and lifted his hand in greeting.

"Here's our charmer," Melva rasped in her graveled voice. "It's the charmers a woman's got to watch out for." She laughed, bringing on a wet cough. She pulled a tissue from her smock pocket, dabbed at the corners of her mouth. As if her hacking reminded her how long it had been since the last cigarette, she flipped open the box and, with the tips of her long, scarlet-painted fingernails, plucked out a Salem.

"How do," Jaybird Hawkins said, as Donnie Ray passed him. A retiree from the General Motors plant, Jaybird sat at a stool three before the one Donnie Ray had staked out as his own. The old man liked to talk, relating gossip about people that Donnie Ray didn't know, much less care to know.

Donnie Ray reached for a newspaper folded on the bar, let Jaybird see he had reading, not talking, on his mind. Donnie Ray's preferred seat offered a clear view of the front door to his left and, to his right, two swinging doors at each corner of the wall, each leading to the kitchen. A mirror ran the length of the bar, providing a view of anyone behind him.

Common sense told a man to never sit without covering his back, forgetting this had gotten even the otherwise savvy Bill Hickok killed.

No matter how tough you were, you could never let your guard down, never trust any damn body. He'd warned Shayne a million times.

Loretta held up the coffee carafe, and he said he only wanted water. His nerves still jangled from the shot of adrenaline that had found no relief when Florida had taken off.

"Chili's extra good today," Loretta said.

Jaybird's stool squeaked and swiveled, and he cleared his throat. Donnie Ray asked Loretta to make his order to go.

"You're lookin' a might peaked," she said. "How's about a fried egg sandwich on the side?"

He nodded, and she pushed through the swinging door nearest her. A moment later Loretta pushed open the far swinging door and stuck out her head. "Melva, you need to get back here."

"What now?" Melva waved one hand, cigarette dangling between two fingers.

"We got us a situation."

"Like what?" Melva said.

"Best come see for yourself," Loretta said.

"You're the one always itching to take over running this place, Retta. You handle it." Melva tapped her cigarette on the ashtray.

Donnie Ray grinned. That old lady didn't take any shit. Last week, he'd been in when some drunk at the bar kept muttering about all women being bitches. Melva sucked in on her Salem and shot dragon smoke out of her nostrils. In her been-smoking-for-over-sixty-years voice, she announced, "I guess that makes you a son of a bitch."

"It's that Ben Meyers," Loretta said. "Says he *needs* to see you and won't talk to me. Got some girl with him."

Melva stubbed out her cigarette, giving the butt a vicious twist into the heap of ashes. "Jesus H. Christ." She tapped the fingernails of one hand on the Formica tabletop. Clickity-click, click, click. "Well, don't just stand there with your ass in the kitchen and your head in here, Retta. Haul them in here."

Donnie Ray sipped his water without shifting his eyes from the mirror. The swinging door pushed open, and a young guy strutted in with a beautiful girl by his side. The girl clutched a ratty suitcase and glanced over her shoulder before setting the case down so that it rested between her feet. Nobody was taking that thing from her.

Tall and slim, she wore her mass of long black hair pulled back into a slightly off-center ponytail, the way girls were wearing them these days, emphasizing the oval shape of her face and symmetrical features. She was young, but her features were drawn, weary and apprehensive. Her eyes darted to every face in the room, studied it, moved to the next. She was running or hiding from something. He'd bet on it. He didn't want to take his eyes from her. He didn't usually like sketching people, but he'd like to give this one a try.

She lifted her eyes and met his in the mirror. She straightened her spine, stared hard, and arched one eyebrow slightly as if demanding to know why he was staring. She reminded him of a cat that had once strayed into the parking lot of his apartment. His headlights had beamed on the cat. Instead of fleeing it had paused, turned slowly and glared, as if daring him to continue. He'd never seen the cat again. He sometimes wondered if it had dared the wrong person, one who was not as charmed as he was by its fearlessness and lack of good sense.

He reached for his glass, tilted it before it lay completely against his mouth. Water dribbled down his chin.

"So, Ben, you going to introduce her already, or you planning on just standing there looking the fool?" Melva said.

Loretta, now returned to stand behind the bar near Donnie Ray, stared intently, her lips rolled back tight against her long teeth into a line that turned down at the corners.

"This," Ben said to Melva, "is the solution to your problems."

Donnie Ray had lifted his eyes to the news running on the TV above the bar, but his attention returned to the mirror.

"Seems I got problems coming and going today," Melva said.

"Right," Ben said, ignoring the sarcasm. "I remembered how you were looking for someone to help around the apartment. You know, on account of you and Edward feeling kinda sick and stuff, and see, I think my friend Rosie here is just the thing."

"I haven't been sick a day in my life," Melva said, one boney shoulder hiking up inches above the other so that her smock looked like it hung on an uneven wire hanger.

"Sure, sure," Ben said. "I only meant . . . come on, you know what I mean."

"You got a last name, friend?" Melva said to the girl.

"Rosa Linda del Río," the girl said.

"And they call you Rosie," Melva said.

"It's easier," Ben said.

"That right?" Melva said. When the girl only shrugged, Melva flicked an ash into the ashtray. "You better learn to speak up, girl, unless you want people walking all over you."

"When people get to know me," Rosa Linda said, "some of them say I speak up too much."

"That a fact." Melva grinned and took a drag on her cigarette.

Ben darted around the girl, planting himself between her and Melva. "Rosie's the daughter of a friend of Kathy's mom, long passed, as you know. Anyway, Rosie's come looking for a fresh start, and Kathy's mom's friend lives out in the country, and you know there aren't any jobs out there. So, me, I says to Kathy, I'm thinking . . . " He paused to tap one temple. "I'm thinking, just the ticket for Melva and Edward. Here, Rosie can work and have a place to stay. You said the helper could live here. I remember you said that. Good for her, good for you."

Jaybird had twisted around to face the ongoing drama. "You got something to say, Jaybird?" Melva said. He ducked his head but turned only halfway back.

"Now then," Melva said, returning her attention to Ben. "That's got to be the most twisty-turvy tale I ever heard." Her chimp-round eyes narrowed behind her thick glasses. "Where's Kathy?"

Ben dashed to the door and called out for his wife. Kathy appeared with a sleeping Jude's legs straddled around her waist, his head resting on her shoulder. "Jude needs changing, Ben," she said.

"Just a minute." Melva held up a hand and waved it. "I know you could hear Ben from in there. You vouch for this gal?"

"She can't stay with us. We don't have room." Kathy stared over Jude's head at Ben.

"I didn't ask you that, Kathy."

Kathy shifted her weight. "Yes, I vouch for her."

"Good enough," Melva said.

"Well, I never," Loretta said. "Why not call the police, Melva? Have them check the girl out."

"Thank you very much for that piece of wisdom, Retta," Melva said. "But if you can tear yourself away from my private conversation, you might be able to hear that bell ring when customers walk in."

"Try to help a body," Loretta said, with a snap of her dish towel, "and what do you get? Heartaches, that's what." She wiggled her fingers at the working men that had taken a table by the door. "Be right with you, gents," she called. "Glad to see somebody wants me around."

Melva studied the girl. "We had a gal helping out, but she was lazy. It's not like there's a lot to do. I got somebody coming in to do heavy cleaning. Me and Edward just need someone to tidy up. The pay's not going to make you rich, but room and board's worth quite a bit on its own. You'll get wages on top of that." She waited until the girl nodded.

"You got any experience cleaning, caring for others?" she asked.

Rosa Linda told about helping her own grandparents before they died and about a job at Green Valley Nursing Home in Marigold, Texas, after high school. "I can give you their phone number," she said, "if you want to call long distance. They'll remember me."

Melva pushed an order pad and pencil to the end of the table. "In case I decide to do just that," she said.

"Melva," she said to Rosa Linda. "Everybody calls me Melva."

"OK," Rosa Linda said, "and you can call me Rosa Linda." She offered her hand to shake, but Melva ignored it, picked up her cigarette case, and flipped it over, side to side.

"Melva don't shake," Loretta said, her eyes triumphant

with her knowledge. She had returned to the bar to pull three draft beers. "Hurts the bones in her hands." She winked at Donnie Ray, as if expecting confirmation.

Jaybird leaned sideways toward Donnie Ray. "Fancies hisself a ladies man, Ben does," he whispered. "He'll be back sooner than later, you'll see."

Ben laid his hand on Rosa Linda's shoulder, and she rolled it off. "I'll be back in a couple days," he said, "to see how you're doing, my friend."

"What'd I tell you?" Jaybird whispered to Donnie Ray.

"Better you should worry about your family," Rosa Linda said.

One of the customers at the front dropped some coins into the jukebox, and Donnie Ray could no longer overhear Melva's conversation with the girl. Good, he thought. He couldn't believe he'd been pulled into eavesdropping.

Within minutes, Loretta sat the bag with his to-go order on the counter. "I wrapped you a hunk of cornbread. Still piping hot," she said, and winked.

Donnie Ray turned to leave when the girl stopped next to him. Her earthy scent whispered beneath a cloud of flowery perfume.

She lifted her chin. "What? Do you think you know me or something?" the girl said, a challenge in her voice that he didn't understand.

For a second he was taken aback. Finally, he said, "No."

"Oh, you were staring so much I thought maybe you had something on your mind."

She held his gaze. She'd outlined her hazel eyes in black, and her eyelashes were long and spiky with mascara. Too much perfume, too much make-up. With all her natural beauty, what did she have to cover up?

"Well, OK then," she said, when he didn't respond. She smiled, her dimples softening her face. She rolled her tongue inside her cheek, dislodging a wad of gum. She turned away with a pop-snap.

Christ, Donnie Ray thought, she was nothing but a kid.

CHAPTER FIVE

"Too old for you, missy — he's got to be thirty if he's a day," Melva said, "and double that in experience." She motioned for Rosa Linda to follow her to the kitchen.

"So you know him?" Rosa Linda said.

"Donnie Ray Camper's his name, working temporary next door at Powers. He's a moody one, all charm one minute, next thing he keeps to himself, can't get a word out of him."

Melva turned a stiff neck to look up at Rosa Linda. "Let's get something straight right here and now. I'm not putting up with some man-crazy bobby-soxer."

Bobby-soxer? Rosa Linda's lips twisted to one side with her repressed smile. "No, Ma'am," she said. "I'm just interested in people, that's all. I did some acting in high school, and our teacher used to tell us we needed to observe others. You know, so we could really get into their heads."

Melva's expression was skeptical, so Rosa Linda added, "I'm a people watcher. That's it. I'm not interested in what's-his-name."

Donnie Ray had been trying to hide his obvious interest in Rosa Linda, making her suspicious at first. She had studied him in return to see if she recognized him as one of Cisco's friends or workers. She'd seen Enon's car turn off miles back, so she was certain — well, almost — that he was back on the highway to Chicago. But maybe Cisco had not believed, after all, that she'd left for New York and had sent someone to bring her back? But based on what Melva had said, Donnie Ray wasn't involved with Cisco.

"Acting," Melva said. Good thing you dropped that after you graduated. That's no job for a serious person. Well, come on, don't just stand there if you want me to show you around."

Rosa Linda held open the kitchen door for Melva. At the table, the old woman's voice had been deep and full of authority, a person accustomed to having her way, so Rosa Linda had expected a taller woman. But when Melva stood, the top of her cap of layered curls, the color of pale lemonade and the texture of spun sugar, barely reached Rosa Linda's chin. Melva's smock hung loose and boxy over her angular frame, and when she walked, she favored one side, causing her stooped shoulders to tilt like a weighted seesaw.

Rosa Linda would lay low with the Kopps for a while, see how things went. Donnie Ray sounded interesting. Not boring. Her nearness had turned his breathing uneven, despite his stone face. And he was handsome like the drawings of the romantic heroes in the graphic novels her mother devoured. More than his face, his hands made Rosa Linda's heart linger, bruised with scarred knuckles. The hands of a street fighter. More than once, she'd had "heartbreaker" thrown in her face, but she didn't have to worry about hurting this guy. He had faraway eyes. And her heart was safe because she'd dump him before he knew what happened. No man would have the opportunity to throw her away like so many of her relatives had. No attachments for her. Keep looking forward. Run, Rosa Linda, run.

For the moment, though, she had bigger issues to think about. The day had gone crazy on her — and the sun hadn't yet set.

"Got somebody for you to meet, Geneva," Melva said, inside the kitchen. As Melva waved in the direction of the tall, rectangular slab of a woman standing at the stove, the diamond on Melva's right ring finger caught the light, a broken rainbow of colors. The stone on her left hand was equal in size and brilliance to this one. Rosa Linda's Aunt Sylvia was forever bragging that her husband had bought her a full carat engagement ring, but each of Melva's rings was at least twice as large. The diamonds in her ears were a little smaller but heavy enough to stretch the old woman's flabby earlobes. Wasn't she afraid of being robbed?

Geneva glanced over one beefy shoulder. She nodded and returned to her stirring, head pulled back slightly to avoid the steam wafting up from the pot.

"Geneva's not bad once you get to know her better, which you might just do, *if*" — she emphasized the word and paused to give it effect before repeating it — "*if* me and Edward decide to keep you on."

"And me," Rosa Linda said, "*if* I think it's the right position for me."

Melva grunted.

"I don't need no extra help," Geneva said, staring into her soup. "Bob's got the pots and pans detail. Any more in here's a crowd."

"For chrissakes, don't get your bloomers in a twist," Melva said. "Nobody's going to interfere with your kitchen." She pointed to the man standing at the dishwasher. "Bob," she said, introducing him. "Hard worker, but don't give him complicated instructions, or he'll get frustrated."

Bob blushed. Small, round, and soft, he was middle-aged but had the sweetly sly smile of a mischievous child. "My mom named me after Bob Mitchum," he said, his face reddening even more until the color blended with his already ruddy cheeks. "He's a movie star."

"You wouldn't know him," Melva said to Rosa Linda. "From the forties and fifties."

"I do know," Rosa Linda said. "I used to watch the AMC movie channel with my nana. Mitchum was one of her all-time favorites."

"Now, where did you say she lives?" Melva squinted.

"I didn't, but she *was* born in Texas before she married my grandfather and went to live in Arizona. They're both dead now."

"That's right," Melva said, "you don't have nobody."

Rosa Linda's head ached from exhaustion, and she couldn't remember exactly what she or that silly Ben had said, so she said nothing and smiled.

Melva motioned for Rosa Linda to follow across the kitchen to an inside door, feet from the stove. "Here's the way to my castle," Melva said. "That's Sugar yapping on the other side."

Melva opened the door a crack and pushed in the toe of her white nurses' shoe. "Get back," she ordered. Then in sweet baby-talk the old woman said, "Come to Mommy, Sugar," and with a grunt, she bent at the waist and opened her arms. The Chihuahua jumped and almost slipped out of Melva's grasp. Rosa Linda suspected that neither the woman nor the dog would be able to carry off the feat much longer.

"What a cutie," Rosa Linda said.

"Horse poop," Melva said. "She's got the rheumatism. Her hair's mostly gray and she's lost a good number of her teeth. Just like Mommy and Daddy, right baby?" She stuck out her mouth and chin for the dog's tongue-lick kisses.

"You like dogs?" Melva said.

"Who doesn't?" Rosa Linda said. When Mami and Papi would send her and her brother Sergio for what they called "little visits" with the relatives, she and her brother were always separated to make the visits less of a burden for the host.

When she was allowed to stay with her parents, Pelón, half coyote and half mutt, was Rosa Linda's constant companion. He sweated and farted at just the idea of being put in a car. No "little visits" for Pelón, so she was forced to leave him at the pound. Rosa Linda refused the company of dogs after Pelón. She would never be disloyal to the memory of the best friend she'd ever had. She cursed herself for loving him, for thinking she wouldn't have to leave him behind.

Rosa Linda reached out to pat Sugar's head. "Ay," she said.

The dog snarled, and she pulled back her fingers before Sugar could snap at the tips.

"It takes her a while to warm to anybody new," Melva said. "Dogs and people are no different — trust has got to be earned."

Melva informed her that Sugar had regular visits to a professional groomer, but Rosa Linda would clean up any accidents the dog might have in the apartment. "Mostly she goes outside — I usually take her but sometimes you'll need to. Now that she's old, though, she can't always wait. But like I told you, your main thing is tidying up and looking after Edward. He's not all he used to be, either. Forgets."

Rosa Linda nodded. Melva looked pretty old to her; how much older could Edward be? Maybe Melva woke up each morning, avoided the mirror, and pretended her body remained as young as her spirit. Rosa Linda liked the old woman for the possibility.

"Well, this is my castle," Melva said. She paused. "I just said that didn't I?"

"It's easy to forget things," Rosa Linda said (and thought, especially lies).

"Don't patronize me, missy."

They stepped into a carpeted hallway and, indicating the door they'd just come through, Rosa Linda said, "Is that the only door in and out of this apartment?"

"That a problem?"

"Do you keep it locked when the restaurant's closed?" Rosa Linda said.

"Of course. We've never been broken into yet. The alarm system's on the blink, but I'm talking with another company about a whole new system."

Rosa Linda was getting a choking feeling, like Melva's castle might turn into Rapunzel's tower.

"If you're through interrogating me about security . . . ." Melva waved her arm back and forth, indicating the hall. "At this end is the bathroom you'll use and the two bedrooms, kitchen's down there with a utility room and, at the far end, the living room. Not much but everything we need." The door to the bath was ajar, and a faint scent of lavender wafted out. Rosa Linda imagined herself sinking into a tubful of scented bubbles.

"Next to your bathroom," Melva said, "is the guest room, the room you'll have." She reached around the inside wall and flipped on the switch. A queen-size brass poster bed made up with a bedspread, pale lavender with a print of small bouquets of purple violets, took up much of the space. The drapes on the windows of the outside wall were of matching material. A TV sat on a chest of drawers across from the foot of the bed.

"Wow." The exclamation had slipped out. Rosa Linda didn't want Melva to think that she'd never had a nice bedroom of her own. Better dead than pitied.

"Hard work, that's what'll get you ahead," Melva said. "Me, I've worked like a dog my whole life for every damn thing I own. Well, go on in. Try out the bed. New mattress and box springs. And yes, there's a lock on the door.

"The window I want kept closed. Not much of a view. There's a small meat-processing plant down the alley. It attracts some big-ass rats of the four-legged kind. At two in the a.m. the two-legged variety get out of the bars. Some of them are pretty wild. Especially that traffic from the Peeping Tom. Sherrill keeps them in line when they're inside but once they're out, it's not his concern."

The claustrophobia wrapped tighter around Rosa Linda, like mummy sheets. She suspected that Melva, accustomed to giving orders, would expect Rosa Linda to ask before coming and going. She was her own woman now, but fate had brought her here for some reason, and she planned on sticking around. But only until she got her bearings. She would keep that window to the outside world closed — until she needed to open it.

"You ever going to let loose of that thing?" Melva pointed at the suitcase. "Put it in the closet. Up on the shelf there's a box with some wigs and another with clothes, shoes, sweaters, just odds and ends. You're welcome to them, although with that head of hair you got, I doubt you have need of the wigs. I will say that unless you got some warmer clothes packed, you're going to be thankful for the sweaters."

As they walked down the hall, Rosa Linda mentioned casually that she watched TV late at night, and since their rooms were adjacent, she wondered if that might wake up Melva or her husband? Melva told her that Edward was deaf without his hearing aids and that nothing could wake her after her sleeping pill did what she paid it to do.

Melva cast a narrowed eye at her but continued with her tour. She pointed out the kitchen, where she would expect Rosa Linda to prepare coffee and a light breakfast for the three of them.

"Help yourself to anything in the icebox or cabinets," Melva said. "Something special you want, just write it on the list stuck on the fridge door. Me and Edward take our other meals out front at my table, and you're more than welcome to join us."

In the living room, a VCR player sat below the TV in a small entertainment center, and what Rosa Linda guessed to be a hi-fi cabinet stood against one wall. Her dad preferred old vinyl to cassettes, but he had both. Glass and porcelain knick-knacks sat atop some of the furniture, but she had no idea if they were of any worth. The big painting hanging over the hi-fi seemed out of place in the tasteful beige room.

"You like that?" Melva said.

Rosa Linda was startled. She'd apparently been staring. Melva eyed her, and Rosa Linda wondered why the nervousness over a cheap picture of a bowl of fruit with untrue colors. Her nana used to buy such pictures at the Woolworth Five & Dime in Nopal. Her Uncle Tomás back in Oklahoma hid a wall safe — stuffed with cash and jewelry — behind a cheap picture of the last supper.

The top of Edward Kopp's pink dome peeked over an overstuffed reclining chair aimed at the muted TV console. The camera panned to a live audience that laughed open-mouthed at something said by a male host wearing a lot of tan pancake makeup.

Melva snatched the remote control from the side table

and switched off the TV. Edward's closed eyes fluttered, as if sensing the absence of a companion. "Huh?" His huge hand, resting on the tabletop, jerked, knocking the ashtray full of ashes and a burned-out cigar.

"Jesus H. Christ," Melva shouted. She reached in Edward's front shirt pocket and adjusted the control for his hearing aid. "Turn that blasted thing on."

Edward yawned behind his hand and pushed his chair into a sitting position. "Who's this pretty gal?" he asked. Big and aiming to please, Edward reminded Rosa Linda of Baby Huey in the comic books, but old.

"This is Rosie," Melva said. She plucked the cigar butt from the ashtray. "How many times do I have to tell you, no smoking when you're alone. You want to set yourself on fire?"

She turned to Rosa Linda. "See why I need you to keep an eye on him? Somebody's got to run the business, and I can't be everywhere at once."

"She's as cute as a bug in a rug, isn't she, Melva?" Edward said.

Sugar whined, and Melva placed her in Edward's lap. "Sugar's the only one that wants to hear your old-man sweet talk." While the dog licked Edward's face, Melva told him there were going to be some changes made. "Rosie here wants to come and stay with us. What do you say about that?" She nodded at Rosa Linda. "Tell Edward a little about yourself."

"Like what?"

Edward eyed the remote control on the table, and Melva picked it up, slid it into her smock pocket. "Nothing interesting to tell," Rosa Linda said. "I used to stay with my grandparents in Texas and Arizona. Now they're all dead." Rosa Linda didn't mention all the other little visits with relatives. Or her stay and engagement with Cisco, or the next possibility of her Aunt Bea in Chicago. (If Enon was in Chicago, so what? Easy to get lost in a big city.) Better to keep things simple.

She was about twelve the last time she'd visited Bea. One night Bea brought home a man she'd met at the corner bar. This wasn't unusual, but this time Bea forgot that Rosa Linda was sleeping on the sofa. Bea and the guy, too hot with passion to make it to the bedroom, tumbled to the living room floor, groaning and licking.

Out of the dark, they heard a surprised gasp followed by a giggle. That very night Bea called her brother and said, "This kid of yours has got to go." Bea was sure to be over that incident. Anyway, Rosa Linda was a grown woman now.

"Nothing interesting about me," Rosa Linda said to Melva. "Alone and doing my own thing." She shrugged.

"To your credit," Melva said. "That's how it was for me. Made my own damn way in this world." She dropped the cigar butt back into the ashtray and handed the glass dish to Rosa Linda. "Dole out the cigars. And watch him like a hawk when he's smoking." She pointed to the tiny black pinpoint burns on his shirt front and tie.

"I'm hired?" Rosa Linda said.

"Mind you, it's temporary until we see how it works out. I've known Kathy and Ben since they were knee high to a grasshopper, and they both vouch for you."

"Cool," Rosa Linda said.

"*Cool*, the girl says," Melva said. "You do right by us and we'll do right by you. The moment things go south, I'll pay you a week in advance, and you're out. But after a month's time and things work out, you'll get a nice raise. Agreed?"

Rosa Linda said she'd take it, and Melva said she could tell right off that she was a smart girl. "I got to get back to work," she said, her voice brusque once more. "You rest. You look bushed. And don't be cracking bubble gum out front. I never put much store in being a lady, but the sound gets on customers' nerves."

* * *

Rosa Linda bounced gently on the cushy mattresses before dropping back onto the bed, her legs bent, feet planted on the floor. Fate was strange. Here she was in the bedroom of her dreams, yet only this morning she'd been close to death. Enon and his weird eyes. And his suggesting that he and she were alike. No way, not even close. She rubbed her own eyes as if to erase the memory.

She thought of the boxes on the high shelf in the closet, and grinned. One box of clothing and one of wigs. Perfect. She loved getting in costume, becoming someone else.

In grade school she'd always been chosen to be in school plays, even though she hadn't volunteered. When she announced the news to her parents, her mother Roxana never failed to curl her mouth and turn up her nose as if Rosa Linda had just farted. And Roxana always found an excuse to not attend the play — an important errand, a headache, a broken nail. Papi stayed with Roxana. Rosa Linda always figured she'd been chosen in grade school for being pretty, nothing more. But in high school, Mr. García, the drama teacher, singled her out in the hall and invited her to try out for the school's play, insisting he could tell she had a gift for the stage. At first, she had refused.

After all, for all her parents years of striving for Roxana's stardom, her mother had found only bit parts in the movies. But Mr. García persisted, and Rosa Linda was Laura in *The Glass Menagerie*. Rosa Linda was hooked — she'd found the way to live many lives, to run from one identity to another.

High school ended — she'd promised Nana on her deathbed that she would graduate — and with it, she tried to be the mature person her parents said she had to be. "No more Nana and Tata left to spoil you," her mother said. "You're an adult now, baby girl." After graduation, Rosa Linda drifted from one job to another, staying longest at the rest home. She decided to go back to her grandparents' vacant cottage in Nopal. No more aimlessness. She would make plans for her future. But she'd met Cisco and fell into what seemed to be an easy solution.

Cisco was a good man. Lots of girls would consider her lucky to have inspired such love. But he had loved who he wanted her to be — the Madonna/housewife his mother had wished for him. The woman who would give him children and support him in his growing trucking business. It didn't matter what Rosa Linda said or did, he would not be distracted. Cisco yearned for his illusions, and she yearned for something she couldn't define.

A firm knock on the bedroom door interrupted her thoughts. Rosa Linda blinked in the dusk. Her legs cramped, and for a moment she thought she had been sleeping on the short sofa in her grandparents' tiny house in Nopal.

"You awake?" Melva called from behind the closed door.

Zombie tired, Rosa Linda went through the motions of dinner with Melva and Edward that evening, but she couldn't have said what she ate. Later, she showered (leisurely bubble bath would have to wait for another time) and unpacked. Tomorrow would be a new day.

Rosa Linda snuggled deep beneath the covers with the faint scent of lavender from the soap and lotion in Melva's — no, her — bathroom. Cisco's money, left under the lining of her suitcase, tucked deep inside the closet, gave her a warm sense of security. She would save and add to her stash before taking off, destination to be decided. Guilt nibbled at her conscience. "I promise to pay you back, Cisco," she whispered. She reached inside the neck of her T-shirt for the ojo de venado. She would kiss it to seal her oath. She remembered Enon and closed her empty hand.

Outside, the wind whistled and rattled the glass. The outside wanted in.

CHAPTER SIX

Block glass windows shielded the inside of the Bottoms Up from prying eyes — locals preferred keeping themselves to themselves. Outsiders entered the shadows and noxious cigarette smog at their own risk. Smart strangers escaped from the sudden silence and hostile stares after one quick drink (to leave sooner would be considered an insult). Those few who did stay on for a second round soon heard comments out of the darkness: Who the hell's he? What's that flukie duke want down here? Think you're better'n me? What're you looking at? Once the questions were asked directly, the visitor had stayed too long.

Tonight, like most, tales of heartache and life gone haywire blared from the jukebox. New singers like Kim Carnes with her "Bette Davis Eyes" and George Strait and his "Amarillo by Morning" were added to the old standbys. But at the Bottoms Up, loyal Holler folk stayed true to rebels Johnny Cash and Willie Nelson. Many a shot glass had been lifted in salute to the likes of Patsy Cline, Hank Williams, and Charlie Pride while on a quiet night the new classic, "Desperado," could bring patrons to their feet in respectful reverie.

Tonight, Charlie Rich's baritone asked, "Did You Happen to See the Most Beautiful Girl in the World?" and Donnie Ray thought of Rosa Linda. He hadn't returned to the restaurant since that day. He'd seen her walking by Power's three times this last week; she'd glanced in at him — or at least into the building.

She had a way of lifting her chin as if she were looking down her nose at her surroundings. Rosa Linda (he loved the sound of her name and had practiced pronouncing it in the sanctuary of his room) was the kind men fell in love with. Other men. He would not allow himself that weakness. And so, he'd avoided her, called in his orders, had Bob run them over to him. The Bottoms Up was his kingdom. Here lay no worries about Rosa Linda.

He reached for a bottle of whiskey, poured himself a shot, and downed it. The days had moved slowly this week, too much time for remembering Shayne.

"Surprise, babe." Tara tapped her car keys on the bar. "I got something for you."

He hadn't been answering his phone or taking calls at work, so he wasn't surprised to see her. "You know," he said, turning and staring meaningfully at the covered bowl on the bar, "that hash brown casserole you left on my porch was raided by a possum."

"Possums in these parts?" Tara said. "I don't believe it. There ain't no woods around here. Anyways, what am I supposed to do if you won't answer the door?" When he didn't answer, she continued. "This here," she said, "is banana pudding. Your momma tells me it's one of your favorites, so don't tell me it's not." She inched the bowl toward him with her index finger.

"I can't eat all that," he said. That pudding had commitment written all over it, yet he was almost tempted to take a taste.

"Here now," Arlie said, and sat a beer on the bar. "This one's on the house, Miss Tara."

Donnie Ray turned to washing glasses. "Tell you what, Tara," Arlie said, "Donnie Ray's busy. I'll put this up in the office fridge, and later we can all have a little."

Donnie Ray focused his attention on the customers drifting

in. For a while Tara followed him with her woebegone gaze, but when he refused to make eye contact with her, she moved toward the end of the bar. Not more than an hour had passed when her laughter, loud enough to announce what a good time she was having — caught his attention. Some guy had taken the stool next to her, his back to Donnie Ray. Tara was leaning into him, as if he were the most interesting man in the world. Good for her, he thought, maybe she'd found a better man.

"Hey, Donnie Ray," Tara yelled, and waved. "My friend here needs a drink."

The guy glanced back over his shoulder, and Donnie Ray poured himself another shot, knocked it back. There was something vaguely familiar about the stranger, but, no, he looked like a hundred other guys he passed on the street.

"Ask Arlie to get it," Donnie Ray said.

"He's busy," she said. Her new friend suddenly glanced up, stared directly at Donnie Ray. When Donnie Ray held his gaze, the stranger didn't blink.

It had been some time since anyone in the Holler had challenged Donnie Ray. He placed his shot glass in the sink. "You look like you've got something to say," he said.

"Not me. Thirsty, that's all." The stranger lowered his gaze to his empty beer glass.

"Aw, come on, Donnie Ray," Tara said. "He ain't doing you no harm. Forget it, OK? I'll find Arlie."

"Just passing though," the man said, "and that there's a fact."

"Keep passing." Donnie Ray's voice remained calm.

When the stranger stood to leave, Tara said, "Well, if he's not welcome, I'll just leave, too. You hear me now? I'm walking out that door with my new friend." She hefted her quilted purse. "You don't have a hold on me, Donnie Ray Camper."

Donnie Ray held her gaze for a moment then turned away to draw a draft for a customer.

"Problem?" Arlie said, now standing by Donnie Ray.
"Some punk."
"Tara leaving too?"
"She's free to do what she wants. What do I care?"

Arlie rested his hands on the bar, studied them for a moment. "Yeah, you're right. You're hitting the bottle kind of hard for so early in the night. Maybe pace yourself?"

"You my dad now?" Donnie Ray straightened the glasses on the tray beneath the bar.

"Nah . . . look, I'm not trying to tell you what to do, but that gal's driving me nuts, always calling, etcetera, etcetera. If you and her are finished, why don't you just cut her loose?"

Donnie Ray had been wondering about this himself, so he said nothing. Arlie held up both hands. "OK, OK, I know it's none of my business. But let her down easy, won't you? She's a good kid. I hear Tara and her mom's doing really good business at the Ladybug. And did you hear about the playground?"

"I heard," Donnie Ray said.

"But it's not all hot air like with some. That girl's organizing, getting folks all riled up. Them biddies have been burning up the phone lines calling down to City Hall. A regular shitstorm of calls." He chuckled.

"We've seen it all before."

"Not like this," Arlie said. With a cloth, he wiped circles on the bar. "She's one of us, and she's got fire in her eye."

"One of *us*. Fuck. You used to talk all big about the Holler, about preserving the neighborhood."

"Oh, I get it," Arlie said. "If the Holler's gone to hell, it's all Arlie's fault."

"You're only down here these days to make money. You lock up at night and drive back to your house with the picket fence in the goddamn suburbs. You're a traitor — make a few bucks and you can't get out of here fast enough."

"It was Lisa's idea, the kids, better schools . . . ." his words trailed away. He glanced at a customer, waiting to order. "Look, Donnie Ray, you're looking for a fight, and I'm not going to give it to you."

* * *

Business picked up as it always did on Fridays, and Donnie

Ray kept busy serving drinks, restocking booze, and watching for agitated slights, real or imagined. The regulars or semi-regulars knew him well enough to know when he meant business, so coming around the bar and giving them a cold stare usually did the trick.

Near closing, Tara returned, sidled onto a bar stool. "I forgot to tell you about Spike," she said, as if their conversation from hours ago had not been interrupted. He wanted to ignore her but was interested in the dog. Unlike people, animals could be trusted. Loyal to the end, they didn't come up with backstabbing schemes.

Spike, she said, had bruises and scratches but no broken bones or permanent injuries. "I'm going to keep him in a playpen at work. Of course," she said. "When he's OK on his own, I'll have to just run down to the apartment and check on him while I'm working. You want to come and visit him tonight?"

"Where's your fuckface boyfriend?" he said.

"Aw, now, you know he ain't my boyfriend." She sighed. "OK, so I did leave right after him. You pissed me off; I never had a mind to *be* with him. All I done was tell him I was driving down to the Southern Belle. If you want to follow me in your car, I says, why, what's the harm? He's a lost soul, wanting somebody to talk to, that's all."

"Last call," Donnie Ray said. "You want something before you leave?"

"And you know what? Down to the Belle, he mostly asked about you. Not like he was looking for a fight with you," she said quickly. She gazed into the distance, trying to find the words. "He asked if you had a girlfriend or wife. I told him no, that me and you was working on getting back together. Anyways when I got up to dance with my friend — Mary Clemmons, you know her? — why he just disappeared. He told me earlier he wasn't sticking around, says Mad River ain't been none too friendly." She pursed her lips. "Do you reckon he's gay? All them questions, I mean."

Donnie Ray stared at the wall clock. "It's been a long night."

Tara tossed her hair off her shoulder. "Anyways, I got a

meeting tomorrow with my committee about that playground." She swung her purse and slapped it back on the bar. "Oh, uh, well, I thought I should tell you. I seen your mom. She came into the Belle late with her new boyfriend."

"Last call," Donnie Ray said. He didn't realize he was grinding his teeth until pain shot through his jaw.

"She needs you, Donnie Ray. The anniversary of Shayne's death . . . it's getting to her."

"We're closed," Donnie Ray said.

CHAPTER SEVEN

After two weeks at the restaurant, Rosa Linda had come to understand Melva's philosophy. "Stop spinning that wheel of fortune you're always talking about," she advised over and over, "and think about what it is you want from life. Put a name to it, dammit, and go for it." Rosa Linda wasn't certain if Melva repeated it so often because she wanted to bring home her message or if Melva simply didn't remember what she'd said. Maybe a bit of both.

"Yes, ma'am," Melva would say, "without a clear plan — and hard work — I never would've amounted to a hill of beans. Neither will you. Mark my words, missy. You've got the gumption, now get the job done." Gumption was one of Melva's favorite words.

"I see," Rosa Linda might mumble. Melva didn't seem perturbed by her lack of enthusiasm. After all, Melva hadn't gotten to where she was by giving up.

And hadn't Melva persuaded Rosa Linda just last night about the pies? She was having dinner with Edward and Melva, as usual at the back table in the restaurant; Rosa Linda enjoying a hamburger and fries while the Kopps had the daily special.

Melva glanced up from the plate of cabbage rolls and

mashed potatoes (half portions for her) and said to Rosa Linda, "You need to get up at dawn tomorrow."

"Somebody's going to be mother's little helper," Edward said.

"I'm telling this," Melva said.

Edward swallowed his chuckle with a gulp of iced tea. He glanced at Rosa Linda, tapped the side of his nose with his forefinger. This now familiar gesture signaled to Rosa Linda that something was being said or done to which she should pay close attention.

"So . . . why am I getting up early?" Rosa Linda asked and dragged a French fry through the puddle of Tabasco sauce she'd poured on her plate. Melva had mentioned the pies before, so Rosa Linda knew where she was going with the comment, but Melva was telling this, after all.

"I don't know how you eat so much of that shit," Melva said, shaking her head. "Why you can't use ketchup like everybody else, I'll never know."

"That's the way we do it where I come from."

"You're here now, so better get used to our ways."

"Hmm." Rosa Linda shook a larger puddle of Tabasco onto her plate.

"You mind looking at me when I'm talking?" Melva's voice rose at the end as if it were a question, but Rosa Linda understood that it was only Melva's bow to good manners. She let a French fry fall dramatically from her hand into the hot sauce.

"You seemed to have settled in just fine," Melva said. "Got your schedule down. I imagine you're ready to switch things up a bit."

So far Rosa Linda had it pretty easy. She was always up on time, brewed coffee and toasted English muffins in the apartment kitchen, placed a banana next to Edward's plate for the added potassium his doctor recommended. She had breakfast with the couple, and while they lingered over their second cup of coffee Rosa Linda laid out Edward's clothes for the day and made certain that he changed into them. If she didn't, he'd cram the clean shirt under the bed and put back on the stained one. Edward said he could remember back in the day when changing, like taking a shower, wasn't required daily.

"Back in the good old days," Melva would tell him, "you weren't burning your shirts with cigars or catching crumbs on that big gut of yours."

At first, Rosa Linda didn't really get why Melva was so strict about his appearance. Mostly he watched his game shows on TV with Rosa Linda, and she laughed at his corny jokes (she preferred corny ones herself) during the commercial breaks. She kept him out of trouble, kept track of his cigars and made certain he didn't turn off his hearing aid when Melva joined them. But Melva also insisted he come out to the front to speak with the customers, and she told Rosa Linda that he had to look sharp. "If a man looks good," Melva said, "he'll feel good, like he's still somebody."

Rosa Linda nodded. If something should happen to Melva, she worried about what might happen to the old man.

"As you know," Melva said, pushing her half-full plate away and reaching for a cigarette, "tomorrow's my day for pie baking. We put on our aprons and get our hands dirty, so set your alarm. You're joining me for your first lesson."

"OK," Rosa Linda said. What the hell? It wouldn't hurt her, and the old lady's face was shining like the beacon of a lighthouse. Now that Melva and Edward were comfortable with her, Friday night, once they were asleep, she would slip out her bedroom window and find some real excitement. She could tell Melva she was going out, but the old lady might stay up waiting for her to return and hassle her about her appearance or behavior. When she first arrived in Mad River, she'd welcomed the comfort and safety of a nest. All was quiet. Now the nest was beginning to itch.

"You'll do it, then?" Melva asked.

"Sure," Rosa Linda said, "why not?"

"Why, ain't this a hoot," Loretta said. She stood sentry behind the bar and in front of Jaybird. "Hear that, Jaybird?"

"How's that, Retta?" Melva cocked her head to one side.

Jaybird, not taking his eyes from the television screen,

mumbled, "Uh-oh." Edward's fingers slipped into his shirt pocket.

"Next thing you know," Loretta said, still staring pointedly at the side of Jaybird's head, "Melva'll be taking our little princess up to the Crown of Glory with her for a shampoo and set."

"Loretta, you got something to say, spit it out." Melva tilted her head back as far as her stiff neck allowed and blew a ring of smoke. She closed one eye and watched Loretta through the hazy cloud.

"Far be it from me to tell you anything, Melva," Loretta said. She whipped a damp cloth from beneath the counter, rubbed circles on the bar. "Mind you, some might think it a tad strange that after all these years of not inviting me to help with them pies — me, your trusted friend that's proven herself to you time and time again, don't you know — and then, well . . . some little nobody just drops in here out of nowhere far's I can tell, and you start treating her like she's your kin?" She folded the cloth in her hand, giving herself time to catch her breath.

Rosa Linda chewed her last bite of hamburger. Loretta had decided to hate her the moment she walked in through that kitchen door, and no matter how nice Rosa Linda tried to be, Loretta seemed convinced she was intent on taking her position as Melva's right-hand woman.

More than once, Rosa Linda had overheard Loretta complaining to Melva that something was off about that girl and no good would come of her sticking around. Now, Rosa Linda sat back and listened, almost hypnotized by how the light bounced off Melva's diamonds.

Melva ground out the cigarette she'd just lit. "Retta, since when," she said, measuring her words, "have you ever been interested in helping with those pies? You've always been too busy doing this or that. You got plenty of family to worry about." Loretta opened her mouth, and Melva held up her hand to stop her. "I'm old, and I decided — because by God, I'm Melva Kopp, and I run this place. I want Rosie to help me. Period."

Melva snapped open her newspaper. "Rosie, you know the plan."

"Sure," Rosa Linda said. She had no interest in baking or cooking or any of the other homemaking chores that she'd been taught along the way. These skills only led to serving others who soon took all that work for granted — and then demanded more. Her nana was forever cleaning and cooking. When relatives came to visit, they sat at the kitchen table, waiting for Nana to serve flour tortillas hot off the griddle; Rosa Linda had other ideas for her future. Unlike her grandmother, she was paid cash for the household chores she completed, a temporary means to an end.

*   *   *

"You ought to comb your hair like that all the time," Melva said, when Rosa Linda shuffled, not quite awake, into the restaurant kitchen. "First choice is to lop off that mess but barring that the braids will do. Looks like a little Swiss gal."

"Like Frida Kahlo." Rosa Linda had pinned her braids in a crown atop her head in the style of the artist.

"Who?" Melva asked but without waiting for an answer shoved a long white apron at Rosa Linda. "Here," she said, "put this on."

"She's a famous Mexican artist, a strong woman, like me — like you."

Melva barked a laugh. "More power to her. If us gals don't learn to do for ourselves, who will?"

"But she took too much shit off a man in the name of love," Rosa Linda said. "That's not me." She'd had a dream about herself and Cisco last night, getting married. He walked into the church, not handsome like a Mexican movie cowboy but with the frog-face of Diego Rivera, Frida's philandering husband. When she woke up, she braided her hair in support of Frida.

"Learn how to make and sell a product," Melva said, "and you won't need to take anything off of any-damn-body.

Now, let's get to work." She had already tied on her own apron, strings wrapped around her narrow midriff and tied in the front.

Leaning one hip against the counter, Melva placed her finger against her pursed mouth, vertical smoker's lines deepening above and below her lips, and tapped. "Shit," she said, and enumerated the ingredients before her: apples, lemons, frozen cherries, bananas, eggs, milk, flour, spices, brown and white sugar, shortening.

"What's wrong?" Rosa Linda said around a yawn.

"This getting old business is for the birds." Melva shook her head. "Something's missing, but what?" She pursed her lips tighter, and the lines around her lips deepened. Melva's finger lifted, pointed upwards in an *aha!* gesture. "Peanut butter. All these years I've been doing this, now I forget peanut butter?"

She angled a look at Rosa Linda. "You'll find out one of these days. And that day'll come sooner than you think. Youth disappears in the blink of an eye." She snapped her fingers inches from Rosa Linda's nose. "Better start now on making money, securing that future."

"I've still got time before I have to get serious," Rosa Linda said. She knew the old lady was right, had known it when she'd gone to Nana's vacant house to think out her future. But then came Cisco. Why did she get involved with him? Why was she always messing things up?

"OK enough of this horse poop," Melva said. "Get me one of those big jars of peanut butter from the basement. Over in the far right-hand corner. You know, where those metal shelves are?"

Rosa Linda nodded. She'd gone over every inch of the restaurant and basement while Melva and Edward slept. Any cubbyholes she'd missed were those locked up with the keys Melva kept in her pocket during the day and on a bedside table at night. One morning, she'd forgotten them and cursed about having to return to the apartment. Rosa Linda had offered to retrieve them for her and picked them off the table where Melva told her they'd be. By this time, she had already peeked under the painting hanging in the living room and just as she suspected, found a wall safe beneath. Before seeing the safe, she'd hoped that somehow it would be locked with one of the accessible keys on Melva's pocket rings. But no, it was a combination lock.

Rosa Linda often pressed an inverted drinking glass to the wall between her bedroom and the Kopps'; one night she heard Edward laugh and chide Melva for forgetting to put her earrings away in the safe. Melva had answered that she was too tired to go back to the safe, that she'd keep them close to her.

Now Rosa Linda headed toward the basement door at the end of the kitchen, only feet from the outside door. It swung open, almost hitting her. "Ay, sorry," Rosa Linda said, apologizing even though she was the one hit.

Loretta patted her freshly salon-styled hair. "Glad to see that mop's out of your eyes," she said, then glanced around Rosa Linda into the kitchen. "Melva?" she called out.

"I was out this way, had to stop over to the daughter's to pick up some stuff, and thought I'd pop in. Baking pies?"

"Jesus H. Christ," Melva said. "Do not start on that again."

Rosa Linda shut the basement door behind her. She clomped down the steps as loudly and quickly as she could, grabbed a gallon jar of peanut butter, kitty-toed to the top of the stairs, and pressed her ear against the door.

"Like it or not," Loretta said, her voice growing fainter as she moved deeper into the kitchen, "it'll behoove you to hear me out."

"Don't have time for chit chat," Melva said. Rosa Linda had no trouble hearing her booming voice. "Got to get these pies done, so Edward can get me to my beauty appointment on time. As you well know."

Rosa Linda had learned a lot over the years by pressing her ear to doors and walls. For example, her parents' private discussions, usually about some new disappointment regarding her mother's career, or about Rosa Linda and how she'd been an unwelcome surprise that left her mother with stretch marks that pretty much ruined her chance at becoming Hollywood's next big sex symbol. After a while, Rosa Linda came to hear many reasons for her mother's failure to rise above bit parts.

Loretta had lowered her voice again, and Rosa Linda couldn't make out what she was saying. But the urgency of her whispers emphasized the sibilants, creating a hissing, snakelike sound.

Melva's crepe-soled work shoes squished across the kitchen. If she came too close, Rosa Linda was prepared to open the door, as if she'd just made it up the stairs.

"Let me get this straight," Melva said, "you're interrupting my work to tell me that I need to watch out?" The refrigerator opened, and Melva's voice muffled slightly. "If I stopped what I was doing every time somebody acted strange around here, I wouldn't get a goddamn thing done."

"I know," Loretta said, her voice coming closer, "how important those diamonds are to you. You've worked like a dog your whole life to get them. And mind, bought them yourself, never asked a man—"

"OK," Melva snapped, cutting her off, "that'll do for the boot licking. What's your proof?"

That viejita didn't take it from anybody, a real chingona. But what was Loretta complaining about this time? Rosa Linda pressed her ear more firmly against the wooden panel.

"Why else would a girl like her be taking this kind of work?" Loretta said. "She's after something."

"That's your proof?"

"All I'm saying is she's been eyeballing those rocks of yours since that first day she come here and last night, why, she was staring at them like she was downright hypnotized."

"Everybody ogles my diamonds. Including you. That makes you a thief?"

"I — I can't believe you just said that," Loretta stammered.

"You've had your say, now drop it." Melva's raspy voice sparked.

Rosa Linda's heart pounded, the steady boom-boom of a bass drum in her ears. Had she really been so obvious?

"Do as you will," Loretta said. After the door closed, Rosa Linda counted to ten and stepped out of the basement.

Melva held up a pitcher of cold water from the refrigerator, her bony wrist wobbling from its weight. "Here," she said to Rosa Linda, "take this and that peanut butter to the counter. Let's see if we can't get some pies made."

"Starting with the crust," Melva said. "We'll make it first then put it into the ice box to get nice and cold — that's the secret to a flaky crust, and of course lard. Meanwhile we get on to making the fillings. See? Plan your time. When you set out on a journey, you got to know your destination and the steps along the way to get you there."

"Hmm."

Melva slipped off her rings, dropped them into a cup on a ledge over the counter. Her movements were slow and calculated. Rosa Linda touched each ingredient on the counter, as if memorizing them, making a point of not paying attention to Melva's actions.

"You know, everybody's got to eat," Melva said. She dug the pastry blender into the lard and flour, paused, and handed the tool to Rosa Linda. "Your turn."

As Rosa Linda cut the fat through the dough, Melva said, "Thing is, not everybody can cook — or has the inclination. A body who knows what she's doing in the kitchen can make a go of it anywhere. Us gals have to learn our worth."

Like Melva, Nana had tried hard to teach Rosa Linda domestic skills, but she'd taken her training even further and taught her how to sew. Nana gave her a doll and taught her how to create her own patterns. She pinned tiny pieces of paper to the material for sleeves, bodices, and collars, sewing them together on her Mighty Girl Sewing Machine. Rosa Linda sewed on lopsided sleeves and bagging waistlines. Nana instructed her on the perfect flour tortilla, a stretchy and nearly transparent circle. Rosa Linda's were oblong and brittle. "Oh, well," Nana would say, and laugh. Then they'd belt out one of Miguel Aceves Mejia's rancheras.

"You ever think of running a restaurant?" Melva said.

"Not really," Rosa Linda said. At least Melva wasn't suggesting that she find a good man and get married.

"I got my start," Melva said, "slapping together cold sandwiches, lunch meat and cheese on store-bought loaf bread. That and nickel beer — alcohol's where you'll make your profits. I was like you with nobody to help start me off. My tables and chairs were mismatched things. That's all I needed. That and lots of elbow grease. People need nourishment of the body but, hell, there's more to it. You think all those working men couldn't have made a damn sandwich for themselves? Or stocked up some beer in their ice boxes? I ask you, what brings them in?"

"They don't want to eat alone?"

Melva cackled. "Everybody's looking for a little company, even those who mostly want to be alone. Mind you, your real profits are in the booze, but the other stuff keeps them coming too."

Melva had her stir in a bit of water, and when Rosa Linda instinctively moved to knead as she would for tortilla dough, Melva shot out a hand to stop her. "Hell, girl, you want pie dough or shoe leather? Roll it in a ball and take it to the refrigerator to chill."

Rosa Linda turned to walk away with the cloth-covered bowl without even a glance at the cup on the shelf. Maybe it wasn't a test of her honesty. Maybe the old woman really would forget all about those rings. The earrings were still hanging on Melva's lobes as low as overripe fruit, but the rings alone would bring plenty. If she went to Chicago, she could get an apartment of her own.

"Earth to Rosie." Melva clapped her hands.

"Sorry, I guess I'm still a little sleepy," Rosa Linda said.

Melva instructed her to squeeze a little lemon juice on the apples to keep them from browning, and added, as if it were a minor yet related detail, "You taking precautions to make sure you don't get pregnant?"

Rosa Linda stared at the old woman. Both her grandmothers had avoided the subject, as if sex, to their knowledge, had not yet been invented. Even her mother, who always wore clothes to accentuate her breasts, hips, and behind, didn't discuss sex with Rosa Linda. The few times Roxana had taken Rosa Linda shopping for school clothes, she picked out articles that covered as much as possible, making Rosa Linda look like a Puritan. When Rosa Linda got to be a teen, her mother continued to want her daughter to wear dresses with Peter Pan collars and Mary Jane shoes.

"Don't look so shocked. You think I don't remember what it's like to be young with all the juices flowing?" Melva said. "I didn't think about it back then, either — and before you know it I was in some filthy back alley getting business taken care of."

Melva told her she'd be glad to make an appointment for her with a gynecologist and take some preventative measures. "We don't want you going through what I had to."

"We'll see," Rosa Linda said. And what was with this "we" business?

*   *   *

Powers Pool Hall had a bar running along the left-hand wall with three pool tables in the center of the small room. At the back right corner of the room, sat a stool and a high table, and a calendar with Vargas-style pin-ups hanging on the wall behind. A stack of paperbacks, sketchbook, and pencils waited on the table for Donnie Ray during lulls in business.

Donnie Ray glanced at the wall clock. Bob was late with his phone-ordered grilled ham and cheese sandwich and chili today. He didn't feel like waiting behind the bar, getting drawn into the bullshit being slung by Leland and two old-timers who had been nursing the same beers for the past fifteen minutes.

Leland, who occasionally helped at Bottoms Up, had discovered where Donnie Ray was temporarily working and started popping in, convinced that his friend needed the company. Donnie Ray had been a year ahead of Leland in school, and they'd first met on the playground. A ring of boys at the far edge were hooting and shouting "Gimp." Like some of the other kids, Donnie Ray ran over to watch. He'd seen Leland around the neighborhood, knew about his arm, withered by polio. When he saw Leland get punched then struggle back to his feet, snot and blood pouring from his nose yet determined to go down fighting, Donnie Ray jumped in. He was all for letting a man fight his own battles if the fight was even. Leland had followed him around ever since.

When the bar conversation deteriorated to digestive problems, Donnie Ray threw up his hands in an I-give-up gesture and walked out from behind the bar to the far pool table by the plate glass window. "What do you say, Donnie Ray?" one of the old men called out.

Donnie Ray gathered the balls on the table, said, "You guys figure it out. I got work to do." It was his mom and Dee that had his nerves jangling, not the lonely old guys at the bar, and he didn't want to take it out on them.

Charlotte and Dee had dropped in at Bottoms Up last night and started harping on Shayne's memorial again. For a year they'd tiptoed around the subject, but they were adamant about having a memorial and that he would be involved. His mother counted on him. Before Shayne died, Donnie Ray had thought his heart was so hardened by life and its disappointments that nothing could affect him. He hadn't figured on Shayne getting himself killed.

He'd been the one who had arranged for Shayne's viewing and funeral, but in the end, he hadn't been able to view Shayne's coffin, and at the burial, he stood tombstones away from the other mourners. He'd slipped around a massive oak and vomited booze and bile until he expected his insides to come up. He couldn't even say Shayne's name out loud, not unless he was talking in his sleep.

While Charlotte and Dee were speaking to him at the bar, he'd made constant excuses to fill orders or clean up or drop more quarters in the jukebox. When they suggested dinner on Sunday, he agreed quickly. Anything to get them out. Yes, he told them, he promised to show up.

He finished racking the balls, glanced around for something else to do, but earlier he'd already stocked the bar, laid out the chalk, straightened the cue sticks.

He stepped to the picture window and closed his eyes. Without warning, Fred Dunlap's face appeared in his thoughts, on the inside of his eyelids. If the son of a bitch had ever come down to the Holler, he wouldn't have left alive. Donnie Ray could have killed him as easily as Dunlap had murdered Shayne. No one in the Holler would have seen or heard a damn thing — they never did when one of their own had business to take care of. But Dunlap was too smart to come slumming to the Holler again the way he'd done the night he'd met Dee and charmed her with his natty suit and his bulging wallet.

And Tim Elkins. Another motherfucker he'd like to stomp. The reporter for the *Mad River Daily* had written the initial article on Shayne's death. What was left of Donnie Ray's heart had split wide open when he had read the headline: "Successful Businessman Kills High School Dropout in Self Defense."

Dee had been so proud of her muckety-muck boyfriend, his big house with the swimming pool. Shayne belonged to the Holler; he should have stayed home.

Sweat rolled down Donnie Ray's face. He wanted to forget and yet was terrified that he might. With the back of his hand, he swiped at the sweat stinging his eyes. When he opened them, the girl from Melva's stood on the other side of the window. Her eyes were wide with an expression he couldn't quite read. She stared at him through the smudged glass.

A breeze blew stray strands of the girl's braided hair across her face, and she pulled them back with her fingers. He wondered how long that thick mass of hair would be if set free. He fixed the image of her face in his memory. He could sketch people from a picture, but when he tried to capture someone from life, he failed.

She held up a brown paper bag.

The buzz of conversation from behind him had stopped.

"Hi," Rosa Linda said, and stepped through the doorway. No one answered, but she smiled, revealing a slight overbite, the edges of two front teeth peeping between her full lips.

"Lunch." She swung the bag slowly.

"Where's Bob?" Donnie Ray asked.

"I'm headed to the shopping center," she said, "and, like, you're on my way."

She motioned with her chin in the direction of the high table. "Should I put it there?"

Donnie Ray followed her, aware of the three pairs of eyes watching from the bar.

"Hmm," she said, glancing at the stack of books. "Buffalo soldiers? What a coincidence. They used to have a soldier's camp in a town not far from where I lived. There's nothing there now, not even a plaque, but I've stood right where it used to be. The viejos say the ghosts of some of the soldiers are still there. In fact, my great grandfather was a buffalo soldier."

"Yeah?" Donnie Ray asked and studied her face for African influence. He'd already finished reading the book but brought it to leaf through the photos again. The black soldiers intrigued him. History hadn't said that much about them. At least he hadn't known about them.

"Camp Little," she said, "on the border. The buffalo soldiers were stationed there. Over by where my grandparents lived."

"What's a buffalo soldier?" Leland said. He'd walked over from the bar and stood next to them.

"U.S. Cavalry," Rosa Linda said.

"How about you stop breathing down my neck," Donnie Ray said to Leland, and he mumbled that he was just trying to make conversation and shuffled away.

"Do you even remember me?" the girl said. "Rosa Linda? From Melva's?"

"I remember," Donnie Ray said. He took the hand she offered, but she quickly slipped it from his grasp. He was surprised by the warmth and softness of her hand.

"She could come to the Bottoms Up tonight," Leland called out from the bar.

"Bottoms Up?" she said.

"Thanks for the lunch." Donnie Ray pulled his wallet out.

"Where's this Bottoms Up?" she asked.

"Take the Logan Avenue bus toward downtown," Leland said. "Get off—"

"Not for you," Donnie Ray said to Rosa Linda.

"No?" She shrugged. "Maybe you can lend me that book when you're finished?"

"I just started reading it," he said, and laid his hand on it as if it were the Bible.

She ran a finger across the cover, barely brushing the edge of Donnie Ray's hand.

"Hmm," she hummed.

He followed her to the door and braced himself against the door jamb, watching her, wanting her to leave but having difficulty pulling away. His flesh still tingled where she'd touched him.

She held her head high as she walked away, light on her feet like a dancer. She possessed a natural grace, but he recognized poor trying to make do: the flowers on her sundress at first glance pink, were really a faded red; the rundown heels on her flats, cracks in the black patent leather.

Donnie Ray turned to go back inside, but something across the street stopped him. The sun bounced off a shiny surface across the street behind the overgrown bushes and near the dumpster to one side of the Shipwreck. More than once, he'd spotted rats, fat, and daylight-brazen, scampering in and out of the trash. Donnie Ray shaded his eyes to the glare, shifting to one side to get a better view. It appeared to be the windshield of a car. If the driver was dumping trash, he was taking his time.

"Jailbait?" Leland whispered behind Donnie Ray.

Donnie Ray whirled around. "Damn it, Leland. Do not sneak up on a man. That shit's going to get you killed one of these days." Donnie Ray lowered his fist. "And get your mind out of the gutter. It's not like that. She's a nice kid. Nothing more to it."

When Donnie Ray had first arrived at Powers, he had resented the new space, the new faces, but slowly he realized with surprise that he could enjoy the near anonymity. He hadn't brought a detailed history with him, and none of them had histories as far as he was concerned. The people in Powers and Melva's expected little from him, he less from them. But it hadn't been long before the Holler, in the shape of Leland, had found Donnie Ray. Maybe Arlie had the right idea when he'd gone far enough to leave the Holler behind him.

CHAPTER EIGHT

Rosa Linda felt Donnie Ray's robin-egg-blue eyes on her back. She didn't need to go to the strip mall, but she didn't want him to think she'd made a special trip outside just to deliver his lunch. What was his deal anyway? All she wanted was someone to hang out with. So far, she liked being with the Kopps; they reminded her of her grandparents. But she couldn't hang out with grandparent types.

The strip had interested her at first, but she'd been there several times and had visited each store more than once: a grocery market (Melva did all the food shopping), a bank (not for her — better keep her savings where she could get to them fast), a laundromat (the Kopps had better machines and no hitchhiking cockroaches), an Elder-Beerman department store (not for her budget). The thrift store, as big as a warehouse, had been like finding a treasure chest. She'd bought a few items with ideas for outfit combinations that, with the help of Melva's wigs, would turn her into completely different characters.

She had hoped for some promising conversation with Donnie Ray, but he didn't want to play along. A strange sensation waved over her, as if someone were watching her. Maybe Donnie Ray had returned to the doorway of the Powers now that she was in the distance. She flipped a braid over her shoulder. She would turn full around and let him see she'd caught him staring.

The car, brown and heavy, was behind several cars, keeping its distance. When she stopped and stared at it, the driver made a sudden and sharp turn into a parking lot. She hadn't seen his face, but she recognized the car. She wanted to return to Melva's, but she'd have to pass the car. Only yards ahead of her, railroad tracks cut across the road like a scar on Frankenstein's monster. To the left, tracks disappeared into a dense wooded area, a reminder of the lush vegetation that had once dominated the area.

Adrenaline pumped. Run, Rosa Linda, run. Her feet pounded toward the woods. She'd hide where the car couldn't go. She prayed Enon wouldn't risk jumping out of the car and chasing her; she'd already learned that witnesses scared him off. She glanced over her shoulder. The car remained idling in the lot. The edge of the woods, only a few feet away, held dark promise.

She crashed into the thicket, catching her sleeve on blackberry thorns. If he'd waited for the other cars to drive on by, he might now be coming for her on foot. She had to put as much distance as possible between them. She yanked at the material until it tore away from the brambles. She stumbled backward. She couldn't catch her balance and rolled down a hill. A fallen tree stopped her from tumbling into the puddled creek bed, nearly dried out from lack of rain. She stayed on the ground even though something sharp poked her in the back. She listened. Cars whooshed by on the other side of the trees, but no one turned in. She sat up and brushed the small sticks and leaves from her clothing. From behind her and around the creek's bend, faint voices traveled.

Maybe kids playing Robin Hood, or berry pickers (Melva had told her the woods were full of them) or maybe workers. Curious, she crept slowly toward their voices. She hunched behind a tree, held her breath. Three men sat on the ground, one lit a rolled cigarette and passed it around. The skunk smell of cheap pot wafted in the air. She stepped backward, and a branch snapped beneath her foot.

"We got company," the shortest one said, standing.

One man crooked his finger, wiggled it, gesturing for her to join them. She turned and scrambled back up the hill. When she reached the top, she gave him the finger and headed toward the tracks.

The men guffawed, but there were no footsteps tramping behind her. "Just trying to be friendly, sweetheart," one shouted at her back.

When she made it to the crest of the hill, she paused to catch her breath and turned to make certain no one followed her. The men were trudging back to the woods, and one turned to look up the hill.

"Come on down, Pocahontas," he called to her, "smoke the peace pipe with us."

She waggled her braids at him, and shouted, "Not even in your dreams, gentlemen." He laughed and, waving her away, slipped back into the shadows with his friends.

At the edge of the woods, she peered up the street toward the lot. The car was gone. She looked in the other direction. No sign of the old brown car. She was picturing the car in her mind when a detail came back to her. Enon's plates were from Florida; she'd noticed that when she'd first walked toward his car with her suitcase. The car she'd spotted today didn't have Florida license plates. When he'd dropped back from the car in front of him, she'd gotten a glimpse of his plates. They were white and red. What a fool she'd been. The driver was probably looking for an address, pulled over to check a map, or something. It's not like there weren't hundreds, thousands of cars that looked like Enon's. She ran up the street, twirling, shouting, for no reason in particular "¡Ajúa!"

Rosa Linda left the humid outside and entered the coolness of Melva's. She paused. Once her eyes dark-adapted, she searched the room for Enon. Por si acaso, just in case.

"Here I am, pretty gal," Jaybird called out from the far end of the bar. "You looking for me?"

"Hmmph." Loretta stood at the end of the bar, one elbow propped on the edge. "At her age, I looked every bit as good."

"How about," Jaybird said, "I buy you two beauties at Bubble-Up?"

"Not at the bar, you're not," Loretta said. "She ain't twenty-one. Leastways, I don't think she is. I mean, what do we really know about her?"

"Law still says eighteen, don't it?" Jaybird said.

"Melva don't like her royal highness sitting at the bar. Reckons Miss High and Mighty is suited for finer things."

Jaybird slid off the stool. "I don't guess it'll hurt me none to scoot away from the bar this once."

"Can't stay long," Rosa Linda said, taking the chair he pulled out for her at the closest table. She didn't have the patience for Loretta's insecurity today; she had other things on her mind. What she needed was bus information and directions to the Bottoms Up. From what Leland had said before Donnie Ray shut him up, she started out on the bus line, but did it go close enough to the bar? One way or the other, she had to get away for a bit or she'd go mad.

Loretta smacked the bottom of the glass onto the table, causing the fizzy soda to splash out. "I hear you took over Donnie Ray's lunch. Well, let me tell you something, little girl, that man's out of your league." She yanked her order-taking pencil from behind her ear, poked it through her bouffant hairdo and scratched her scalp.

"He doesn't think so," Rosa Linda said. "He says I should take over his lunch every day."

"Is that so now?" Loretta tried to smirk, but the muscles around her mouth twitched with anger.

"Jaybird," Loretta said, "I ain't had time to tell you about the ruckus we had this morning." She was panting with anger. "Seems Melva's rings went missing during the pie baking with her little pet here."

Jaybird looked to Rosa Linda for explanation, but she only shrugged. Better let Loretta get it out of her system before her body shook itself into a full earthquake.

"Yes, sir," Loretta said, "this one goes back to the apartment after they finished with the pies, just as innocent as you please. Anyways, I was in the area off and on, so I stop back in when I knew they was done. I wanted to see Melva before she went off to the Crown of Glory. Well, sir . . . . " She paused and took a jagged breath. "I says, 'Melva where are your rings?' Now you know as well as I do that she don't never take them off."

"To sleep, she does," Jaybird said. "I've heard her say so."

"Well, sure, to sleep—" Loretta began.

"Or maybe if she's going to put her hands in a mess?" Jaybird said. "I don't believe I'd wear diamond rings while making pies."

Rosa Linda laughed but cut it off before it took her over again.

"Whyn't you let me finish?" Loretta said. "So, I tell Melva, I says, 'First time this has happened. Mighty strange,' I says." Loretta scratched her scalp again with the pencil, all the while eyeing Rosa Linda. "Well, sir, Melva goes straight back to the apartment where this one was. Yessirree, she knew just who to ask about them rings."

"And I," Rosa Linda said, her voice rising over the end of Loretta's sentence, "told Melva to go check the cup on the shelf. I didn't go back with her, so don't say I returned the rings. When Melva saw the rings, she remembered right away that she put them there herself. Some big mystery."

"Oh." Jaybird furrowed his brow. "She just forgot where she put them, that's all?"

Rosa Linda finished her soda with a dramatic slurp. She pointed to the pencil Loretta had stuck in her hair: "You keep scratching with that, you might poison your brain. Lead, you know?"

"You may have some fooled," Loretta said, "but you do not fool me. There's something about you that don't sit right."

"Fooled about what?" Rosa Linda said, curious to know how Loretta imagined her to be. But Loretta only sputtered, the words not coming to her.

Loretta stomped away and shoved the swinging door into the kitchen. Once she was out of earshot, Jaybird shook his head slowly, and told Rosa Linda not to pay any attention. "We all know you're swell," he said. He cleared his throat. "Don't be too hard on Retta, she's a good ol' gal. See, her and Melva's been friends for ages, almost like mother and daughter. Then you come along. I don't believe I've ever known Melva to take to somebody the way she has to you. And it don't help none that the customers like you, too."

"Hmm," Rosa Linda answered.

Jaybird smiled. "See, you got all your life in front of you; Retta, well, this is all for her." He waved one hand in a circle to indicate the restaurant. "She needs to feel like she's somebody, like she's needed — hell, we all do."

"Sure," Rosa Linda said. She was letting Loretta draw her into exchanging insults. She needed some hard dancing to free her mind. "I have something better to talk about," she said. After making Jaybird promise he wouldn't say anything to anyone (not caring if he did but thinking he'd like the idea of being her confidant), she asked him about buses and was glad to know that a trolley stop was only a block away.

"Up Logan a piece and right across from the Tasty Burger Drive-in," he said.

When she asked about the Bottoms Up, he said he knew of it but warned her against going to the area. "It's down in an old part of town some call the Holler," he said. "They don't care for outsiders in those parts. I know that for fact, 'cause when I first come up here from Kentucky, I rented me a house down there. Once I got me a job over to the GM I hightailed it out of that mess. A whole lot of heartache."

"I've always felt like an outsider wherever I go, so that doesn't bother me." She patted his hand. "I'm not going to the Bottoms Up. I heard some people at the thrift store talking about it one day. Just wondered, that's all."

"There's some places near there," he said, "in the Washington Historical District. Lots of college kids. And you can get there on the same bus. I never been but might suit you."

*   *   *

In the kitchen, Rosa Linda paused only long enough to give Donnie Ray's tip to Bob. After slipping the money to him, she hurried toward the back kitchen door. She'd completed her chores and didn't want to hang around while Melva and Edward were both gone.

Rosa Linda headed across the alley in the direction of the park she'd heard about, planning to stay there until Melva returned. She was on guard, the way she'd been when she'd arrived at Melva's that first day and uncertain if Enon had followed her after all. Or one of Cisco's friends. Vigilance was a good thing.

The center of the park had been mowed for baseball games, and she searched the perimeter for a big tree. Melva had told her that the dry spell caused the leaves to fall early, and now she lay on a small pile of fallen dead leaves. They crinkled beneath her, releasing a nutty scent. She closed her eyes. A bee buzzed in the distance, and she imagined it zig-zagging through the tall grasses at the perimeter of the field. She hummed to herself and felt her spirit lifting, flying on and on. But to where? she thought.

After she'd graduated from high school, completing her promise to Nana, she only knew she wanted out of Tia Matilda's house. She wished she could spend some time with her parents while she thought about her future but knew how that would go. She couldn't bear their rejection, so when she tired of her dead-end jobs, she went with her impulse. She had been happy in Nopal with Nana and Tata. She would take the Greyhound to Nopal to the border town, live with the memories of her grandparents while she figured out her next move.

The house had been abandoned since her grandparents' death while Roxana and her siblings decided how they wanted to settle matters. Why shouldn't she get some use out of the house while they bickered?

It was late when she got off the bus in downtown Nopal,

and not one of the town's three taxis was in sight. She ignored the calls from the men who hung out in front of the depot, smoking, spitting on the street, their hands forever reaching down to adjust their privates. Or maybe to assure themselves their manhood still hung safely between their legs.

Rosa Linda had straightened her spine, hefted the weight of her suitcase in her right hand, and focused her gaze on the path ahead of her. When she crossed the avenue, leaving the well-lit downtown area behind her, she walked faster. She kept to the center of the sidewalk, not too close to the street, not close to dark doorways, either. She turned onto Arroyo Street. The steep incline was paved, but she knew that at the crest of the hill the road turned to dirt, and houses became scarcer.

A dog barked from inside a house in the near distance, starting off a chorus of answering barks and howls. Rosa Linda welcomed the sounds. Dogs liked her. If someone bad was lurking in the shadowed doorways, the dogs might scare them off.

At the top of the hill, she stood beneath the last street lamp and peered into the darkness beyond the pool of light. To reach Nana and Tata's cottage, she would have to descend the hill and continue the winding road for at least another mile. How could she have thought this was a good idea? As usual, she'd just acted on an impulse and put her luck in the hands of fate. The electricity and water would be shut off at the house, and she had no matches with her and no idea if there were candles at the house. She shook her head at her own stupidity.

She stepped off the cement and onto the dusty dirt. She'd barely left the halo of light when she heard the engine slowing down behind her. Shit.

The hood of a pickup ticked alongside her, and a man's voice crooned, "Need a ride?" A Chicano accent.

"No, thanks," she said.

After a moment that stretched as long as the dark road before her, he said that he'd meant no disrespect, but that drug smugglers often crossed the border fence nearby. It wasn't a safe place for nice girls.

"Come on," he said, "get in. Let me take you to where you're going."

"I can get there on my own," she said. Then just so he'd know she wasn't aimlessly wandering, she added that her grandparents were waiting for her. If he was smart, he'd take off before her tata came out with his shotgun and mistook him for a javelina or a thieving coyote.

"Ain't nothing down this way but some old ghost house," he said. "The people who lived there died. Oh, wait, you headed there? Didn't you know? Hey, stop for a minute, will you?"

He reached into his pocket. "Francisco Garza," he said, showing her his driver's license. "Call me Cisco. See? I got nothing to hide. I'm telling you the pure truth, that house is falling apart. How long has it been since you talked with your people?"

She told him that it had been a while, and she'd lost contact with them. He apologized again and offered his condolences.

"I was living in California for years and I came back to start my own business," he said. His voice grew stronger with his pride in his achievement, and she understood that he was telling her he was a decent guy, not someone to fear. "You look tired, come with me to my mother's. She knew your grandparents. Good people." He told her that his mother's home wasn't far, that Rosa Linda could take a shower, rest, visit her grandparents' house the next day, if she was determined. His mother, he said, had passed away, but Rosa Linda could be assured that he'd never do anything bad in her house.

He made the sign of the cross and kissed his thumb and index finger. "I swear on my mother," he said. "You're safe with me."

And so she went with Cisco. Fate had stepped in to show her the way. Once they arrived, he explained that with only one bedroom, Rosa Linda would sleep in his mother's bed while he would take the sofa.

She had been touched by Cisco's kindness, his determination to help her, his devotion to his mother's memory — and his good looks didn't hurt. She woke up during the night, tiptoed to the sofa, crawled beneath his sheets, needing the comfort of a warm body close to hers. His arousal, even though he seemed half asleep, was immediate. It wasn't really sex she wanted, but she understood and accepted that, as a man, he would most likely interpret her temporary need for closeness this way.

"You smell like Palmolive soap," he said. As if she would smell of any other when he had been the one to unwrap a bar taken from his mom's bureau drawer.

He hesitated a moment, pushed himself up to gaze down, searching for truth deep within her eyes.

"Are you a virgin? No, don't answer, it don't matter. You're the woman that my mother always prayed I would meet. I was going home tonight, and something made me drive down that road. You are my destiny. Don't you feel it?"

"I'm not the woman you think I am," she said, "and I'm not looking for what you are."

He closed his eyes and smiled.

Afterwards, he stroked her hair, called her "mi alma."

"I'm not your soul," she said. But he talked on, as if she hadn't spoken. They were meant to be together, he said. No matter how many times she told him that night and many more after that she was only passing through, his eyes would go blank. He would not allow the words to register. No doubt he believed his love and kindness would change her mind.

The next day he took her to visit her grandparents' house, but it was, as he had warned her, in ruins. Vandals had pulled away protective boards from the windows and broken in, stolen everything. Now only dust and the echo of her own voice filled the rooms.

She stayed on with Cisco for three months. She had no money. But the truth was staying with him was so easy. How easy to feel loved and cared for. At times she told herself that maybe he was right about fate bringing them together. Another part of her hoped he would tire of her and would set her free, taking the decision out of her hands. He said she was his dream realized and never stopped planning their life together. When he insisted on setting a date for them to go to the county courthouse for a marriage license, she understood that she had stayed too long.

"Dear Cisco," she wrote, "thanks so much for all your kindness. I will pay you back the five hundred dollars when I can. Your knife I took por si acaso. I'm heading to the big city! Maybe you'll see me on the stage someday. Ha, ha. Best of luck. Adios."

Run, Rosa Linda, run.

* * *

When Rosa Linda awoke, her back had gone stiff. She stretched and lifted her eyes. Purplish clouds billowed in the sky. Maybe rain would come tonight. A tiny black bug crawled along her forearm. She positioned the tip of her finger before its prickly legs, and when it climbed aboard, she placed it on a low-hanging tree branch.

Melva stood at the kitchen door, cracked open a few inches, the wind blowing away the curl of her cigarette smoke. "Where the hell have you been?" she bellowed when Rosa Linda was still yards away. "Looks like a storm's brewing."

With one hand, Melva pushed the door wide as Rosa Linda neared, short of breath. "Edward's pooped out from shopping, but he's been asking for you, brought you a jar of honey." Rosa Linda apologized and told her she'd go find him, but Melva flapped a hand. "He's out like a light; you know he can't hold off on his nap."

"Can't I have some time of my own?" Rosa Linda had not meant for her words to be so sharp.

"Excuse the hell out of me." Melva looked away but not before Rosa Linda saw the hurt flash in her eyes.

"I'm sorry," Rosa Linda said.

"I got a parcel for you in the apartment." Melva's tone was all business now. "Left for you in the mailbox, no stamp on it."

Ben, Rosa Linda thought, as she followed Melva into the

apartment. Who else could it be? He'd stopped by to check on her, as he'd promised, a few days after she arrived. Melva had not allowed them one moment alone. She had both Rosa Linda and Ben sit at her table in the restaurant. Before he could say more than hello, she fired up a cigarette, leaned across the table to stare into his eyes, said, "If you think you're coming to my place to sniff around for skirt, you got another thought coming, Mister. I'll not have it."

She went on to tell him that she didn't know what he had in mind when he brought Rosa Linda to her. "But," she said, "the gal's working for me. With her looks and potential she's got a lot bigger fish to fry than some married man out to cheat on his wife."

His face red, Ben jumped up so fast he lost his balance. He grabbed the chair before it fell. "If that's what you think of me, I'll leave right now."

"Fine by me." Melva's gaze held his.

Once he was out of earshot, Rosa Linda and Melva had laughed.

Now Rosa Linda waited outside Melva's bedroom while the old woman retrieved the small, padded manila envelope.

Rosa Linda's fingers chilled as she reached for the envelope. In block letters, all capitals, someone had printed, "ROSA JUST OPHELIA LINDA."

"What's that Ophelia business about?" Melva asked.

Rosa Linda's mouth was dry, her tongue stuck to her palate.

"What's wrong, dammit?" Melva demanded. "Who's it from?"

Rosa Linda ran her tongue over her lips, but dry on drier didn't help. "Nobody."

"By God, somebody sent it. Well, you planning on opening it sometime in this century?"

"Later. Probably one of the customers." Rosa Linda shook her head, trying to clear her thoughts. Her feet felt like anvils, holding her to the floor. She pushed one in front of the other.

"Well, excuse me for giving a care," Melva said, and huffed away.

After shutting the bedroom door behind her, Rosa Linda

perched on the edge of the bed and held the package in her palms. She took a deep breath, ripped off the edge, shook out the contents. Still laced with the cord Enon had broken off her neck, out dropped the ojo de venado. She unfolded the small piece of paper that came with it: Two penciled hearts, one inside the other, and beneath them, printed in all caps, "TWO HEARTS ONE BEAT."

CHAPTER NINE

When Rosa Linda opened her hand, her fingernails had imprinted red slipper-moons into her palm. The talisman had once brought her comfort; now she pictured one of Enon's pale gray irises in the center of the Sacred Heart. He was hitting close to home. Was he now threatening Melva and Edward, too?

Cisco used to kiss the ojo de venado, the side with the Holy Mother, after taking it off before his shower and hanging it on the edge of his mother's dresser mirror. A gesture that irritated Rosa Linda for some reason she couldn't name. One day, she asked him if he really believed in the protective power of a common seed with pictures shellacked on it. "I believe in a mother's love," he answered, so honestly and simply that she'd looked away, embarrassed.

Yet once Cisco placed it around her neck, it became one of her favorite possessions. Roxana was not the motherly type, so how nice to imagine that she had a mother's love watching out for her. She wanted to kiss the ojo now, but knowing Enon had touched it ruined the magic for her. When she tossed it into the waste can, it hit with a clink against the metal. Before ripping up the note, she grabbed a pen from her night table and X-ed out the hearts, and beneath his words she wrote, "In your dreams, pendejo."

Enon knew where she was. What was worse, he knew about the Kopps. She didn't have any right to put them in danger. She had to leave. Forget about saving up more cash. Melva's diamonds glimmered like the promise of a better life. Melva was always trying to help her get ahead; well, the diamonds would help a lot more than lessons on pie-baking. If it weren't for the old woman's arthritic joints, the rings could slip right off. Maybe one day they would. If she lost them when she was out shopping, a stranger would find them and keep them.

Melva had been good to her, but as crafty as that old woman was there was probably some angle behind all that generosity. They weren't even blood, after all. Not that blood meant you could trust a person. Rosa Linda couldn't think of what Melva's angle could be but still . . . And the diamonds were insured, so Melva could buy new ones. Rosa Linda wished she could take them now before she had more time to think about it. But it was only afternoon, Edward was napping and Melva was in the kitchen making a list of specials with Geneva. Maybe she wouldn't have to take the diamonds; maybe the safe held cash, lots of it.

Rosa Linda tiptoed to her bedroom door, cracked it open, and paused to listen for movement before continuing down the hall. Edward lay snoring in his recliner, a small jar of golden honey on the side table next to him. Heat flushed into Rosa Linda's cheeks. He'd fallen asleep waiting for her with her gift of honey by his side.

Faithful Sugar nestled on his lap. The Chihuahua squinted up at Rosa Linda through graying eyelashes, curled one lip and growled half-heartedly. Sugar needed her nap even more than Edward. Her bulging gaze followed Rosa Linda to the large print on the wall, and when Rosa Linda glanced over her shoulder, the dog watched her still. As if that pipsqueak could do anything to stop anybody from doing anything. That's OK, Rosa Linda thought, at least the old dog's got some balls. Attitude could get you a long way, but not far enough to stop Rosa Linda. She carefully lifted the frame off the wall hook, her hands shaking with the thrill of anticipation. Melva kept the night's earnings locked away until she could take the money to the bank the next day.

In high school, Rosa Linda had been good at opening combination locks on the lockers of female students, the ones who were always flaunting their trendy clothing and latest hair and makeup items. How they enjoyed flouncing and preening in front of less fortunate girls. They had so much stuff they had stashes at home and at school.

Sugar yipped once, twice. Rosa Linda held her breath. Sugar was struggling to stand, her two front legs now uncurled from beneath her. Edward shifted, snored. Rosa Linda smiled at the dog, but Sugar responded with another low growl while pushing against Edward's thighs, nails digging into the softness of his old man's bandy legs. Edward groaned, closed his mouth, smacked his lips, turned his head in Rosa Linda's direction. She waited to see if his eyes would open.

When they remained closed, she eased the frame back onto the wall, padded back into the hallway. Better to wait for them both to be asleep at night, Edward deaf and Melva drugged out on sleeping pills. Even if that pesky Sugar woke up, only she and the dog would hear.

She had just shut her bedroom door when, with a long creak, the door connecting to the kitchen opened.

Melva knocked and without being invited opened the door. "You coming out?" She glanced at the envelope on the bed. "You going to show me?"

"It's nothing." Rosa Linda made a tsk sound with her tongue to show her irritation. "Some guy didn't have the courage to ask me out in person. He sent me a card anonymously. That's it."

"Sent a card in a padded envelope — all to ask you out *anonymously*? I felt something hard inside, what was that?"

"Some silly necklace." Rosa Linda wadded up the envelope, tossed it into the trash to cover the ojo de venado before Melva spotted it.

"You look like you got something on your mind. You going out tonight?"

"Whew," Rosa Linda said, "I don't get the connection, but, no. I'm tired. TV and bed are my exciting plans. As usual."

"Jaybird tells me you were asking about bus schedules."

"Jaybird's got a big mouth." She kicked off her shoes. "Is this the Inquisition? So many questions."

"Look here, missy." Melva splayed one hand on her high-sitting hip. "It's not like you're some goddamn prisoner. You want to go out, no skin off my nose. All I ask is you get in at a decent hour. Before me and Edward's asleep. And don't bring home any stray cats."

"I want to watch a little TV. That OK?"

"If you get hungry and don't want to come out front," Melva said, her voice softening, "there's plenty of stuff in the kitchen. We went to Kroger. I picked up chips and dip, Cokes, ice cream, all that garbage young people like, but some healthy things, too. Fruit, chocolate milk." Melva paused, held onto the doorknob with the door open. "Did I ever tell you about Edward's daughters?"

Rosa Linda waited, curious to follow the thread of Melva's mind.

"Two of them," Melva said. "Retired school teachers, spinsters. Live together on a farm in northern Ohio. Raise some chickens for eggs."

Melva paused, and after a moment, Rosa Linda encouraged her. "And . . . ?"

"As you know," Melva said, "I never had kids. Ilsa and Fern Kopp, they figure on getting all this someday." Melva made a small open-hand gesture. "I'd hate to see that."

"I hope it all works out the way you want." Rosa Linda's voice was sharper than she'd intended. She studied her own toes, digging into the carpet. She wished Melva would quit being so nice. Nice wouldn't stop Rosa Linda from doing what she had to do to survive.

Once the door closed, Rosa Linda fell back onto her bed and covered her face with her hands. Jesús, María, José. She needed a distraction, something to keep her from thinking too much.

Jaybird had tried to scare her about Bottoms Up, but he'd

only made the place more attractive. For sure, she wouldn't have time to think about her situation. She'd have to be extra careful that Enon wasn't following her — and she knew how to take care of that. All she had to do was to make it to the bar full of patrons.

She pulled down the wigs from the closet shelf and bent to scoot out the boxes of old clothes. For tonight, would she wear the cap of blonde curls, the angular cut brown wig that fell longer at the shoulders and shorter at the back, or the long dark-blonde style with heavy bangs? As she scooted the boxes and bags about with her foot, her eye caught the gold glint of the waste can to her side. She plucked out the ojo de venado. It wouldn't hurt to wear it tonight. Por si acaso. She wiped the seed on her shirt.

*   *   *

Inside the smoky sanctuary, Patsy Cline's "Crazy" started up on the jukebox, and a regular Bottoms Up customer, Mary Lou, moaned loudly. She held out her glass like a beggar's cup toward Donnie Ray.

"Oh Lord," she said. "Better fill me up, Donnie Boy. That Patsy kills me every damn time." She leaned forward, motioning for him to come closer. He leaned back, away from her perfume, as sweet and strong as decaying flowers.

"A little more vodka this time, Donnie Boy, and light on the orange juice."

When he turned to mix her screwdriver, Donnie Ray glanced at the wall clock to the left of the bar mirror — 10:20 p.m. Arlie added on 15 minutes, meaning it was only 10:05. No sight of Charlotte and Dee yet.

He clamped his jaw, felt the pain, and stopped. He'd finally dropped into the dental clinic when the pain radiating from his jaw and his molars lasted the day through. A shot of Jim Beam usually did the trick, but not lately. He had hoped the dentist would inform him that he had a hidden cavity that needed filling or a tooth that had to be pulled. Instead he learned that grinding his jaws had created hairline fractures in many of his teeth. The dentist recommended he wear some contraption in his mouth while he slept. Instead, Donnie Ray took up cracking his knuckles each time he felt his jaw tightening. His replacement habit was working most of the time, when he was awake.

"You're hitting it pretty hard, Mary Lou." He set the screwdriver on the bar. "Think you'll make it 'til closing?"

Mary Lou, on the far side of middle-aged, preferred younger men and kept an eye out for hardcore alcoholics who had drunk so much by closing that they didn't know, or care, who guided them out. "Come on now, sweetie," she'd murmur, helping them into her car. "Mary Lou knows how to take care of a man."

Lately, when Donnie Ray watched Mary Lou stumble out with her latest prey, he thought of his mom. She'd been tossing back the Pinnacle more than usual since Shayne's death. And his mother's dates seemed to be getting younger. He'd chased off more than one with a flat stare or a veiled threat, and she'd finally gotten the message. She didn't stop seeing the assholes, just stopped bringing them around him.

"Ah," Mary Lou said, her words thick with booze. "You're no fun anymore. Always pissed about something." She slid off the stool with a little hop.

His mother had insisted that she and Dee would be there no later than 8:00 that night. He cracked his knuckles. It was his fault — he should have gone to see them last Sunday for dinner. When he hadn't showed up, Charlotte had called Arlie to make certain Donnie Ray would be at work tonight. The place was packed, the jukebox blaring. Even if they came in, they'd have to shout to be heard over all the chaos.

Why the fuck had he believed that his mother would keep an appointment on a Friday night? When he was a very small boy, he'd believed her drunken rants about the feast she planned to prepare for upcoming holiday get-togethers. Thanksgiving dinners, at their best when she didn't have a steady boyfriend, were the prepared holiday "complete meals" from Kroger. If she was seeing someone, she usually took off with the guy and left her kids to eat peanut butter and jelly sandwiches. At least he and Dee had each other, but Shayne had been so much younger that he'd grown up as an only child in many ways.

He served drinks, rang up bills, cracked his knuckles, and avoided looking at the clock until he couldn't resist any more. 11:30. His eyes shifted to the mural at one side of the clock. Arlie had asked him last year to paint one of those scenes with different breeds of dogs sitting around a table playing poker. He told Arlie that he was a few years late on that trend, but Arlie had insisted. The bulldog, Donnie Ray's favorite, held a hand of mismatched numbers and suits. His eyes, shining brightly from within their frame of loosely folded skin, seemed to be gazing at the clock outside the mural, as if hoping that time could somehow save the inevitability of his loss.

"Watched pot never boils."

Donnie Ray shoved the register drawer shut. "Hey, Tara," he said, happy to see her in spite of himself. She'd been so busy lately with work and fighting the suits that she hadn't been calling him. Or maybe she was losing interest in him. Well, good for her. "What're you having?" he said, his hand already on the draft beer handle.

"Ginger Ale," she said.

"What's with the pop?" he asked when he placed her order in front of her.

"Need a clear head. I got a full schedule tomorrow at the salon." She fluffed her hair. "Like it?"

"I always liked your hair," Donnie Ray said. "What'd you do to make it so big?"

"Looks great, right? I got me a perm. Everybody's getting one; it's the style." She sipped the pop, looked into the middle distance. "They're giving us the runaround down to City Hall. About the playground?"

"What did you expect?"

"I knew you'd say that, but they don't know Tara Fugate." She stirred the pop with her straw. "By gosh, I'm going get ahold of the media: TV, radio, newspapers. Anybody who'll listen to me, or bug 'em till they do. Or you know what?" She hopped off her stool, as if she were taking a stand right then. "We'll protest, that's what we'll do. Everybody's doing it these days, so it must do some good. Leastways, it'll get their attention, make them know us Holler folk are still here and ain't going away." She held up a finger. "Oh, I got something to show you." She dug in her purse and pulled out a Polaroid photograph. She leaned over the bar and turned the photo toward Donnie Ray. "Isn't that the cutest thing you ever seen?"

He chuckled at Spike staring into the camera, his beige fountain of hair parted so that it sprayed to both sides of his head. A blue kerchief was tied around his neck at a jaunty angle. "Looks pretty proud of himself," Donnie Ray said.

Tara pressed the photo in his hand. "You keep it. I've took a whole roll of film of the little rascal. He's grown since you last seen him." She drew back and fell silent. He waited for her to nag him about not calling her or to invite him to come over to her place.

She crinkled her nose and straightened. She'd smelled his breath. "Donnie Ray," she said, drawing out his name. "You're on the job . . . do you think it's a good idea to be drinking—."

"You running this place now?" he said.

"I'm sorry," she said, her tone cool. "I spoke out of turn. Oh, I seen Charlotte and Dee coming out of the VFW. Heading this way, I think."

"How Blue" dropped on the jukebox. "I'm taking that as my cue to leave," she said. "If I stay, Reba'll have me crying. Lord, I love that girl."

"Here I thought you might be meeting up with that asshole you were so interested in last week," Donnie Ray said.

"Ah," Tara said, "you know that's not true." She hefted her purse on her shoulder and turned to leave. "You're just being mean on account of what I said about your — oh, forget it, but you better think about how you push people away. Won't let them love you. It's like in that song. And maybe one of these days you're going to find yourself all alone."

"You sure you want to let her get away?" Arlie said, after the door closed behind Tara.

"You interested?" Donnie Ray shot back.

Arlie lifted his chin in the direction of the door. "Check out the mouse."

At the front door a lanky figure, her shoulders hunched, stood at the elevated entrance.

With one hand she held the door open, half of her body inside, half outside, as if unable to decide whether to make her entrance. Or maybe simply allowing in some light from the outside streetlamp as she grew accustomed to the smoky darkness. She stepped in and sidled to one side, pressing her back against the wall.

She wore a white uniform tunic over pale yellow slacks falling about two inches short of her white tennis sneakers. A large brownish tote bag hung on one shoulder. Her long brown hair hung loose, topped by a crocheted hat pulled down to the tops of her ears. She kept her head lowered and her chin tucked so that her face fell into half shadow.

"Anybody you know?" Arlie said, as the woman felt out a path, one tenuous foot in front of the other.

"Nah," Donnie Ray said, shaking his head slowly as he studied her. She seemed shy, unsure of herself, but at the same time there was something dramatic and intentional about her entrance.

"She's not from around here, that's for sure," Arlie said. "She's wondering about now about why in the hell she came in here." He laughed.

If such an obviously uncomfortable stranger had entered the Bottoms Up on a weeknight when the joint wasn't so crowded, the din of murmuring voices would have hushed and only the sound of country music would be heard, as the patrons studied the mysterious stranger for signs of trouble. But on weekends couples were determined to have a good time and forget the week. They abandoned their tables for the dance floor, hot sweating bodies pressed close, seeking in the grind of their partner's groin the something that would fill the yearning within. Some who had not made it to the floor stared fixedly at the dancers with drunken longing or envy. Tonight, only a few heads turned to watch her.

"I got this," Donnie Ray said when she headed toward the bar. There was something made up about her, as if she were going to a costume party.

"Bubble Up, please," the woman mumbled when she claimed the stool Tara had left empty. She kept her head bent so that he was left staring at the rose at the top of her crocheted cap.

Donnie Ray set the glass in front of her. She giggled and glanced up at him through her lashes, thick and long even without the mascara. The rest of her face was also scrubbed free of makeup, and she looked young and fresh.

"Figured it was you," he said. "You come down here by yourself? Dumb move."

"Ay," she said, "you're not my father. Can't you even comment on my disguise?"

The outside door whooshed open with force, and from the other end of the bar, Arlie called, "Donnie Ray. Heads up."

"Woo-hoo," Charlotte yelled. She waved her arms, shouted, "Gentlemen, your dream girl has arrived."

Donnie Ray recognized his mother's about thirty-minutes-away-from-falling-down-drunk voice, somewhere between that too-high register women used when greeting another woman and the piercing whine of a habitual complainer.

He walked out from around the bar, and Charlotte leaned forward, preparing to collapse against him, certain he would be there to hold her just as he always had. Dee, who had come in with her, grabbed her around the waist. "Take it easy, Momma," she said, her voice not so boozy as her mother's.

Rosa Linda's curious eyes made him even more aware of his mother's behavior. Holler old-timers knew this crude version of Charlotte but were also acquainted with the sweet-talking southern belle his mom could be before the vodka kicked in. For the first time in years, he felt the deep embarrassment he had when he was a kid and had fought anybody who laughed at his mother or mimicked her.

Rosa Linda made a show of stirring her Bubble Up with the straw.

"Best lookin' man in town," Charlotte said. "My son." She struggled to free herself from Dee's arm, but her daughter only held tighter. "Let go, damn you," Charlotte said between gritted teeth.

"Donnie Ray's working right now, Momma," Dee said in her most appeasing tone. "I used to have two sons," Charlotte mumbled, her head lolling back against Dee's shoulder. Her half-closed eyes opened and met Rosa Linda's. She attempted to push herself straight. "What the hell're you looking at? Didn't you burst out of a woman's womb?"

Rosa Linda snorted but covered her mouth and quickly recovered. "Excuse me," she said, "I'm Rosa Linda. Nice to meet you."

"Nice to meet you," Charlotte mimicked in a too-sweet voice, then turned her attention to the music.

Dee glanced toward Donnie Ray. "Friend of yours?"

"Yeah, in fact, I was just about to take her home," he said. Rosa Linda didn't blink, and he nodded to her in appreciation. He owed her one.

"Now?" Dee said. "What about us?"

"It's almost midnight," he said. "And Mom's in no condition to talk anyway."

"You're more like Earl Camper every damn day of your life," Charlotte said. "Never think about anybody but yourself, you stinking turd. You'll take off one of these days. Forget about your own kin, same as he did." Charlotte's words were thick and slurred.

"I waited for this?" Donnie Ray said, directing his comment to his sister.

"Oh my, my, now he's grinding his jaw. See him?" Charlotte pointed at him, and glanced around at Dee, Arlie, Rosa Linda. "Should I be scared?" Charlotte twisted her face to imitate fear.

Suddenly she stopped struggling with Dee and turned to Rosa Linda. "She doesn't look like his type, does she, Sissy?"

To Donnie Ray, she demanded, "Where's Tara?" Her lips flattened into a disapproving line. "I thought you'd keep her. She doesn't expect anything of you, doesn't ask questions. She just sits around looking pretty and batting her eyes at you." Charlotte batted her eyes.

"I tried to get Mom to leave the VFW earlier, honest I did," Dee said.

"Hey, Arlie," Donnie Ray said, "I'm taking off now, like I told you."

"What's a lady got to do to get some goddamn service around here?" Charlotte hollered.

"Come on," Donnie Ray said to Rosa Linda. "Arlie'll get Leland to cover for me."

"Uh, OK," Rosa Linda said. In a whisper, she added, "but I'm not going home."

"Donnie Ray, please, we have to talk," Dee said.

Donnie Ray tugged at Rosa Linda's arm. "There's another exit through the back," he said.

"Bless her heart," Charlotte said, in a stage whisper. "Why, she's homely as a mud fence."

As he guided Rosa Linda through the storage room, he asked how she'd made it to the bar.

"Bus," she said. "I meant to come earlier, but I didn't know the buses ran so far apart." She glanced at her watch. "I thought you might drive me home — after we party." She held up her tote bag. "Dancing shoes in here."

"Let's get you to the bus stop," he said, "before the last one leaves you behind."

"No way," she said. "I need to have some fun."

*　　*　　*

They stepped out into a dark alley, bordered on one side by the backs of business buildings that included the Bottoms Up, and on the other side a six-foot plank fence that ran the length of the alley.

"Fuchi," Rosa Linda said, "what's that smell?" She flapped

her hand in front of her nose. At the same time, her glance took in the dumpster and trash cans that dotted the alley.

"Yeah, it's getting a little ripe," he said. "We need a good rain to wash some of the stink away."

"It's so dark," Rosa Linda said. "Look, how beautiful." Her voice went soft as she pointed to the sky, the sliver of white moon peeking over a cloud of black cotton. "That cloud, it's almost like a short mountain range. See the peaks there?"

"With this breeze, it'll travel across the moon in a minute." With uplifted faces, they waited. Surprising himself, he said, "My little brother collected plastic dinosaurs and when he looked for shapes in the clouds, he always saw dinosaurs. That one, there?" He pointed to a dark shape to the right of the moon. "T-rex."

"Your mother said she *had* two sons. Does she mean he's—"

"Yeah," Donnie Ray said, cutting her off. "I don't want to talk about that."

"Somebody break out the light?" Rosa Linda pointed to the streetlamp. "Same thing happened to the one in the alley behind Melva's."

He turned his head sharply to the right. He held up a hand for her to be quiet. A trash can rattled in the distance. A cat? No, a muffled sound — a human voice.

Rosa Linda pointed to the dark mouth of the alley. "From there," she said.

"Stop." The voice was louder this time. An old man.

Without speaking, Donnie Ray inched toward the sound, Rosa Linda so close behind him she could feel the tenseness in his muscles. Laughter and hoots answered the old man's pleas. "Stop," a gruff voice hollered, and this time a scream followed.

"Shut up," a young male voice said in a hoarse whisper. "Shut him up."

A gust of wind whipped the sounds up the alley. One old man and multiple young male voices. How many, he couldn't be certain.

"Get back inside," Donnie Ray said and shoved her.

"Hey," she said as she stumbled backwards. She grunted, and he thought she must have hit the brick wall of the bar.

Donnie Ray ran down the alley, keeping close to the fence where the matted grass softened the sound of his footfall, covering as much distance as he could, hoping they wouldn't hear him over their own commotion. From between the spaces of the fence slats, the few lights still on in the nearby houses blackened. Mind-your-own-business monkeys who didn't see, hear, or speak evil. Who could blame them?

"Stop, boys, stop," the old man whispered hoarsely. He'd lowered his voice as if hoping his compliance would appease his tormentors into letting him go. It was Boom Boom. His cries were followed by a thud.

Donnie Ray stopped yards away, hid behind the cover of a utility pole and the stray, three-foot tree that had taken root next to it. A huddle of three men stood around Boom Boom, curled on the ground in a fetal position, arms and hands covering his face and ears, like a man protecting himself from an attack by a pack of mad dogs.

Donnie Ray's muscles stiffened. Old fool. Hadn't he warned him about roaming the streets? He crouched. A few feet behind him, he heard breathing — shallow pants. The scent of lavender wafted in the air, and he realized the girl had smelled of it earlier on. He should have known she wouldn't listen. He motioned with one hand for her to stay to one side in the shadows against the fence.

"Wait," the tallest of the three men said, and held up his hand. "Pops wants to get up." Boom Boom struggled to lift himself to all fours, wagging his big gray head as if trying to clear his mind.

As Donnie Ray duck-walked forward, the clouds shifted, and the moon washed the scene in an eerie silver light. He could see them more clearly now: a tall skinny one, a stocky guy with sandy-colored hair, and the third with blond hair that shone a pale straw-yellow in the moonlight. Donnie Ray didn't recognize any of them, but he could see they were in their early twenties.

"Nobody's gonna help you, old man," one said. Another mimicked Boom Boom's calls for help in a high falsetto.

"Aaaah." A prolonged, guttural sound ripped from Boom Boom's throat. He had made it to his knees and lifted one hand inches from the ground. "Donnie Ray," he called.

All of their eyes turned to Donnie Ray. A moon shadow shifted, settled over him.

"Shit," the sandy-haired one said, and tensed as if to run.

"Hold on," the tall one said, and grabbed Sandy's shoulder. "He's alone, and he's nothing." The three of them fell silent, staring, waiting for Donnie Ray's move.

Donnie Ray glanced behind him but couldn't find Rosa Linda. He was glad he didn't have to worry about her getting in the way, yet a little surprised she'd kept back.

He stepped forward and out of the shadows. Boom Boom stretched out his arm farther, causing his body to wobble off balance. The tall one, locking eyes with Donnie Ray, planted a Doc Martin boot on the old man's behind, pushed hard. Boom Boom sprawled forward, collapsed on his side.

Donnie Ray edged closer, eyes locked on the tall one, the obvious leader.

"Fuck you," Sandy said. He sought the faces of his friends. "Right, dudes?"

"Shut up," the tall one said, and to Donnie Ray, "Mind your own business."

Their accents — Ohio but not Holler — told Donnie Ray they were either new to the neighborhood or maybe from one of the surrounding areas. Boys from the Holler didn't challenge him. Not yet. The days where he knew everyone in their area were gone.

"Move out the way, Boom Boom," Donnie Ray said, voice calm, and the old fighter belly-crawled to one side.

"Fuck you, dude," the two shorter men said in unison, causing them to laugh. The tall one said nothing. His arms hung at his sides, hands clenching and unclenching, but Donnie Ray could see the fear in his eyes. The guy was no match for him, he knew, but he never underestimated what desperate move a cornered rat might take.

Scared or not, the tall one was the head of the snake, the

one to watch. Sandy's attempt to intimidate with his big mouth revealed weakness; Blondie was panting open-mouthed, eyes darting behind him and to the side, the two paths of escape.

"Oh, he's a bad m-f-er," the tall one said, and spit. The mucous blob landed a foot from Donnie Ray.

Boom Boom pushed on the ground, trying to roll into a sitting position. "I got your back, Donnie Ray," he said between wheezes.

"Johnny Ray?" the tall one said and snorted. "We got us a John Boy." He slapped his thigh, brayed, "Hee haw." He broke off the end of his word, beer bottle in hand, and charged, bellowing.

Donnie Ray shifted to the left, punched him in the side of the neck, and as he went down, again on the back of the neck with the power of both hands clasped. The punk smashed onto the dirt with a grunt. Donnie Ray kicked him in the ribs.

"Help," the downed man said, holding onto his side.

Blondie looked from Sandy to the open space between two buildings to his right. A quick run through an alley and they'd be on the main drag.

"I got the keys, guys," the tall one said, breathing hard, anticipating their betrayal. He pushed himself up to a slump while still holding onto his ribs.

Donnie Ray started toward the duo. Blondie's eyes opened wide. He backed up, his hands held out. "No, man," he said, then whirled around, stumbled and ran.

Donnie Ray clamped his jaw. He would catch them, and he would stomp the shit out of both of them.

"Behind you," Boom Boom said, and Donnie Ray spun around, fist raised.

A small knot of people ran toward him, Rosa Linda at the front.

"Calm down," Arlie said, trying to catch his breath. He moved slowly toward Donnie Ray. "It's me, Arlie, Donnie Ray. It's me, OK? That's enough, brother. Snap out of it." He gestured with his thumb to the tall one. "Get lost," he said, "while you can." The tall one stumbled out of the alley.

The vein in Donnie Ray's temple pounded. He squeezed his eyes shut, opened them, took a ragged breath, then another. The whiteness diffused into a swirl of fog.

Arlie instructed the two men from the bar who had come with him to help Boom Boom up.

"Out of here," Arlie said to Donnie Ray. "Don't worry. One of the boys'll run him home. We got this."

"Yeah." Donnie Ray felt the adrenaline still surging.

"The girl," Arlie said, "she going with you?"

"Yes," Rosa Linda said. She'd lost her cap and her wig sat askew on her head.

CHAPTER TEN

Rosa Linda had no driver's license but offered to drive anyway. How hard could it be? she thought. Donnie Ray insisted he was fine. She pointed to the front of his torn and blood-splattered shirt. "Not mine," he said. Excitement still heated her blood. She'd missed the beginning of the fight, but she'd seen enough as she ran back with Arlie to know that Donnie Ray was a natural fighter, a survivor. Something primitive had taken over.

She licked her parted lips and enjoyed the rush of the wind blowing through the open window. Donnie Ray's face remained mask-like except for his working jaws. Typical tough guy, she thought. He'd never admit fear or pain. She'd grown up with a lot of men like that. She wondered if they didn't get tired of the roles society pushed on them; she sure got tired of society expecting her to be someone she wasn't.

She patted her chest, felt the ojo de venado beneath the polyester tunic.

"You OK?" she asked, but he stared silently at the road in front of him. Fine, he didn't want to talk. She lay back her head and rested.

In the alley, when she'd first heard the noise, she half expected to come face to face with Enon. And earlier that night, when she dressed to go out, she'd had Enon on her mind. She wanted to change her appearance as much as possible but packed lighter shoes and her makeup in a tote bag for prettying up later on. Her chosen clothing said "nerd." She twisted her hair in large flat swirls secured by bobby pins and covered the pin curls with one of Melva's wigs. "Dutchboy," a label inside called the style, which fell longer in the front and shorter in the back. It looked cuter than she intended, so she wore a cap that looked like it had been crocheted by someone's grandmother.

She rolled her sheet, shaped it into a human form beneath the covers, and where the head should be placed Melva's darkest wig. After she opened her window and pushed out the screen, she held her breath and listened for sounds of voices or car engines. Just in case Enon might be out there, spying, lurking. He wasn't going to beat her at this game of cat and mouse. She slid her legs over the sill and dropped to the ground. She wiggled the screen back into position and crept on tiptoes to the edge of the low brick wall at the border of the Kopps' tiny yard.

Silhouettes shifted in between a pickup and a car. A middle-aged couple were climbing into the car without words. That was the way of it, Rosa Linda thought, people who refused to split up even when they had nothing left to say to each other. Although she had to admit that silence wasn't always bad: Nana and Tata often sat quietly in each other's company, their love so strong, it warmed the air like a cup of Mexican hot chocolate. Like she and Donnie Ray now?

She couldn't imagine herself old. Anyway, she had no patience for that kind of love — easy, slowly developing. When the fun stopped, she wanted out, fast and easy. No one would ever again have the chance to abandon her the way her parents had.

She remembered the stories about the large rats that roamed the alley behind Melva's and the meat processors. Her pulse hammered with the thought that he might have been out there, waiting for prey like one of those alley rats. But she'd outsmarted him.

Now she glanced at Donnie Ray's profile, sharply defined in the light from the passing streetlamps, and admired the clean outline and planes of his face. She shifted in the seat suddenly aware of the soreness in her back from where he'd pushed her into the outside wall of Bottoms Up.

*   *   *

Donnie Ray pushed open the apartment door with one hand and reached for the inside wall switch with the other. From beneath his raised arm came an odor of male sweat beneath deodorant and something metallic. In the glare of the overhead light, the blood on his shirt showed up in technicolor splotches.

"You coming in?" he said, standing to one side. It was the first he'd spoken since they got in the car.

"Nice," Rosa Linda said. The room was tidy, and it occurred to her that his car had also been unusually neat, no dust or stickiness on the surfaces, no scraps of napkins or empty bags. As she had in the car, she detected in his apartment an undertone of cigarette, but subtle, as if the smoker had been here once and moved on. No magazines lying out, no ashtrays, no plants, no breakfast coffee cup on the short counter separating the living room from the kitchenette. No sign of life.

When Nana came into Rosa Linda's room and found clothes thrown over chairs or shoes kicked off in the middle of the room, she'd say that a messy room suggested a messy mind. If that were true, Donnie Ray's apartment suggested a little more order than Rosa Linda liked.

In a far corner, she spotted an object with some character: an old-time portable record player (much like the one her father had) and album covers for vinyl records inside a cabinet with glass doors. Next to his vinyl collection sat a small TV on a metal table with a VCR player on a shelf beneath the set.

"You live alone?" she asked.

"Always." He plucked at the shoulder of his torn shirt. "I got to get out of this." He pointed to her head. "And you, don't you want to take off that thing?"

She laughed and then jerked at the wig; it caught on some hairpins and dangled from one side of her head. She tugged hard but the wig remained caught.

"Here," he said, pulling out two hairpins and handing them to her. He paused, studied her face. "You know, you don't need all that makeup you usually wear. Your face is even more beautiful without it."

"Uh-huh." She'd heard the makeup lecture before. "I don't wear it to look prettier, just different. And bare face just happened to go with this outfit."

"Watching you is better than watching a movie," he said. "Are you always putting on an act, or do I ever get to see the real you?"

He'd stumped her, and she paused to think about what he'd asked. She'd spent so much time trying to be the chameleon who suited her surroundings that she'd lost track of her true self. "Does anyone have a real self?" she asked. "Don't all of us present masks to others?"

"Most of us have some idea who we are beneath the masks," he said. The expression on his face seemed to question his own words. He waved a hand to take in the apartment, and perhaps to brush away the topic of conversation. "Help yourself to something to drink, eat," he said, gesturing toward the kitchen. "I'll take you down to the bus stop after I wash up."

She thanked him without mentioning that the last bus between the Holler and Melva's had been the one that dropped her off.

"In the cabinet," he said, as he walked away, "to the right of the sink. Jim Beam. Pour a couple."

Rosa Linda preferred her Coke straight, but since he was finally treating her like an equal, why not join him for a shot?

The kitchen cabinet interiors were as neat and sparsely

inhabited as the rooms. She pulled out two sparkling clean tumblers and poured whiskey into each, wrinkling her nose at the smell. She'd need something to dilute hers. The refrigerator held a carton of half-and-half, three cans of Coke, four eggs in the egg holder, a stick of butter on a saucer, a loaf of white bread, a small jar of Miracle Whip, a jar of dill pickle slices, a speckled banana, and at the back of the middle shelf, an opened box of baking soda. She had to grin at the thought of the fighter with the scarred knuckles as being the housekeeper who was concerned about odors in his fridge.

Unless, of course, someone else had thought of that little housekeeping tip. Hadn't his mother asked about some woman at the bar, letting Rosa Linda know he had someone in his life? That mother of his.

Just looking at her Donnie Ray's face had gone white except for a red spot appearing on one cheek. Maybe it had been a good thing that his mother came in, priming his anger for the guys in the alley. Well, he didn't have to be embarrassed in front of Rosa Linda. She knew all about parents who tried to find their lost dreams in the bottom of a bottle.

One of the refrigerator drawers lay empty, but the other held a plastic package of Colby cheese and something wrapped in brown butcher paper. She lifted a corner of the paper—olive loaf. She made them each a cold cut and cheese sandwich with Miracle Whip, cut the bread on the diagonal, placed the sandwiches on small plates and set them on the coffee table.

She sank onto the lumpy sofa and sipped her drink of Coke and whiskey. Maybe it would numb the pain in her back. She stretched out on the lumpy cushions.

*   *   *

"Hey, you awake?"

She lifted her head and rubbed her knuckles in her eyes.

Donnie Ray wore a fresh outfit that looked pretty much like what he always wore and smelled of soap. Irish Spring, she guessed. If it weren't for the scratches on his forearm and his knuckles, she wouldn't have guessed he'd just come from a fight against three other men.

He pointed to the glasses and sandwiches. "You didn't have to wait," he said, and sat at the opposite end of the sofa. "I'll be fast," he said, holding the sandwich to his mouth.

"No rush," she said.

Now that he'd showered and his muscles looked less tense, she considered it safe to bring up the fight. "What's the story with that old guy back in the ally?" she said. "You know him?"

Donnie Ray sipped on his whiskey. "Boom Boom," he said. "A friend. Don't worry about it."

"I just didn't understand why you would face down those guys for some old bum."

"Odds don't mean shit if it's your friend. You turn your back on your friends?"

"If you don't save yourself," she said, "how can you help anyone else?"

He took another bite of his sandwich, as if she hadn't spoken, but she wasn't ready to let it drop.

"So," she said, "what if you came upon the same scene, only the old man wasn't your friend? Maybe you knew him, but he wasn't a close friend. Then what? You'd mind your own business, like everybody else, right?"

"He *is* my friend, and what happened, happened" he said. "How about you? You could've just gotten the hell out of there, but you didn't. You went for help."

"Well, yes," she said. "I was afraid you might kill one of those guys."

He stared into the middle distance. He pulled his legs off the table, leaned forward, the muscles in his back knotting beneath his shirt. "Kid," he said, "I'm going to give you some advice. When you sense danger, don't wait for the other guy to strike. Sucker punch. And once you get the son of a bitch down, make sure he stays down. Kick. Stomp. Hit him with all you got. Because if he gets back up, he's going to finish you off. Get it?"

"Uh, OK." She had the sense he was advising someone else.

"I could use another of these," he said, and tipped his glass. "You?"

She shook her head. "But I'll make more sandwiches." She picked up the empty saucers and returned to the kitchen with him.

Outside, the odd car drove down the street, and in the distance a dog barked. Late-night sounds that she'd always loved. When they returned to the sofa, he brought the bottle, poured himself another shot. After a sip, he sat back, and without turning to her, said, "You one of those women who gets turned on by the sight of blood?"

"Why do you even say that?" She snatched her wig off the table. "If that's really what you think of me, I'll leave."

"Quit being so dramatic," he said. He studied his sandwich. "You ever do any acting?"

"My mother's an actress," she said.

"I'm talking about you."

She told him about her high school experience with theater and how her teachers had encouraged her. "But it's a dumb profession. Even Melva told me that."

"So where is she, this actress mother of yours?"

"Both of my parents are in California," Rosa Linda said. "But it's not like my mom's famous or anything. See, that's the thing. She says that the only thing an artist can depend on is rejection. Melva says I should think about getting in the restaurant business."

He drained his glass, set it down. "If you want to be an actress, maybe you should be where your parents are. They must have some connections."

She shrugged. "They're busy. And in the last few years," she said, "it's really hitting her — for Hollywood, she's old. Especially since she wanted to be a movie star more than an actress. Me, *if* I ever became an actress, I want to be like Ofelia Medina. You don't know her, right?" Without giving him time to answer, she explained. "She's Mexican. How about Meryl Streep?"

"I've heard of her."

"I'll watch any movie she's in."

"I mostly watch movies on that," he said, and indicated the VCR.

Rosa Linda suggested that he try the foreign film section at the video store and search for Paul Leduc's film starring Medina as Frida Kahlo.

"She's a great artist," she said.

"Yeah, Kahlo had guts." He grinned slyly. "Didn't think I knew her work, right? She didn't let anything — not any of the shit life threw at her — stop her from going for her dream. But as far as the art, I prefer her husband's work. Diego Rivera. Did I pronounce that right? What? You didn't think a good ol' boy like me would know anything about artists?"

"I did not think that. Well, maybe a little," she said, and they both laughed.

They fell silent again, and Rosa Linda, usually not minding quiet but now afraid their connection would break, blurted, "That first day at Melva's, you know that story Ben told about how I got to Mad River? That was a lie."

"You're kidding," Donnie Ray said, in mock surprise. "Do you always talk this much?" The skin at the corner of his eyes crinkled, as if he were preparing to fully smile. He settled back on the sofa, set his feet on the table.

The alcohol had loosened her tongue and she almost fell into a confessional mode. She wanted to tell Donnie Ray about Cisco and his money and explain that she'd never taken money from anyone before. OK, those snooty girls at school. And a few times when she visited her cousins or friends, secure in parent-run homes, she might take a souvenir, an aunt's lipstick, a cousin's cassette, a friend's blouse. Little things that wouldn't be missed, or at least not until long after she was gone. But that had been different than with the mean girls. How could she explain the urge that came over her to tuck away those pieces of friends and relatives. She didn't understand it. And Donnie Ray probably wouldn't understand about Cisco and the money. Better to keep some things to herself.

She told him that one day she'd taken her life savings and

let fate decide where she would go. She'd ended up in Mad River. "That's the short version," she said.

"And now?" he said.

She shrugged. "Maybe I'll go to Chicago someday. Or New York City. Maybe I'll become an actress." She glanced at him hopefully, and he didn't let her down.

"Go for it, kid," he said. "You want to travel and experience life, do it. You're young and think you have forever to decide. But life is short. Remember Frida."

"Yeah, it's like something is always after me, pushing me on and on. It's like . . . like in my head . . . ." With her finger, she traced a figure eight on the coffee table, as if searching for the words.

"Rosebuds and maggots," she said. "Inside my head I have rosebuds and maggots."

He snorted. "Quite an image," he said.

His hand lay in the space between them and with her fingers she grazed his swollen knuckles. "Want me to get some ice for that?" she asked.

He jerked his hand back as if she'd touched a flame to it. "Look," he said, "I don't know what you're expecting from me, but I got nothing to give." He stood. "A girl like you, you're made for dreams. Time to get you to your bus."

She tapped the face of her wristwatch. "Too late. No more buses tonight." She patted the sofa, said as casually as she could, "Maybe I could spend the night here."

"What'd I just tell you? Let's go."

"Sleep, I said — nothing more. You don't have to be so hard. I just need a change of scenery."

"Not going to happen." He held out his hand to pull her up in the same way he'd done for Boom Boom.

She flipped her hair off her shoulder. "Mind if I use your bathroom first? Or would that mean I'm expecting something from you?"

The door to the room next to the bathroom was ajar, and she figured it to be his bedroom. She hesitated.

"Not that one," he called out from the living room. "See

the door to your right, the open one with the light on, with the sink and tub in it? That'll be the bathroom."

"Ha, ha," she said. One toothbrush hung in the porcelain wall holder, and a bar of pale green soap — she'd been right about the Irish Spring — lay on the sink. She opened the metal door of the medicine cabinet over the sink, found Gillette shaving cream and a razor, a spray can of Arrid deodorant, and Head & Shoulders shampoo. No medications, not even an aspirin. No makeup, perfume, or tampons to suggest a woman's presence. She pulled back the plastic shower around the porcelain tub. No shelf to hold a girly bubble bath.

She peed quickly, and when she stepped out into the hall, she heard the water running in the kitchen. No doubt Mr. Clean was already washing the plates and tumblers. She crept into his bedroom. A beam of moonlight shone through the window, and the shadows of the tree branches outside created the illusion of a spider web across the bed. Too narrow for more than one to sleep comfortably. A monk's room, she thought. She glanced to the side and spotted the bicycle on the wall. She couldn't imagine such a tough guy riding a bike, not unless he'd had his driver license taken away. But he drove his car to work.

She cocked her head. The water in the kitchen no longer ran. She backed out of his room, her feet making squeaking noises on the linoleum as she hurried down the short hall, entering the living room at the same time he did.

"I happened to get a look in that room as I passed," she said, "and I was wondering whose bike is that on the wall?"

Donnie Ray's jaw muscles worked. "Now that lie is flat-out stupid," he said. "You can't just happen to see that wall from outside of the room."

She lifted one shoulder, dropped it.

"My little brother's," Donnie Ray said. "The other son my mom mentioned." His words sounded forced.

"Oh." She waited for him to continue, and when he didn't, she asked, "What happened to him?"

He clamped his jaw, and the skin around his eyes and mouth

tightened. He shook his head silently, as if not daring himself to speak. At the front door he paused, twirled his keys on one finger. "Time to get you home. Think you can manage to not talk anymore tonight?"

"Sure. I like my own company."

*   *   *

Rosa Linda whispered a good night to Donnie Ray and carefully closed the car door. As she darted across the small square of dry grass to her bedroom window, she paused. Had someone said her name? She squinted back at Donnie Ray, sitting military-straight behind the wheel of the car, then toward the swaying branches of the trees across the alley. Only the wind swaying the treetops.

Donnie Ray had insisted on waiting for her to get inside, so she had to explain to him that she had no key and had to go in through the window. She wouldn't want to wake up the old folks, she said. Now she knelt before the sill and nudged up as slowly as she could with her free arm. She waited, strained to hear if Sugar stirred from Melva's bedroom. She doubled over the sill, tumbled into her room. From inside, she watched the taillights of Donnie Ray's car blink red as he turned back onto Logan.

Undressed and in bed, she stretched her legs between the sheets. She snuggled deeper beneath the covers, listening. The surrounding bars had closed, the last good timers had made it to their cars. How she adored the night, a magical time when she could be alone with herself.

From the highway beyond the Shipwreck, trucks and cars whizzed by. How she ached for that freeing sensation of driving through the darkness, being inside the mini world of the vehicle, separate yet a part of the world beyond. Soon, she'd be back on the road.

Outside the wind howled. She strained to hear the branches of the nearby trees. Tall, dry grasses whooshed in harmony. Snap.

Rosa Linda held her breath, strained her ears. A deer? She'd been hoping for a sighting. Geneva said that she'd spotted a doe and its fawn outside of the restaurant once when she'd come to work. Years ago, the area had been densely wooded, but with the years, Geneva told her, more houses, more businesses, and most of the surrounding forest had been chopped down to accommodate progress.

She flipped back the covers and tiptoed to the window. The wind had increased, blowing in additional clouds, filling the night with mystery. Maybe tonight they'd finally get the rainstorm that everyone had been waiting for. She loved sleeping with the windows open, but she'd catch the devil from Melva if the carpet or bedding got wet. She thought of Donnie Ray's brother. She'd kept her promise and stayed quiet on the ride, but that didn't mean she didn't have questions. They would meet again; she would know his story — his and Shayne's.

It wouldn't be so bad to stay here in Mad River for a while. During one of her talkative moments, Geneva had told her that the trees would soon be a riot of colors as they began to prepare for their winter's sleep. "A regular patchwork quilt," the older woman promised, "stitched by God's hands."

Rosa Linda wanted to believe that Enon had left the ojo de venado as a good-bye, letting her know that he was moving on. But she remembered his eyes and knew she was deceiving herself.

CHAPTER ELEVEN

Rosa Linda stood at the opened kitchen cabinet, staring at the package of English muffins, her mind in the Holler. Only yesterday she had stood outside the Bottoms Up studying the block glass on the bar's windows that prevented her from peeping in. Once she stepped inside and the door closed behind her, it was as if she'd entered a new world. The cigarette smoke and country music swirled around her, and something else she couldn't describe enticed her. Maybe it had been a sense of home — somebody else's home — inviting her in and rejecting her at the same time.

Then, snap, just like that, here she was back at the Seniors Home. She reached for the muffins. Melva and Edward were speaking to one another, their voices still low and froggy with sleep.

"You need some help over there?" Melva's voice had raised. "Or you too busy daydreaming to get the job done?"

Rosa Linda popped the English muffins into the toaster. When she went to bed, she hadn't been able to let the memory of the night go and reran the details in her dreams. Even if Enon were out there in the darkness, he wouldn't have recognized her in her getup. She'd never go out as the same character twice. And Donnie Ray, the way he'd exploded.

Scary. Then so tender later when he'd spoken about his brother. Flying the trapeze without a net definitely had its thrills.

"Oh, for Pete's sake," Melva said, and scooted her chair back.

"I've got it, I've got it," Rosa Linda said. She placed the plate of toasted muffins and a jar of honey in the center of the table.

"Always tastes better when *you* butter," Edward said to Rosa Linda.

"Your arm's not broke," Melva snapped. "From now on, Edward Kopp, you butter your own damn toast just the way you've been doing since I've known you." She snatched up a muffin, cut off a bit of butter, slapped the knife back and forth across the surface. "See?" she said. "Nothing to it."

Rosa Linda patted Edward on the shoulder. His mild flirtations didn't come to anything. He never followed up by touching or whispering sly double meanings. It was like having her grandpa back when he'd wink at her and call her his little Yaqui princesa. She and the Kopps were falling into a cozy routine. That was another reason for staying on — she needed time to save more money. She had time.

"By the way," Melva said, "did you hear anything outside your window last night?"

Rosa Linda spread honey on her muffin, and cocked her head slightly, as if thinking back. "No, I don't think so. Why?" She tried to not hold her breath.

"I got up to take my sleeping pill, forgot to take it, and I thought I heard some rustling, like somebody sneaking around on the fallen leaves. Around about the time the bars close, I think."

"I might've heard a deer," Rosa Linda said, thankful to speak the truth.

"Maybe one of those drunks from one of the bars couldn't find his car," Edward said, and laughed.

"Maybe," Melva said. "But keep your ears sharp at night, Rosie."

Rosa Linda reached for the plates, and Melva barked at her to wait.

"There's something I want to say. We could use some help in the kitchen, on weekends for now. Geneva keeps saying 'no' but meantime the orders pile up while she keeps taking breaks to ease those bunions of hers." Melva poured herself a cup of coffee from the old electric percolator that she'd bought ten years ago and insisted on using. "It's a good opportunity to learn the ropes."

"We-e-e-ell," Rosa Linda said, drawing out the word. She didn't want to be rude, but she also didn't want to give the old woman any false hope about her being interested in any long-term job at a restaurant.

"Should I take that for a no?" Melva said. The hurt in the old woman's voice scratched at Rosa Linda's heart.

"Let me think about it," Rosa Linda said, and stacked the dishes.

"You're in an all-fired hurry today," Melva said dryly.

"It's only that I have too much to do." She pointed to the burn specks on the front of Edward's shirt. "Why didn't you wear the one I put out for you?" she said. When he looked at her with shame in his eyes, she wished she could take the words back. They expected too much from her.

After making the beds, tidying the apartment, and playing a few hands of gin rummy with Edward — letting him win to make up for her sharp words earlier — she left him snoozing in his recliner.

In the restaurant kitchen, she peered over Geneva's shoulder into the simmering pot. "What kind of soup today?"

"Potato-sausage," Geneva said. She shifted her weight the way she did to let folks know they were invading her space.

"Yummy," Rosa Linda said. "Donnie Ray order some for lunch?" She had started the night in costume and in character, but, with Donnie Ray, she'd soon dropped the act, and felt comfortable with him, almost trusting him. And she found she wanted to know more about him. Their relationship was developing. Into what, she wasn't certain. He wanted to keep her at a distance physically, as if he wanted to keep things platonic. Yet, his breathing grew uneven when their bodies were near.

"I have no idea," Geneva said. "I ain't keepin no diary on who eats what." She stirred crumbled sausage that she'd fried crispy in a huge iron skillet, then scooped up the meat with a slotted spoon and dropped it into the simmering pot. The plop-plop splashed up hot liquid, warning Rosa Linda back.

*   *   *

Outside, the dry wind had torn a smattering of yellowing leaves from one of the trees lining the avenue. A leaf landed on Rosa Linda's shoulder, as gently as a butterfly. She plucked it off and slipped it into her pocket. Later she would press the leaf — a keepsake of this pause on her journey. When she stepped inside Powers, a silence fell over the room just as it had the other time she'd ventured in. She scanned the area. Maybe Donnie Ray was taking a bathroom break.

"Can I help you?" a man behind the bar asked. Wiry and olive-skinned with pale green eyes, he reminded her of her friend Paco back in Texas, but his accent was definitely Southern.

"Where's Donnie Ray?" she asked, walking to the bar. Two guys playing pool at a table by the wall had paused when she entered, and now they resumed their game.

"Not here," the bartender said. "And I don't give out personal info, sweetheart. I'm Kelly Powers, owner of this joint. Something I can do for you?"

"I need to talk to him," she said.

"Don't know nothing about that," Kelly said.

Rosa Linda started to turn away but thought she'd try a different tact. It was always easier to solicit information from someone who thought you identified with them.

"By the way," she said, "are you part Mexican, or something?" She smiled. "I am myself, and you look so much like one of my uncles."

"Me?" The man laughed. "Nah, my mimaw's full-blooded Cherokee, maybe that's what you're seeing."

"Ah," Rosa Linda said, "I'm part Yaqui. Well, I won't take any more of your time. Or do you think he'll stop by later?"

Kelly studied her face, as if looking for possible trouble. He drummed two fingers on the edge of the bar making up his mind. "What the hay," he said. "It ain't no secret he'll be down to the Bottoms Up tonight. Working, that is, not socializing. You want more information, you're not getting it from me. Not even if I do look like your uncle."

*   *   *

Donnie Ray began with broad strokes, an outline of her face, oval-shaped, faint lines for eyes, nose, mouth, all separated by standard distances for symmetrical features before tackling the details. Too symmetrical, too much like a comic heroine, a Lichtenstein minus the dots to make it trendy. No hint of the ephemeral something that attracted him to her. She was pretty, sure, but his interest was driven by something much deeper than lust.

He flipped the page, angry at what he could not do. His hand worked quickly, drew intricate curves and hidden places: a human brain. Inside the coils he sketched delicate rosebuds, some petals nibbled by the maggots, white and insidiously small, slithering around the buds, plopping out of the curlicues of the brain. He searched among his colored pencils and selected the palest pink. Only the rosebuds would have color to contrast them more sharply with the black ink. He held the tablet at arm's length and studied it. Then slapped the pad closed. He would not allow himself to fall in love. She was a kid who yearned for the world. She wasn't meant to be caged. There were places for her to visit before finding a home. And he wasn't the traveling kind. He liked his routines, his home, and yes, even the Holler, warts and all.

He picked up the pad again and opened it to a blank page. He plucked a Kool from the pack on the table, and lit it with his Zippo, the one Shayne had given him. The image of his next drawing came to him, and he rested the cigarette in the ashtray. He drew the bike in motion — no longer the still-life it had become — wheels whirring so fast the spikes blended into a blur of action. The Hulk riding again.

He had bought the BMX for Shayne two years before he died. Shayne had asked for a bike for two Christmases and two birthdays before that, and their mother had promised him one each time. When it didn't show on Christmas morning, Charlotte, in baby talk, said Santa hadn't made it this year but for sure the next. Donnie Ray told his mother to quit making promises she wouldn't deliver, but she'd cry and shout, accusing him of driving her to drink with his lack of faith in her. Finally, when Shayne was in middle school, Donnie Ray, without saying anything to his mother, bought the bike himself. He'd chosen a model too big for Shayne, wanting to make certain he'd be able to ride it for years to come.

He'd taken the bike over to the duplex where Shayne lived with Charlotte, and off and on with Dee when she was between jobs or boyfriends and needed a place to stay. That Christmas Dee was away, hoping that the newest of her long line of boyfriends, this one married like most of them, might make it over Christmas morning. She said she'd be over later for with the prepared dinner she would buy at Kroger's deli. Donnie Ray knew that their mother would be sleeping late, since she'd gone to a party with some of her coworkers from the electrical supply company.

By 10 a.m. Donnie Ray couldn't hold back any longer, so he squeezed the bike into the back seat, stopped at the Hole-in-One for a dozen donuts and at Willa's for fried egg sandwiches. He'd banged on the door until Shayne stumbled down the stairs, wearing only his briefs.

Donnie Ray told Shayne he needed help getting something out of the back seat, and Shayne, running his fingers through his sleep-tangled hair, pulled on his jeans, all the while grumbling that he didn't see why a person couldn't wait for a decent hour before coming around demanding favors. When he saw the bike, Shayne tried to hug Donnie Ray, but he'd pushed him back and told him not to go mushy. Now, he wished he could relive that moment. But he'd grown up without familial hugs and went stiff when any of his family members tried to hug him as an adult. Now, he wished he would have hugged his brother.

Donnie Ray closed the pad and rubbed his eyes, grainy from lack of sleep. The night before, Arlie had let him know that Kelly felt strong enough to start working Saturdays at Powers, so he expected him to start earlier at the Bottoms Up tonight.

The phone trilled. It had started ringing at 10 a.m. and each time the caller let it ring twenty times. Charlotte or Dee maybe. Or Tara. He stared at the phone, willing it to stop. God, he wanted a drink. But he'd awakened with a hangover and made a deal with himself not to drink until after six.

He cracked his knuckles, slowly, one at a time. A hard grain of pain had settled in his chest after Shayne died, and it grew inside him, roots spreading like a cancer that was slowly devouring his insides. He didn't talk about the way his brother died but couldn't stop thinking about it. He had let Shayne down, and so had Charlotte and Dee.

He eyed the kitchen cabinet from where he sat on the couch. The phone trilled. He cracked his knuckles.

*   *   *

Rosa Linda unhooked the towel wrapped sarong-style around her and stood before the bedroom closet. Who would she become for tonight's adventure? She positioned the wigs on the bed. Maybe the straight, blond-streaked hair that fell just below her shoulders and bangs that covered her eyebrows. She couldn't imagine Melva ever having worn this one. She'd go full smoky on her eyes, bring out the green highlights. No dreary drudge. Tonight, she would not be cheated out of dancing.

She'd been thinking about that line of clubs the bus had passed last night. It had cut down a busy street, Washington, off Logan. Bars and restaurants lined the street, but what caught her eye was the large magenta neon sign outside a building: Free Will, it flashed. Donnie Ray was out of the picture for tonight. She'd enjoyed talking with him, but he ran hot and cold. He'd listened to her, really listened, as if he cared about her. But, when she'd touched his knuckles with her fingertips, he'd jerked his hand away. Was he not interested in her as a woman, or was he playing hard to get? Well, Rosa Linda del Río didn't chase men. She didn't have to. Whatever it was that Donnie Ray wanted from her, well, he'd have to decide and come to her. She'd decide if she was interested.

On the second story of Free Will, long naked windows revealed a twist of bodies inside the club, shaking and gyrating to music that she couldn't hear from inside the bus. Many of the people milling outside on the sidewalks looked like college students, and she remembered Jaybird informing her that there was a university near the historical area.

During the ride home, she had wanted to ask Donnie Ray if he'd ever been to the club, but he'd already made it clear he didn't want to talk. When she thought about it, she couldn't picture him among those wildly gyrating bodies. He could never allow himself to look so foolish. But she could and she would.

Once she'd chosen her outfit and wig, she picked out big rings she'd bought at the thrift store, two for each hand. She wore the two largest, a steel skull and sharp plastic star, on her right hand. In her shoulder bag, she dropped a car rearview mirror she'd found in Melva's basement.

Tonight, she would tell Melva she was going out. Sneaking out had added to her fun, but once was enough; Melva and Edward were employers, not her grandparents. Better to get that clear. Besides, she wanted to leave earlier tonight when Melva would still be up.

"I see," Melva said, and reached for her Salems. "At night out all by yourself — smart move for a young lady. Mind telling me where? In case you don't return, I'd like to know where the police can start looking for your body."

Rosa Linda sighed. Honesty was not paying off. "Rick's Flicks."

"What the hell's that?"

Rosa Linda remembered passing by the cinema. At first, she'd taken it for some sort of porn place, but then saw Terrence Malik's artsy *Days of Heaven* advertised on the marquee.

"An art cinema near downtown," she said. "They're showing something I want to see. After, I'll go for a burger. Maybe I'll meet some other kids there. Who knows?"

Melva huffed out a stream of cigarette smoke. "Not that it's any of my goddamn business. But I'll tell you something that is, missy." Melva pointed at her with the cigarette dangling between her two fingers. "I said it before, and I'll say it again: Do not, and I mean do not, bring home any stray cats. Male or female. And don't cock that eyebrow at me. You know exactly what I mean. This is my house — paid by years of my sweat and I — Melva Kopp — will decide who does and who does not come into my home."

When Rosa Linda rolled her eyes, Melva added, "Do I make myself clear?"

"You don't have to worry about me," Rosa Linda said. Melva's shoulders were at a higher tilt than usual, and the irritation building inside Rosa Linda puddled into resentment. The old woman meant well, she knew, but all this drama was what she was trying to avoid. This was why she needed to save money, get out, and have a life of her own. A sense of family was nice, but with it came all the ties that bind and all the bitching. She needed a place where she made the house rules.

Melva puffed her cigarette, turned her face away. "I'll hold off taking my sleeping pill until you get home, so I'll hear you when you knock."

"You could give me a key," Rosa Linda said.

"I'll wait up."

* * *

Rosa Linda pressed her forehead against the cool glass of the bus window. The residential areas passed by, houses were aglow from within, yet yards and sidewalks remained abandoned and deserted, as if the night had frightened people to take refuge inside. Not until the bus neared Washington Street did individuals emerge. At first a few, but as she peered out to view the length of the street, she noticed many more milling about on the sidewalks. She reached up and pulled the cord to signal she wanted to get off.

The neon and lighted signs vied for attention, all blinking flirtatiously to lure onlooker inside. Young people gathered in groups, shouting to be heard above the raucous and steady buzz of activity. The day had been overcast, and the wind gusts blew heavy. The TV weatherman had predicted that the long-hoped-for rain would finally arrive tonight.

Rosa Linda decided to walk up one side of the block, cross over, and loop back to the other side of the street before selecting her first bar for the night. A mix of stores showed remnants of the Holler: a Goodwill store; Brownie's, a used bookstore that reeked of mildew and mold even with the door locked for the night; two vintage stores, one with a poster in the window that promoted a spiritual advisor; two adult stores, side by side, one with covered windows boasting of peep shows and the other with a display window with two mannequin torsos, one wearing skimpy red lingerie with black fake fur around the collar and the other in pleather bra and panties. Rosa Linda took a second look. The torsos wore women's clothing but had large male bulges in the crotch. She laughed, and thought, Why not?

Next to an empty storefront, Free Will's magenta neon hummed. Students stood in knots outside on the sidewalk as they had when she'd seen them from afar, but now the DJ music boomed. She had stepped into the scene. Her pulse pounded in rhythm to the music, currents of electricity vibrating through the soles of her feet. Three young guys huddled against the outside wall, watching her.

"Hey, beautiful," one called, "here's where you want to be."

The doorman checked her ID, slipped a magenta band around her wrist to indicate she was between the ages of eighteen and twenty-one. No soda for her tonight. She wanted a buzz to set her free for dancing. When she ordered a rum and Coke, the bartender pointed to her band, and asked what kind of beer she'd like. "You choose," she said, and accepted the bottle of near beer. It would do.

"Here, I'll get that," a man next to her yelled above the music and voices. He waved a couple of bills at the bartender.

She shook her head and paid. She was here to dance, have some fun. Not to find a man. He shouted something about "no strings attached," but she gestured toward her ear to indicate she couldn't hear. She wiggled a good-bye with her fingers, prepared to push through the crowded room.

The constant beat of the music stirred something inside her. She couldn't make out the lyrics nor did she care to, but Chaka Khan's strong voice and the thumping beat of the music shook the floorboards. Her feet found the rhythm, and it pulsated up her legs, into the sway of her hips, into the shimmy of her shoulders. The music belonged to her; she belonged to it. A hand grabbed hers, pulled her away from the bar. Young, fresh-faced features reddened with alcohol pushed inches away from her face.

"Dance," he yelled. He pointed to the dance floor, a sea of heads away.

She held her bottle aloft with one hand, allowing him to clasp the other, as he wove them through the crowd. When they made it to the crush of writhing bodies on the dance floor, the tune had ended but another started up. She spied the stairway leading up, gesturing for them to ascend.

"The windows," she shouted.

Madonna's "Borderline" started up, and the energy inside her bubbled. She laughed, feeling like one of those balls in the bingo machines, poppity-pop, pop-pop. Upstairs, flashing lights lit up the dancers, breaking their movements. She pulled him toward the windows. Let the world see her, envy her energy, her freedom. And she was free. Free to do as she pleased.

From the window glass, her reflection gazed, wild-eyed, back at her, and behind her the orgasmic, twisting bodies. Outside, she knew, people were watching, just as she had. She would stand out from the others. A shining star. The old "Miss You" by the Rolling Stones came on, and she closed her eyes, allowed the music to inhabit her, stopped trying to recognize songs.

"Hey, hey," her dancing partner was shaking her by one shoulder.

She opened her eyes, still so much inside the music that he seemed far away. She had no idea how long they'd been dancing, but she was aware now of how warm and damp with sweat she'd become.

"You're something," he said, "me, I gotta take a break." He breathed through his mouth, and with two fingers swiped sweat off his forehead.

"Go on," she said. "I want to finish this song." She felt suddenly thirsty and lifted her hand to take a swallow of beer. She studied her empty hand, had no idea what she'd done with the bottle, and didn't care. She laughed. This is what she'd been needing, the self-hypnotic trance that came upon her when she danced. She needed no drink, no partner. It was just her and the music.

"I'll be back," her partner said. She nodded and closed her eyes, seeking the beat again, but she couldn't fall back into it immediately.

His breath blew warm into the shell of her ear a second before she heard his whispery voice. "Just Ophelia."

She jerked alert. With one motion, Enon encircled her upper arms with his hands and pressed her back to his chest. The scent of Old Spice cut through the smoke and sweat, filling her senses. The chill at the base of her brain that she had never forgotten returned.

"You ain't nobody without me." Enon pressed his mouth to her ear. In spite of her dance-warm body, she shivered. "And you ain't so fuckin' smart," he hissed, his spit spraying on her ear.

She pushed him backward into the dancing bodies; they tilted back, throwing him off balance. She slammed the sharp edge of her clunky heel onto the top of his foot.

"Shit," he shouted, and his hold on her relaxed. She twisted around and brought her knee up hard. The angle prevented a solid hit to the groin, but enough to double him in pain. Sweaty bodies danced around him.

She wedged herself next to him. Gave him a short, hard jab to the side of his head with her right fist. It was an awkward blow, but still solid enough for her to feel the sting clear to her elbow. The star had broken off her ring and punctured the skin at his temple. He crab-stumbled backward to the wall.

Rosa Linda smashed forward through a circle of dancing girls, stumbled, fell to the floor at their feet. The girls laughed. Rosa Linda pushed up on one knee.

"Break dancer," one of the girls hollered, pointing at her. "Give the woman room, dammit." The circle of girls pushed back, opening enough space around Rosa Linda to allow her to grab a sturdy girl by her calves and pull herself up.

"Yo, bitch," the girl yelled, "get off me." But the circle had closed again, and the girl joined her friends, all of them waving their arms above their heads.

A huge man, SECURITY, written across the chest of his black T-shirt grabbed Rosa Linda by the arm. "Hey, what's going on?" he shouted.

She glanced over her shoulder to where Enon had been, but lights flashed, and she saw only light-broken pieces of gyrating bodies.

"No problem," she told Security, "I'm leaving."

She pried space between wedged bodies and headed to the stairs, all the while glancing over her shoulder for Enon. It had happened so fast; she should have kept her senses sharp, but why be alive if she couldn't let go now and then? The hand she'd hit him with still tingled, and she shook it, open-handed.

The scent of Old Spice lingered like toxic fumes, but maybe it was only the memory following her. She felt his cold gray eyes watching her, waiting for the right moment. She imagined him shoving up against her in the crowd, silently sticking Cisco's knife into her, *Un Recuerdo de Mexico* slicing through her guts. If she screamed, who would listen, who could differentiate the sounds of violent death from the frenzy of good times fueled by alcohol? If she dropped to the floor, dead, how long before anyone noticed that blood, not red vomit poured from her?

She stopped every few steps to scan the crowd below. Maybe he waited inside for her; or maybe he'd left. She only knew that the walls of Free Will were closing in, the heat and smell of too many bodies. She was breathing open-mouthed by the time she reached the first level.

"Dance?"

She twisted to face the male voice, swinging her purse back, ready to hit.

"Whoa." The stranger stepped back onto another guy's foot. "Fuck," the guy shouted. "Fuck you," the first one hollered. One pushed the other, and they grabbed for one another.

Above the crowd in front of her, a refrigerator of a man, standing a head taller than the others shoved toward the ruckus. "Take it outside," he yelled.

A mass of people turned in unison, and not wanting to be involved in the brawl, propelled as one toward the exit. Rosa Linda hunched down, riding low in a current of hot flesh toward the front door. The river broke at the doorway, and spit Rosa Linda onto the sidewalk.

As she caught her footing, her eyes darted in every direction. She touched the ojo de venado beneath her blouse for luck. She swallowed great gulps of air, suddenly exhilarated. She'd escaped again. But this time, the thrill seemed to have lost its edge. This wasn't a game anymore. She wanted it to be over. Maybe she was getting old. She laughed, swinging her arms, her shoulder bag still bumping on her hip, as she weaved through the roaming pedestrians. She wondered about their lives, the young ones who looked so healthy and cared for. How sure they were of themselves with their parents as safety nets, their planned lives laid out before them. Or, in spite of their well-bred exteriors, did chaos live inside them, too?

She breathed in slowly through her nose and released through her mouth, and soon stilled her racing heart.

Across the street and some yards down, she could see a café with tables on the sidewalk. Rather than run, she intermittently walked and trotted to what she would now see was a coffee shop and bakery, University Grind. A glass case inside by the cashier displayed an array of pastries and sandwiches. She felt suddenly famished. But if Enon passed by, searching for her, going into the well-lit coffee shop would be tantamount to making an entrance onto a theater stage. However, he might've crawled off to nurse his wounds; she certainly got in some good licks.

She kept to her side of the street and continued past the University Grind. Rich smells of dark coffee and sugar rolled across the street, but she kept on. From behind, footsteps shuffled toward her, coming fast. She spun around. A tall man, dressed in a raggedy overcoat stretched an arm toward her.

"Hey, blondie," he said. "I want a muffin."

"What?" She continued walking backwards away from him.

"I'm hungry," he shouted. He pointed at the coffee shop. "Buy me a muffin, girl."

Rosa Linda fished in her purse for her wallet. "Here," she said, and pulled out a tightly rolled five.

She wedged the edge into a nearby parking meter for him to come and retrieve it. He looked harmless, but now she was on alert, taking no chances. "My last five for you, Muffin Man. This is so you'll bring me luck."

"If I had any motherfucking luck, girl, you think I'd be asking you for a muffin?" He laughed, rotten, broken teeth telling the story of his life. He waved the bill. "Bless you, child. What comes around, goes around," he called, and jaywalked toward the coffee shop.

At the end of the block patrons straggled out of Rick's Flicks, and she sprinted to catch up with the art film patrons. In spite of the chill in the air, all the physical activity heated her, causing her scalp to perspire beneath the wig. Slowing to a trot, then a stroll as she neared the people, she casually followed a group of three who turned left. She was thinking it would be nice to belong to a group like that, coming out of the cinema, not a care in the world, when the woman in the group turned to stare at her over her shoulder.

Rosa Linda nodded a greeting, but instead of responding, the woman nudged one of the guys. The three of them glanced at her and stopped. She was afraid they were going to confront her, but they all climbed into a Honda parked on the street at a meter.

"Wish I had a muffin," Rosa Linda said, as she passed the car. The door locks clicked shut.

She was off the main drag now, and the streets were as abandoned as in those dystopian movies where the hero believes he's the only survivor until, out of the destruction, another being appears. She thought of turning back toward the lights and the crowds, but she liked the dark solitude of a nighttime street.

God, the wig itched. She paused to scratch, wishing she had one of Loretta's pencils for easier access through the net. She'd risk the lead poisoning for a good scratch. Ahead a car was parked on the opposite side of the street a half block ahead. One more block beyond the car, she would reach the ally at the back entrance of the Bottoms Up. She stopped, hands on hips, wondering how she'd landed here. Without thinking, she'd walked right to the place she really wanted to be, where she hoped she could belong but knew she never would.

A car screeched to a halt next to her and, leaving it running, Enon hopped out of the driver's seat and onto the sidewalk. He grabbed her closest arm, and yanked so hard she heard something pop in the socket. "Quit your play-actin', bitch," he hollered. One side of his face was already swollen, dried blood caked where she'd punched him. The steel skull had done its job.

She pulled back with all her might, tried to dig her heels into the concrete. He covered her mouth with one hand. "Me and you," he said, grunting as he held onto her. "We found what we was lookin' for." She sank her teeth deep into his palm. He screamed, saliva bubbling at the corners of his mouth.

From the other end of the street a man's voice yelled, "Hey, motherfucker, I see you!" It was the Muffin Man. He yelled something unintelligible and loped great loose strides toward them.

Enon's eyes darted to the Muffin Man and back to Rosa Linda. She broke free, swung her shoulder bag with all her might. The full weight of the rearview mirror hit Enon in the chest, and he wind-milled backward, hitting the car door.

"I'll be back," he said. "Always." He slid back into his car, leaving behind the smell of burning rubber. The Muffin Man stopped midway to Rosa Linda, bent an arm to his waist, and made a courtly bow before turning and ambling away.

She ran, her feet slapped, slapped on the hard pavement—soles in flight. A second car whizzed by from behind her, a drunken voice yelling something at her. She lifted her hand, middle finger up, and kept going. That didn't worry her; it was Enon, she could sense him. She could almost smell Old Spice.

In one last burst of energy she broke for the alley behind Bottoms Up. Once inside the dark mouth of the lane, she slipped on something slimy and fell. The sound of her ragged breaths ricocheted off the brick walls of buildings lining the alley.

"Please, please," she whispered to the darkness. "Please, please."

A car door opened behind her. Enon cursed, and a thud followed. He had slipped in the same slime. Only he didn't make it upright as quickly as she had, because another curse and another wet slap to the ground followed.

If she tried to cut back to the bar, he'd stop her. She sucked in her breath, and forced herself through a space in the fence where a plank was missing. She turned in the opposite direction from Bottoms Up, cut across a vacant property, hid behind its locked-up old garage. She clutched the catch in her side. Her panting filled her ears, and she wondered if she would be able to hear Enon if he came upon her.

When she exited from the back streets, Donnie Ray's building sat waiting for her, but there was no light in his apartment. She crawled up the stairs, knocked softly on the bottom board of the door. She knocked harder. She crawled into the darkest corner of the small balcony and waited.

CHAPTER TWELVE

The Ohio night breeze had cooled, transporting Rosa Linda to the past and desert nights. By merely closing her eyes, she lay not on the back balcony of Donnie Ray's apartment but in the scoop of the boulder behind her grandparents' house in Nopal, Arizona.

She bent her legs, held them tight against her chest. Her head resting against the rock shelf, she gazed up at the vastness of the sky. All those stars, each a wish waiting to be claimed. She drifted into sleep, and her thoughts evolved into a dream.

Wind howled and swept down from the hills of the Sonoran Desert, breaking around mesquite trees, cactus, boulders. A column of dust formed in the distance. She sensed the soldier's presence before she spotted him, walking toward her, arms outstretched. His cavalry cap sat low on his forehead and a kerchief covered his nose and mouth against the biting grit. Only his eyes were revealed: black, intense, Denzel Washington eyes. The buffalo soldier's gaze shifted in her direction.

He stopped, as if waiting for her to meet him. Just as she was wondering if she should walk out to him, he whispered, but the words were lost on the wind. His shape broke into dots, the way human forms did in time-travel movies, and as the sand beneath him shifted, his footprints were lost to memory. Her ancestor, Rosa Linda was certain.

The story was that Nana's mother fell in love with the handsome soldier in his uniform, and even though it was against the law for races to intermarry, they did what their hearts demanded. The law wasn't so concerned, Nana said, because her mom was more Yaqui than Spanish, and her father's blood was mixed with that of white slave owners from the past. But Nana's handsome father was killed in a skirmish on the border, and she and her mother lived the rest of their lives with only his ghost to remind them of a love that had been.

Rosa Linda is suddenly with Nana, sitting on the front porch, Nana in her rocker, she on the stoop. Both eye the heavens. They're waiting for a shooting star.

"Make a wish, make a wish," Rosa Linda pleads.

"That's for the young, mi amor. My wishes lie at the bottom of a well gone dry," Nana says. She laughs, but Rosa Linda feels sad.

Below, a car pulled into the parking lot, and Rosa Linda's eyelids flipped open. A car door slammed shut and she pressed her hand to her mouth and nose, as if to quiet her breathing. A step creaked. "Who's there?" she said.

"What's going on?" Donnie Ray said.

He slid the key into the lock and opened the door. "What're you doing here?"

"Hey, I'm sorry to bother you, OK? I needed a place to hide. This is the only place I know around here where I feel safe. Some guy, he followed me from the club, the Free Will on Washington." Once she said the words, she felt silly, the seriousness of her statement leaking like air hissing from a balloon.

"Followed you here?" He glanced at the steps, the parking lot.

"Yes, well, no, not *here*. It's only, I don't know . . . ." She searched for the reason. "I feel safe here," she said, and shrugged.

Once they were inside, she asked for something to drink. Her mouth felt suddenly dry as the desert.

"I bought some pop today, look in the fridge," Donnie Ray said. "Now tell me what gives."

"It's no big deal," she said, as she pulled a can of soda from the refrigerator.

"You weren't curled up on my porch like a kicked dog for nothing."

She sat at the counter now, and he sat next to her. "OK," she said, rolling the cold can between her palms. "You're right. Remember when I told you about hitchhiking? Well, I left out part of the story."

"No shit."

She told him about meeting Enon at the Buckeye Diner, about being so tired and sleepy that she'd accepted his offer to take her to Chicago. She held up a hand to stop Donnie Ray before he could answer. "Don't lecture me," she said, "I'm impulsive, not stupid."

"Are you out of your mind?" he said, then answered himself. "You're crazy."

"*You're* crazy," she said, hurt that he would fall to insults when she was opening herself to him.

"Screw you," he said.

"No, screw *you*."

She remembered the two guys at the Free Will and laughed.

His jaw tightened, but when he leveled his cold blue stare, she folded her arms and stared back. His mouth twitched, and he lowered his head. She could see he was about to laugh, and then they both laughed in unison.

After a moment, he said, "Well, now that we cleared that up."

"Anyway, I do have an aunt in Chicago."

"I'm listening," he said.

She told him about falling asleep, waking up to Enon, the details of the too-vivid colors in the trees and sky, the heavy oppression of the closed air inside the car, the smell of Old Spice, the knife at her throat. A mask fell over Donnie Ray's face, and the stonier his expression, the faster her words tumbled out of her mouth.

"That's it," she said, and dusted her hands, as if ridding herself of dirt. "Now Enon's found me. And he just won't stop. Too weird."

"A knife," he said, "no gun?" He walked toward the window, gazed outside before returning to sit next to her on the sofa. "He found you tonight, and what?"

She told him about receiving the ojo de venado in the mail, what followed at the Free Will.

"You're telling me," he said, studying her as if she were an escapee from a mental institute, "you knew the guy was watching you, and you went out alone?"

"Ah, come on," she said. "Don't tell me you'd hide away like a prisoner because of some idiot. Anyway, I only go out in a disguise."

"That's working out great." He clamped his jaw tightly, white lines forming at the sides of his mouth.

"OK," he said, after a moment of silence. "Average height and weight, nothing out of the ordinary, except for these weird eyes, almost no color, that sums him up?"

"How do you know?" she said.

Donnie Ray flicked the Zippo.

"I think he's been down to the Bottoms Up. Some jackass hanging around. I'd like to wipe that smirk off his face. You call the cops?"

"The cops, you think they're going to believe me?" she said. "No way. They'd say I was asking for it by hitchhiking, getting into a car with a stranger — who didn't, by the way, actually rape me or stab me. So they'll say they can't lock a man up for what he's thinking. And if they did find Enon, his word against mine. I'm telling you, the police will say they can't do a damn thing. If, *if* they even believe me — which they will not."

"Christ," he said, "you ready to take a breath? Look, I didn't say you *should* call the cops. Keep your mouth shut. Something happens to him — Enon? — they don't come looking for you." His eyes focused on something in the distance, his thoughts turned inward.

"I'm sorry," she said, "to get you involved." They were the right words to say; she hoped she meant them.

"You're safe with me," he said. Then with a grin, he tapped her head. "Doesn't that damn thing itch?"

As she was unpinning the wig, she blurted, "Do you trust me? I trust you."

"Like you knew you could trust Enon when you got in his car?"

"Oh, see, here it comes," she said. "It's all my fault for getting in the car."

"Settle down." Donnie Ray got up to pull the Jim Beam and a tumbler from the cabinets. He hesitated, then held up another glass to her, but she shook her head no. "Don't assume that you can trust any damn body until you see the proof, that's what I'm telling you. All you need to do is turn your back one time — that's all it'll take."

"OK," she said. "I get it, OK?"

"How about the Free Will?" he said. "Anybody see you guys together? Anybody who can connect you to him?"

She shook her head.

"I mean, it's pretty dark in that place, except for that big old disco ball, flashing off and on people. Well, I did fall on the floor in the middle of some girls, but nobody really pays attention. You know how it is — you get into yourself, your own world. Then a fight started, and I got the hell out. Like a lot of other people, so it wasn't like I stood out for running." She paused. "If something should happen to Enon, it's like you said, the cops aren't going to come around questioning me— or you."

She studied Donnie Ray's face, but his expression revealed nothing. She asked, "Do you think something might happen to him?"

"Sometimes a guy gets his obsessions beaten right out of him. He forgets all kinds of things and considers himself lucky to get the hell back to where he belongs. Sometimes, a really stubborn guy might disappear. Things happen."

She nodded slowly. She didn't want Donnie Ray to get in trouble. Then again, he talked as if he knew how to handle sticky situations. And Enon was exhausting her. Look how he'd behaved at the little diner. When he saw there might be a threat to himself with those other men, he'd scampered out of there like a dog with its tail between his legs. All Donnie Ray would have to do was shout "boo" in Enon's face. Nobody had to get really hurt.

"He followed you to the Holler, right?" Donnie Ray switched off the kitchen light and peered through the slats of the blind. "What kind of car does he drive?"

"Old and brownish — oh, wait," she said. "He did say a Buick, I think. But I don't know much about cars, and I didn't get his license plates." She also explained that Enon had followed her in his car into the alley behind Bottoms Up but not to the apartment.

"Oh, and," she said, "he changed his plates. I distinctly remember he had Florida plates when I met him. But last night the plates were changed." She sucked in her breath. "He's been following me all along."

"That car was out front of Melva's the day you arrived to town," Donnie Ray said.

"I didn't go to your work tonight," she said quickly, "so don't think I was trying to get you involved. I was just trying to hide in the alley. I didn't have time to make it to the front of the building." She paused, and added, "Would that've been the wrong thing, I mean to go inside?"

"Hell," he said, "I wish you'd run right in with him behind you. I can tell you now, that asshole would've disappeared into the back room so fast he wouldn't know what hit him. And nobody would have seen a goddamn thing. Those are my people in there. And those who aren't, they got the good sense to know when to shut down."

"Maybe they could just scare him," Rosa Linda said. She remembered how there'd been something sad about Enon, and she couldn't help but wonder about what had happened in life to turn him the way he was. But then, she remembered the cold blade of the knife against her skin.

Donnie Ray held an open hand to the side of his mouth, motioning for her to be quiet.

"What?" she whispered.

He switched off the light in the front room, opened the door a crack and stepped outside. Inside, her hearing followed the squeak of each one of the wood-swollen stairs as Donnie Ray crept down and then back up to the landing. When he returned moments later, he switched on the lamp.

"The neighbor's old hound dog's nosing around the trash cans," he said.

"But I don't think Enon saw me come up here," Rosa Linda said. "If he did, he would've done something before you got here, no?"

"You should've told me about this guy before," he said.

"Since you're so worried and everything, can I please stay here tonight? I'm telling you, this guy has worn me out," she said.

He told her he'd get her a pillow and a blanket, and she pointed to the phonograph across the room by the TV and VCR. "Could we listen to some music?"

"After I take my shower," he said. "I'll put on the records."

She understood. Her father didn't allow anyone to touch his phonograph or his precious collection of vinyl records, either.

"Thank you," she said. "You don't know how much I appreciate—"

"Yeah," he said, and walked away. When he returned, he handed her the set of white sheets, and a man's T-shirt, soft from many washings, fell off the stack of linen. He wasn't looking her way, so she picked it up, and scrunched the worn cotton to her nose. She wished it smelled of Donnie Ray rather than of a recent bleaching.

"It's all I got. But don't put it on yet. And the sheets, put them on later too. When it's time to sleep."

She wanted to laugh but knew better. What was with these tough guys and their prudishness? Cisco had been the same way. Once he had decided she was the nice girl his mother had wanted for him, he treated her as if she were the Madonna. His tender-handed reverence had irritated her, made her feel somehow guilty, scared her, as if she were a fraud. She'd become determined to show him that his image of her was a fantasy.

Donnie Ray left for his shower, and she considered calling Melva to let her know she wouldn't be home. But she couldn't bear the thought of the complaining, the accusations. Melva might have stayed up, but old age wouldn't allow her to stay awake all night. No, Rosa Linda would stay right where she wanted to be tonight and face Melva tomorrow. She rested her head on the pillow, and a faint smell wafted up. Beneath the laundry soap of the pillowcase, a hint of women's perfume with staying power.

* * *

Donnie Ray opened a glass cabinet filled with rows of vinyl record albums, all in their covers. "I don't have any of that modern shit," he said, glancing back at her over his shoulder.

"I see that," she said, "not even one cassette. Is that Patsy Cline in your hands?"

He turned the cover front toward her.

"The *Showcase* album," she said. "My dad's got that one. He's wild for Patsy. He likes the old stuff — but then, he's kind of old himself. He's old enough to be my mom's dad."

Donnie Ray slipped the record out of its cover, and handling it carefully by the sides, placed it on the turntable. He walked easily — the whiskey had mellowed him — toward her. His bare feet were pale, clean, with long toes and high arches, as well-shaped as his hands but not marked or scarred. Even so she preferred those hands that revealed something of him and his battles in life.

As he had done the last time, Donnie Ray sat at the opposite end of the sofa.

"I still don't bite," she said, smiling to show her dimple.

"I'm just fine," he said, and planted his feet firmly on the worn design of cabbage roses on the linoleum.

The needle scratched into the groove, and Patsy's contralto voice worked its magic. Held by the charm of the singer's rich voice, they fell silent. Rosa Linda rested her head on the back of the sofa, while Donnie Ray sat on the edge with a drink in hand.

"You kind of remind me of Patsy," he said, after a moment. "She liked a good time. Independent, too."

"She was something," Rosa Linda said.

"And like your hero Frida, life threw all kinds of shit at them, and both took up with the wrong kind of men, but they didn't let anything stand in the way of their dreams."

He held up his glass as if toasting. "To Patsy and Frida," she said.

"What's that?" He pointed to her chest.

As she removed the wig, the synthetic hair had caught on the string of the ojo de venado, pulling the talisman outside her blouse.

"This is the scapular thingee that I told you about," she said, "the one Enon mailed back to me?" She explained its significance and started to tell him that her grandmother gave it to her. She didn't want to lie to him, but also didn't want to bring up Cisco. Anyway, Donnie Ray hadn't asked her about where she got it, so why be so eager to volunteer extraneous information?

"Believe in magic, do you?" he said.

"Why *magic*? Anyway, what's wrong with magic? You don't find magic in life? All around us?" Her arms spread wide to encompass the world.

"All religion," he said, "is a bunch of bull to me."

"And you believe that there's only this?" She waved her arms again. "Can't there be something beyond that's bigger only we can't understand? Not a Santa Claus god, or even organized religion. Something spiritual that—"

"Believe what you want," he said, "but as far as I'm concerned, this—" he pointed to the floor with both index fingers — "is all she wrote. And we can't even hold onto this."

"Because you lost your brother." She regretted her words as soon as they came out. "I'm sorry, sometimes I say things without thinking."

"Forget it," he said.

"You know so much about me," she said, changing the subject. "What do I know about you? I'm just trying to understand you."

He lit a cigarette, and watched the smoke dissipating into the air.

She struggled to find something to regain his interest. "Remember," she said, "when we talked about the buffalo soldiers, how I told you my great grandfather was one?"

"And?"

"Well, the camp where they were stationed is gone, forgotten, but the desert will always be there."

"Don't bet on it," he said. "People have a way of destroying everything they touch."

"Why don't you go out there, to the Southwest? My grandmother told me that her father said that as soon he rode into the Sonoran Desert, he knew he was home. He wasn't from there originally, but once he stepped foot in Nopal, he swore he would never leave. Maybe it's the same for you."

He made a dismissive sound, gulped his whiskey.

"Why not?" she repeated.

He swirled the last whiskey in the glass and watched the golden liquid. "What the hell would I do over there?" he said.

"Same thing you do here, work, live. Make your dream reality."

"Hey, here's a question for you: Who comes to Mad River, Ohio, to become an actress?"

"I'm always acting," she shot back.

"I've noticed," he said.

"Ha, ha," she said, "but that's not what I meant."

"Keep it straight with me," he said, "and we'll get along fine." He tapped the side of his glass with one finger before setting it on the table. "Hold on a minute," he said, his voice suddenly heavy and serious. "I got something to show you. Flip the record over, will you?"

When he returned from his bedroom, he handed her a plastic sleeve holding what appeared to be a newspaper article between the sheets.

"Read it."

He didn't sit on the sofa this time but moved away to the shadows by the record player as Patsy sang, "Crazy." He stared at the floor, the expression on his face odd, one that she had not seen on him before. Rosa Linda glanced at the title of the article: "High School Dropout Attacks Local Businessman."

"Hmm," she muttered, "*high school dropout* versus *local businessman*. Gee, I wonder whose side they're on."

She read the short piece that explained how Fred Dunlap, respected local businessman, known for his charitable work with the city's underprivileged had invited a sister and brother to his home, with the hope of mentoring the boy. Shayne Camper, no stranger to the local police, it stated, had attacked Dunlap with a Japanese ceremonial sword that hung on his wall. Dunlap, fearing for his life, had managed to wrest away the sword and turn it on Shayne. Dunlap regretted that he had no other choice but to kill his attacker.

Rosa Linda's hands shook when she laid the article on the table. How might Shayne have told the story? If he'd had the chance. She wanted to say something comforting, but what could she possibly say that wouldn't ring trite?

Donnie Ray's grief filled the air. She tasted salt and, when she touched the wetness on her lip, realized she was crying. She had not thought herself capable of spontaneous and true crying anymore. If she found a need to call on tears for a part on or off the stage, she concentrated and remembered Pelón's face when she left him at the pound.

For several minutes, she had the sensation of being in church, sitting in a pew, eyes closed in meditation, and half-expected the smell of burning candles and incense to fill her with the scent of prayers for and to the dead.

She slowly opened her eyes.

"What really happened?" she asked. She picked up and dropped the plastic sleeve back onto the table.

"People want to feel safe against the *dropouts* of the world." The word caught in his throat with a rusty sound, and he shook his head.

"That guy Dunlap," she said softly, "what happened to him?" Maybe, she thought, he would answer if the question were specific and not directly about Shayne.

He laughed, a bitter sound.

"What do you think? Got off, self-defense, just like Dunlap's cop friends and the newspaper told it before there was even a trial. Retired to Florida right after. At least he didn't get to enjoy it. There was an obituary in the Mad River newspaper. Died of a heart attack not too long after getting settled in St. Augustine." He clenched his jaw so tightly something popped.

"Shit," he muttered, and cracked his knuckles. With a sudden movement, he grabbed the newspaper article and strode across the room. He straightened, took a deep breath, and paused, containing his anger, before tenderly removing Patsy from the turntable. He returned the record to its envelope. "You know where everything is," he said. "I'm going to bed."

* * *

Rosa Linda flipped over the pillow, thankful the other woman's perfume had not permeated through to the other side. She thought about Shayne, imagined the sword slicing through him. She hadn't been able to save her best friend, and Donnie Ray had not been able to save his brother from Fred Dunlap.

She fell in and out of sleep, sometimes blinking in the dark, forgetting where she was. Once the tolling of bells stirred her. The same tune she'd heard when Enon drove her out of Mad River. Enon must have heard the bells then. Had the ringing had any effect on him? Brought back any memories? Did he have dreams? What would a better life look like to him? Had he ever been anything other than a monster?

Thunder rolled in the distance. She peeked out the window, expecting to see the long-awaited rain. But it had only been dry thunder. Enon was out there somewhere, like a faraway storm, moving closer. Old Spice fumes drifted like a fog among the turns of her mind. If only she could click her heels three times and magically transport herself. Poof. One moment in Mad River, then poof in Chicago. Or poof in New York. Why not? Because there was no magic, that was why. Only she could get herself to where she wanted to go.

She wanted to clear her mind. Read. She would read. Donnie Ray had to have a book or two in this room. She opened the small drawer on the coffee table and found *Buffalo Soldiers* and his sketchbooks. She switched on a lamp.

"Wow," she said softly, flipping through pencil sketches he'd done of the Black cavalry soldiers. Their postures, but even more their eyes, seem to speak from the pages, demanding dignity and respect. The drawing of herself was cute, more like a caricature. Then she turned to the page with the rosebuds and maggots. He'd remembered. And, unlike Cisco, he held no illusions about her.

A strangled gurgle came from Donnie Ray's bedroom, followed by a shout, straining at his throat. She'd had enough nightmares to recognize one when she heard it.

CHAPTER THIRTEEN

Donnie Ray drove slowly through the Washington District. He hoped he might be lucky enough to spot Enon or his car, but the streets were Sunday-morning quiet. They were passing Free Will, doors closed and locked, when Rosa Linda pointed out the windows on the second story.

"Last night that place was crazy," she said. "In those windows people were dancing like tomorrow would never come."

"But it did," Donnie Ray said. "Along with the hangovers to prove it." He had talked too much last night, opened up to Rosa Linda. He'd felt close to her at the time, but now the intimacy embarrassed him. He didn't want her to misunderstand. He didn't want to be interested in her. She was the kind of woman — no, "girl," he corrected — that a guy could fall in love with. The kind of love where she had control. No way. But he hadn't any choice but to let her stay for the night after he'd heard about that psycho Enon.

"Only the ghosts of dancing bodies in those windows today," she said, her face turned to the Free Will. Her voice was still fuzzy with sleep.

She'd been sound asleep when he stood next to her for a few minutes this morning, watching her, thinking how she looked like Sleeping Beauty, how he wished he could awaken her with a kiss that would bring her happiness. His insides had ached with the yearning to help her. Just as he wished he'd been able to do with Shayne. He wished he'd done more for Shayne, but his brother was gone. As for Rosa Linda, the best he could do was to let her fly free. She had dreams, and he believed she had the courage to go for them. He couldn't allow that psycho to bring her down. He shook her shoulder, and she awakened with a grouchy, "What?"

"Maybe Enon hit the road," he said. "He's got to get bored like anybody else."

She cleared her throat. "Maybe he hopped away like a big fat toad," she said. "Hit the road like a toad. I'm a poet."

She laughed.

"Treat your enemy like a joke," Donnie Ray said, "and he might be the one getting the last laugh."

"I'm just trying to lighten the mood, you know?" She looked outside. "You get so many gray clouds over here. Makes the light different. I didn't like it at first, but now it's not so bad. It's like I'm a character in an old black-and-white movie on AMC. I wish it would rain, so we could see neon reflected on the wet streets. Don't you love it when they do that in those movies?

"An old-time detective movie," she said. "Picture you and me, Bogie and McCall."

"Don't see it," he said, and imagined the scene from *To Have and Have Not*, Rosa Linda instructing him how to whistle for her, him staring after her befuddled, whistling softly to himself.

She stuck her nose out of the opened car window, sniffed. "Somebody's baking biscuits," she said. "Wouldn't it be cool if movies had scent?"

"Silly," Donnie Ray said.

"No, no, it's been done. For real. Something my dad told me. He went for all the old films and stuff — he told me about when there was a movie with scent. *Scent of Mystery* it was called. Just in case people didn't get it, right? So, the smells came in through the vents, and in the New York City showing, the scent thingee got messed up with the sewer somehow. The critics said that they smelled mystery, and it stank."

Rosa Linda laughed at her own story, and Donnie Ray chuckled, more with her contagious belly laugh than the story. They had stopped for a stop sign, and the laughter drew the attention of two women walking on the sidewalk who eyed them with suspicion before hurrying away.

Rosa Linda was all about excess, a big part of his attraction to her, but that excess also scared him — for her. She was too impulsive, too exposed, and in the wrong company this could get her hurt. Look what had already happened with Enon. She'd gotten out of two encounters; the third time she might not be so lucky.

"You did call Melva this morning like you said, right?"

"Yes, like I said, while you were in your room." Her face was pulled into a pout that irritated him. He could imagine her practicing making expressions in the mirror, deciding which ones would be most effective at getting her way.

He'd mentioned Melva last night before going off to his room, and Rosa Linda said that before going out, she'd told the Kopps she might stay over with friends. Rosa Linda avoided his eyes when she told him this, so this morning he'd insisted on the call.

He lifted one finger off the steering wheel, pointed to Willa's on their right.

"You hungry?" he asked.

She glanced at her wristwatch, her brow knitted. She pulled out her compact and wiped the tears of laughter from her eyes.

"Good thing I'm not wearing mascara," she said. She glanced at him. "Look at you, always dressed the same, comb your hair the same. Don't you ever want to break out of your cage? How can you breathe? I mean we only have one life, so don't you think it's boring to have to live it as just one person?"

"I accept who I am," he said.

"Boring," Rosa Linda teased beneath her breath.

"That's why you better become an actress. In real life, people don't like being fooled. It can get you hurt."

"Sounds like great advice," Rosa Linda said, and gave her eyes an exaggerated roll.

"You're a real smartass," he said. "You know that?"

"Oh, I think I might have heard that once or twice," she said, and grinned. She looked so carefree that his irritation softened.

Inside Willa's, Rosa Linda started toward a booth, but Donnie Ray shook his head.

"I always take the counter," he said. "And you know me, a man of habit."

"Now who's silly?" she said.

Donnie Ray asked if she'd ever eaten biscuits and gravy and said she wouldn't find any better than those served at Willa's.

"Of course," she said, "my granny made the best biscuits and gravy ever." But when she discovered that the kitchen had neither fresh nor pickled jalapeños to give what she called some "bite" to the gravy, she ordered pancakes and bacon.

"Hot sauce won't do?" Big Eric sat at his usual spot at the end of the counter, holding up the bottle of Tabasco by his plate.

After Donnie Ray introduced Rosa Linda to Big Eric, informing her that he was the owner, Rosa Linda said she was glad to meet him, but she was going to have to turn down the Tabasco. "Good for the potatoes," she said, "but not for the gravy."

Eric said, in his booming voice, that he would order a jar of pickled jalapeños to keep on hand, if Donnie Ray promised to bring Rosa Linda in more often.

"You two make quite a couple," he said. "Give the joint some class, know what I'm sayin? Shoot, they'll be comin' in just to get a peek at y'all." He laughed.

"We're not a couple," Donnie Ray said.

"Just friends, right?" Rosa Linda said, and nudged Donnie Ray's shoulder with hers.

The electric shock of her touch shot through his shoulder. Her face was full of fun and mischief. Donnie Ray stiffened.

Emotions were still a bit of theater for her. Shit, he couldn't blame her for being cavalier. Didn't he want to discourage her from getting romantic? He should have just taken her home. Order. He needed to return to ordering.

"Rafi not in today?" he asked Eric.

"Later this afternoon," Eric said. "That boy works too much since he's been on his own." He explained that Rafi's parents had moved to Florida in hopes of better luck. Rafi stayed behind, insisting on graduating with his friends. Promised his parents he wouldn't ask for a cent.

"He's a good kid," Donnie Ray said. "Tell him to stop by my apartment. I want to talk to him about something."

"Sure," Eric said. "We heard about it the other night. Boom Boom. The street's buzzing. You a hero, my man."

"Bullshit," Donnie Ray said. "You woulda done the same."

"Maybe so," Eric said, "maybe so," and picked up his newspaper. "Who's Rafi?" Rosa Linda asked Donnie Ray.

"Nobody," he said, and quickly corrected, "my brother's best friend." He couldn't bring himself to say his brother's name aloud.

*   *   *

Donnie Ray dropped Rosa Linda off at Melva's kitchen door, and this time he drove away not waiting for her to go inside. Rosa Linda continued to wave good-bye after the car had pulled onto Logan, putting off confronting Melva. What a mess. Who had the energy to listen to the nagging, the questions?

In the morning, she had called. She hoped that Melva would be sound asleep by then, after hours of waiting for her. Luck was with Rosa Linda. No one answered the phone. She left a message, in a cheery voice, saying that she was fine, with friends, and she would be home in a bit.

With her fist, Rosa Linda banged on the kitchen door. She waited a moment and pounded again to make certain Melva could hear her from the apartment. The door swung open.

"No need to break down the goddamn door," Melva said. "We're up — it is morning, you know. See how the sun's come up?"

When Rosa Linda walked in without answering, Melva straightened.

"What's going on here, young lady?" she said. "I demand some answers."

"I called," Rosa Linda said.

"Not until this morning. And then I was in the bathroom. You didn't even give me a chance to answer the phone."

"What?" Rosa Linda said, trying to imitate Donnie Ray's calm under stress. "All of sudden, I don't have Sundays off?" She stood in the middle of the kitchen now, facing Melva. The hollows around her eyes were more sunken than usual, and her face hung in weary folds.

"Sneaking around like a common thief in the night." Melva pointed to Rosa Linda's shoes, each hooked on a finger.

"They're dirty, see?" She waved them. "I didn't want to mess up the floor."

Melva blinked behind her thick lenses. "I almost called the police," she said, her voice thick with emotion. "I pictured you out there, hurt or worse." She pulled a balled-up tissue out of her robe pocket and lifted her glasses to dab at her eyes.

"Oh, don't." Rosa Linda draped an arm around Melva's shoulder, but the old woman shrugged it off, and snapped, "Watch you don't break a bone."

"Quite a hullabaloo in here." Edward shuffled in, the leather soles of his house slippers brush-slapping across the vinyl tile kitchen floor. Sugar, cradled in the crook of his arm, lifted her head to bark half-heartedly, as if feeling the need to add her say.

"Come to Momma." Melva stretched out her arms, but Sugar buried her head deeper into Edward's robe.

"Now, now, Mother," Edward said. "She just now got settled, that's all."

"Don't patronize me," Melva said.

Rosa Linda wanted to work up an anger to match Melva's,

storm into the apartment, pack her things and take off. Things were getting messed up, too much unproductive drama. But Edward caught her eye, tapped the end of his nose.

"Mother's been worried about you, Rosie, that's all. Why don't we all go into the kitchen and have breakfast," he said, his face breaking into a smile, unlit cigar clenched at one side, "How about we all have some more of that local honey I got the other day. That ought to sweeten us right up."

"We just ate, Edward." Melva stared hard at him. "You playing dumb, old man, or did you really forget?"

"Did I like it?" Edward said and snorted.

"Play the fool in front of those daughters of yours, see how funny they think you are. And if something happens to me, they'll have you carted away to the funny farm in no time flat so's they can get ahold of everything I've worked for."

Rosa Linda patted him on the arm and winked. "I thought it was funny."

"I guess you also thought it was a big laugh to give out my private phone number, without so much as mentioning it to me," Melva said to her.

"What're you talking about?"

Melva studied her face, trying to detect the truth. Apparently satisfied, she said, "Some guy called here this morning, maybe thirty minutes or so before you got here. Asked me if Rosie was home."

"What did you say?"

"Well, what I wanted to tell him was one thing, but I was so worried about you — and he was really polite, seemed concerned about you. And he did have my number." She paused for a second, giving the last sentence its emphasis. "So, I asked him who he was, and if he'd seen you today or last night?"

"And?"

"He said that he'd bumped into you last night, but you had to run. He was hoping he could catch you today. Then he kinda giggled, or I guess that's what the weird sound was, and I wished I hadn't even spoken to him. Then he hung up."

Her face tightened. "Something bad happened last night, Rosa Linda?"

"What's this?" Edward asked.

"Nothing that concerns you, Edward," Melva said. "You go on back and watch one of your programs."

"Uh-oh," Edward muttered. As he turned away, he reached his fingers into his shirt pocket and adjusted his hearing aid. Reality muted.

"Everything's OK, Melva." A dull hammer pounded behind Rosa Linda's eyes. For sure Enon was bringing it to the Kopps now.

"It wasn't Donnie Ray. I recognize his voice; this guy sounded more southern, or something. After I got to thinking about it, it seems he might've been disguising his voice."

"I wrote your number down when I first got here, in case I needed it and forgot," Rosa Linda said. "I went to a couple of places last night. Maybe when I pulled money out of my wallet, the number fell out. It's nothing for you to worry about. Really."

"Maybe it's the same anonymous customer who left you that note?" Melva said. She narrowed her eyes. "Donnie Ray's the one who brought you home though. Don't lie, I was watching through the blinds in the living room. I saw the car. I hope that's not getting out of hand."

Rosa Linda wanted to answer with a wisecrack, but Melva had never looked frailer, and she didn't want to give the old woman a heart attack.

"It's not like that," she said. "Me and him, we're friends." The words warmed her.

"I hope so. Don't make young and foolish decisions. Don't lose your chances for success on account of some man. And for chrissakes, I hope you're using protection against that AIDS business."

"Hey," Edward shouted from the living room. "Retta just pulled up."

Rosa Linda opened the door and waited for Loretta to make her way to it. "It's Sunday," she said. "Did you forget?"

"No, smarty pants, I did not forget," Loretta said. "Melva was in a tizzy last night, worrying herself sick over you. So excuse me, if I care enough to come over and check on my best friend." She squeezed past Rosa Linda without touching any part of her.

"I'll be in my room," Rosa Linda said to Loretta's back. "In case you all decide you want to execute me or something."

Rosa Linda peered out her bedroom window at the yellowing dry grass. Through her closed door, she could detect the murmurings of Loretta's consolation, and the sibilant hissings of Melva's angry responses.

She lay on the bed, one bent arm shielding her eyes. Things were getting complicated, too much emotion and expectations. She felt like that old pressure cooker of Nana's that would wobble and shake as it spit steam. Once the lid hadn't been screwed on tight enough, and the top blew right off, shooting out a slab of tough meat to the ceiling. She'd hoped to stick around and make more money before leaving to whichever city she finally chose for a destination (she kept hoping fate would reveal the right choice to her), but that was no longer an option. Melva would never stop trying to control her freedom. And that was the least of it. Enon had attacked her, and now he had spoken with Melva. More would be sure to follow. Last night, it had seemed a good idea to have Donnie Ray handle Enon, but she hadn't been able to get the story of Shayne out of her head. She'd seen the pain in Donnie Ray's whole body when they talked about his brother.

Why cause him more pain?

Yes, she had to leave. If she was serious about the acting, why not Los Angeles, like Donnie Ray had suggested? He was right — look toward Frida and Patsy. At least the part of going after her dream with all her heart.

And what he said about her parents was probably true— they must've made some connections by now, and why not introduce their daughter around? Rosa Linda hadn't spoken to them in months. Maybe they were worried about her. She laughed. That last thought had crossed the line. But it *was* time for them to help her out.

Rosa Linda gathered the change that she'd been saving in a mug on her dresser. She'd use the phone booth in the restaurant, try phoning collect first, but take coins in case. She crept out of her room so Melva and Loretta would not hear her.

She put the call in and waited, almost afraid to breathe, while the operator connected with her parents' line. After the phone rang ten times, she asked the operator to keep trying. When she heard her father's voice at the other end, she released her pent-up breath with a whoosh. He was always easier to talk to.

The operator asked him if he would accept the call from Rosa Linda del Río, and she shouted over the operator's voice, "It's me, Papi," before she was shut out of the exchange.

Soon the operator returned, and in a flat voice, informed Rosa Linda that her party would not accept the charges. Rosa Linda asked her if he had said why, but the operator only repeated her statement and disconnected.

Rosa Linda sat on the stool inside the booth, her warm forehead against the cool glass of the folding door. He wasn't going to get off that easily this time. She swiped her coins off the shelf. Her hand trembled, and she had trouble fitting her index finger into the rotary hole. Moments later when she deposited the requested coins, she dropped the dimes a couple of times before finally fitting them into the slot.

Roxana answered this time, but not until the twelfth ring. "Yes, what is it?" she said.

"Hi, it's me, Rosa Linda." She smiled even though her mother could not see her. "How're you guys doing over there?"

"Well, we were sleeping," Roxana said. "That's what people do at this time."

"Oh, sorry, time change."

"Maybe you should call your fiancé and let him know where you are."

"Who?"

"Oh, already you forgot Francisco Garza? Well, he hasn't forgotten you. Came out here to L.A. a couple of weeks ago. You made the man turn loco. Leaving him a note, stealing his money, taking off like you didn't make no promises to him. Oh, he told us all the chisme."

"But in my note, I told him I went to New York City. I'm not trying to make trouble."

"Mierda. You and your dramas. I saw that note — said you were going to the big city to be an actress. So, of course he thinks Hollywood. New York, I say, she meant New York. For the stage, sabes? You know? He called me a liar. Imaginate, imagine. Finally, your father talked to him, man-to-man, sabes? That got him to listen. He's back in Nopal. You better call him, chiquita, and set things right."

"Sure, sure," Rosa Linda said. Now she was glad her mother hadn't asked her where she was calling from. The less information Roxana had to give Cisco, the better. "In the meantime, if Cisco calls, tell him I'm OK. And I'll be calling him."

Her mother remained silent. Rosa Linda took a deep breath. "What I really wanted to ask you—"

"Not to come out here, I hope. We only have the one bedroom. And times are tough. I haven't had more than bit parts since forever. Too old, they're saying. Pendejos, what do they know? I look better than women half my age. Your dad's still doing odd jobs here and there, so many that he doesn't put in enough time on my career." In the background her father defended himself.

"Yeah?" Roxanne shot back at her husband. "Then why you're not getting me jobs, eh? You saying it's because I'm too old?"

"You're still beautiful, Mami," Rosa Linda said. Would her mother go to the grave fishing for compliments?

"I know that," Roxana said. "Mira, look, I'm sleepy, m'ija. Why don't you call at a better hour. We'll talk."

"I'm serious about wanting to be an actress," Rosa Linda blurted, before her mother could hang up.

"Let's talk, but another time, sabes?" The phone clicked.

"Sure," Rosa Linda said to the mechanical hum in her ear. "I understand."

*   *   *

Donnie Ray spotted the Channel 2 van parked in front of the playground from blocks away. People piled out, and as he drove closer, he recognized the blonde woman as one of the channel's reporters, Seana McAllister. In person, she was shorter and thinner than she looked on the screen. Inside the playground, a group of women carried black plastic bags they were filling with trash. McAlllister was saying something to the women and making a downward motion with her hands. The women stopped what they were doing. Tara broke away from the group and walked toward McAllister.

Donnie Ray pulled to the curb a block away, but didn't turn off the ignition. That Tara. He had to smile. She'd done it. She had the media's attention. Let City Hall ignore her now. Ha.

She waved her hands as she spoke to McAllister, gesturing toward the equipment, the small picnic area. The cameras followed Tara as she guided them around the playground. Maybe Tara was going to pull it off.

When Donnie Ray pulled into his apartment's parking lot, he spotted his sister's car. Talk about persistent women.

"There he is," Charlotte said, waving from the passenger side of her car. She and Dee slid out. By her steady movements, he guessed his mother hadn't started drinking yet.

"We hope we're not interrupting anything," Charlotte said. "We don't hear from you these days, so we figured maybe you got a new girlfriend. You're always so interested in the new ones — at the start anyway. Just like a man." She tried to wrap her arms around Donnie Ray's waist.

"OK, that's enough," he said and released himself from her grasp. Donnie Ray couldn't remember his mom ever hugging him as a kid, but since Shayne had died, she suddenly decided that would change. Well, she was too late; her touch made him squirm with embarrassment.

Dee carried a white plastic bag in her other hand. She held it up.

"Sweet rolls," she said.

Donnie Ray started up the wooden steps, Charlotte on his heels.

"Oh Jesus," she wailed.

Without turning around, Donnie Ray paused. "Now what, Mom?"

"Your hands." She reached for one of his, hanging at his side, but he pulled away. "Did you see this, Deirdre?" she asked.

"Is that from the thing with Boom Boom?" Dee said.

"I'm telling you both right now," he said, once they were inside. "Don't make a big deal out of nothing." Others fussing over him caused him an uneasy embarrassment that he seemed to want to cover with anger. Then he felt bad for being angry, which made him angrier. Better for everyone to keep their distance and their emotions in check.

"Aw Lord, look, they got his face." Charlotte's voice rose to a keen. "Your beautiful face."

"It's a nick," he said, "from shaving. Christ."

Dee reached out to touch his face, and he jerked his head back. "Knock it off, dammit. Since when did we become this touchy-feely family?"

"Just the other day I heard this woman on TV talking about how we all got to get in touch with our feelings and share them with other folks," Charlotte said.

"That train's already left the station as far as the Campers are concerned," Donnie Ray said. He wondered if that was true. Talking to Rosa Linda had been nice, but then a body could be a little freer with a stranger, someone who was just passing through.

Dee placed a hand on her forearm. "Leave it, Momma," she whispered. "We need to talk about other stuff, remember?"

Donnie Ray did a quick scan of the room, glad that he'd taken away the sheets that Rosa Linda had folded and stacked with the pillow at the end of the couch. She'd left his sketchbook on the table by the door, and he, without comment, had tucked it back inside the coffee table drawer. The *Buffalo Soldiers* book he'd placed there was gone, but maybe he'd put it where it belonged with the stack in the bedroom. He'd check later.

"Just look at this apartment, will you, Deirdre," Charlotte said, following his gaze. "Neat as a pin, always was, and him a real man, mind you, not one of those homosexuals. You kinda expect that from them, don't you? All prissy and neat-like."

Donnie Ray exchanged glances with his sister, and Dee pleaded with her eyes. He would ignore the remark. Even if he didn't, Charlotte would claim that she didn't know what he meant, that she wasn't giving Shayne a dig, and why did he always think the worst of her?

"You see Tara down to the playground?" Charlotte said. "She actually got the Channel 2 News out on a Sunday morning. And her from right around here. One of us. That girl knows how to shake things up. You got to give it to her."

"I saw her, and yes I know how great she is."

"Momma," Dee called from the kitchen, "we're not here about Donnie Ray's love life." She had taken out plates for the cinnamon rolls and now started the coffee.

"I swear, I'm not talking about his oh-so-secret love life. I'm just saying that if a TV crew comes anywhere near the Holler, it's to show you all the progress they're making down in the Washington District. Now us Holler folk have our own little cheerleader."

"Won't it be great to have us all sit down to a nice family breakfast?" Dee said too brightly.

"You mean like back when we were the Waltons of Walton Mountain?" Donnie Ray said.

"Here comes Mary Ellen," Dee said. She carried the three plates, two held in one hand, the third in the other.

"Oh my," Charlotte said, "you will insist on looking common, showing the world your waitressing skills, won't you? No one's ever going to mistake you for the lady of the manor."

Dee's smile faded. "I'll get the coffee and fixings," she said, "only this time I'll carry them in on that Pepsi tray. Real lady-like."

They ate in silence, each one barely nibbling at the rolls. Donnie Ray didn't want to hurt his sister's feelings, so he forced down the sweet bread in spite of his full stomach.

"In three weeks, it'll be a year since Shayne died," Charlotte announced. She pushed her plate to one side. She clutched her throat and made a sobbing noise. "My sweet baby."

Donnie Ray ground down hard on his teeth. She'd forgotten how ashamed she'd been of Shayne while he was alive. When Shayne was born, she'd told Dee and Donnie Ray the same story she told the neighborhood: In the dark of night Earl Camper secretly returned, pecking on her bedroom window. Peck, peck, like he was a regular cock of the walk.

Paying heed to her heart rather than her brain, she flipped back the sheets and welcomed home her rolling stone husband. While she slept, that wily Earl had climbed out the window and hit the road again. No moss grew on that one. Nine months later, Shayne. She may as well have told everyone a leprechaun had snuck in between her sheets.

By the time Shayne was one year old, Donnie Ray noticed how his brother, with his thick auburn hair, bore a marked resemblance to a lanky trucker that used to drop in after midnight for booty calls with Charlotte and sometimes stayed over into the morning.

"We figured we'd all meet over to the house," Dee said. "Us three, and a few close friends. I'll get one of those big poster boards and an easel. We'll stick on some pictures; we could all just tell stories about . . . ."

She paused for a sip of coffee, settled the tremble in her voice. "I'll tell a story and so will Arlie, Leland, a few of the others from around here. Momma's going to try. Maybe you could ask that Spanish friend of his, the one with the name like a Ninja Turtle?"

"Rafael," he said. "Yeah, I'll ask." He cracked his knuckles. He would try to get through this. He didn't need a memorial to remember, but his mother and sister did. He had to try.

"I abhor that sound," Charlotte said, looking at his hands. "When did you pick up that nasty habit? It is so common."

"A Walton kind of memorial," Donnie Ray said. "No stories about queers and hidden muscle men magazines." He side-eyed his mother.

"Maybe you could say a few words, Donnie Ray," Dee said. She squeezed her mother's forearm.

"For sure no stories about sisters who stand by and let their brother get killed protecting her?" Donnie Ray said. The words had just popped out of his mouth. The anger bubbled inside him. But it wasn't that simple. Beneath the anger, what? Remorse? Guilt? Pain? Despair? Crack, crack, knuckles of his other hand.

Charlotte's eyes had widened after his remark, and strangling noises came from Dee's throat.

"Shit," he said. "Forget it."

"Not likely," Charlotte said, her hand at her throat.

"Oh, Donnie Ray," Dee said. Tears shimmered in her eyes.

Donnie Ray jumped up, knocked his knee against the coffee table. In the bathroom, he turned on the faucet full blast, anything to cut off the sounds of crying. Women and children crying tore him up, but he couldn't show his pain. Always so easy to fall back on the more manly anger. But he'd finally spit out the accusation that he'd kept locked in for so long.

He stared at himself in the medicine cabinet mirror. His eyes burned, and he pinched the bridge of his nose. When Shayne was little, he'd burst into tears over every hurt. Donnie Ray told him that men didn't cry. Not ever. What a fucking stupid thing to say. But hadn't he been told that a thousand times when he was a kid?

When he returned, Dee and Charlotte sat huddled together at one end of the couch, both looking up at him as if expecting him to—to what? His stomach tightened. He'd never lifted a hand to either of them.

"You will apologize to me and to your sister," Charlotte said. "Right now."

Dee, who was blowing her nose, shook her head no. She cleared her throat. "We already have it pretty much planned," she said, and stood. "I'll write the information down and drop it in your mailbox. If you think of anything, call me."

He felt his sister's gaze, but he didn't look up until she and his mother, their backs to him, started toward the door. Dee's shoulders hunched. He loved her and didn't want to hurt her. His mother pushed his buttons, made him want to force her out of that damn southern belle bit, pretending everything smelled of morning dew on magnolias. Life was shit, why couldn't she admit it? This is what came of dredging up the past.

CHAPTER FOURTEEN

Rosa Linda tucked Donnie Ray's *Buffalo Soldiers* inside her suitcase, a keepsake, snapped it closed, and slid the case beneath the bed. She sat in the dark on the edge of the bed. The time had come. Run, Rosa Linda, run. First, hunt for money or diamonds, then call a taxi. She would decide on her destination when she arrived at the station, either bus depot or airport, depending on how much she found.

She tiptoed to her door, had her hand on the doorknob when she heard the Kopps' bedroom door creak. She stopped, pressed her ear to the door. Edward's heavy breathing lumbered down the hall away from the bedrooms. She peeked out, saw the soft glow of the refrigerator light pooled on the hall carpet. Edward sneaking that second helping of vanilla ice cream that Melva had denied him, she guessed. Let his wife worry about his high cholesterol.

Finally, his bowl and spoon clinked in the stainless steel sink, and Edward crept back into his room. There had been no running of water, no closing of cabinet doors. That dirty bowl would give him away tomorrow morning. He'd catch hell from Melva. Rosa Linda wouldn't be there to take the blame for him, like she had before when he made his late-night snack runs to the kitchen. Didn't matter. If things went as planned, Melva would have more than ice cream to worry about tomorrow.

While Rosa Linda waited for him to fall back to sleep, she softly scratched her forearms and daydreamed about what it might be like if Donnie Ray were leaving with her. Both of them in his Chevy, windows rolled down, wind whirling around them before returning to the outside with traces of themselves, a loose hair, a flake of dry skin, a thought, a memory. But it would only be her.

Everyone had hopes and dreams, but he was satisfied visiting the Southwest from the sanctuary of his apartment, leafing through musty books or staring at filmed images on the screen. She marveled at how they'd met, at how they'd connected. When she'd told him she trusted him, she was not a little surprised to realize she was probably telling the truth. He wasn't trying to play her. Others had told her she was a natural actress, yet hearing the words from him helped her believe in herself. Maybe because he happened to tell her when she was ready to hear and accept. Timing, that's what made the difference.

Enon could go to the devil. She wasn't like him like he thought. OK, maybe they were both outsiders, a couple of tumbleweeds looking for a place to land. And maybe he was searching for someone who understood him completely and loved him anyway. Well, it wasn't going to be her. She was not about to ride around the country, picking up hitchhikers and threatening people. Ha. She had places to go and things to accomplish. Now was the time to show him, show them all. So what if she tried and failed? Had fear of failure stopped Frida or Patsy? No way.

She was on her own; she would survive by her wits as she always had. But this time she would have the advantage of a nest egg. Why shouldn't she have some financial backing like others her age with parents? Melva understood how that was. And the old woman had insurance, she told herself again for the umpteenth time. And for Melva and Edward's safety, she needed to be gone. Now. Wasn't Melva always going on about making a plan, setting goals?

The wind sighed at her window, and beyond came the familiar sound of the odd car whooshing by on Logan Avenue. On the interstate, behind and above the Shipwreck Tavern, cars and trucks whizzed by.

Earlier tonight, she'd stayed with the Kopps until they retired to their bedroom, noticing that Melva didn't go beforehand to the safe with her diamonds. Rosa Linda didn't know when another opportunity might arise. It had to be a sign — this was her chance to get hold of those diamonds.

She opened the door, placed one foot onto the hall carpet. From the kitchen Melva's Felix the Cat clock ticked faintly, his swinging tail marking time; farther down in the living room the old grandfather tocked with the confidence of age and wisdom. Tick-tock.

She hesitated outside the Kopp's bedroom. Edward's snore alternated with Sugar's wheezes, a duet punctuated by Melva's muffled cough. The harmony did not change, so she gently twisted the doorknob and stepped in. No turning back now. Edward slept on his back and closest to the entrance— Melva had told her that he said this way he'd be first in line in case of intruders. If nothing else, his bulk hid Melva from immediate view.

Edward farted, rolled to his side so that he now faced Rosa Linda. Had that last helping of ice cream given him indigestion? She squinted at him, but his eyes hadn't opened. If he awakened and snaked out a hand to grab her, she'd explain that she heard his troubled sleep and came in to check on him. Because of her pills, Melva wouldn't awaken to put doubts in Edward's mind.

Rosa Linda cat-pawed into the bathroom. There was little chance she would find what she wanted there, but she couldn't not try. How much easier it would make things if she could find the jewelry without having to go near Melva.

Melva was still upset about Sunday, but at least Rosa Linda had convinced her that nothing bad happened. She'd simply gotten carried away and had selfishly forgotten everything but the good times. She hadn't heard from Donnie Ray or Enon.

She knew Enon was out there. No deluding herself about that anymore. But maybe he wouldn't figure out that she'd left until she was long gone, and maybe by then he'd get tired of the chase and roll back onto the highway, follow it wherever it took him. Enon would no longer be a threat to the folks that had helped her in Mad River. She thought her leaving was really for the benefit of others.

She ran her hands across the bathroom vanity, hoping for jewelry taken off during the bath and forgotten. Next, on top of the toilet tank, around the rim of the bathtub, the soap dish. No luck.

In the Kopps' room, she slunk toward Melva's side of the bed. The old woman lay on her back with Sugar curled up against her shoulder. Sugar's head lifted an inch, her protruding eyes catching a bit of light. The dog stared at Rosa Linda, accusing. She held her breath, waited for the dog's usual growl. Instead, Sugar lowered her gray-whiskered chin back onto her paws and her eyelids drifted closed. The old dog had chosen an odd moment to trust her.

Melva lay as stiff as a corpse, reminding Rosa Linda of Nana when she rested, arms crossed, among the folds of white satin in her coffin. A deep sense of loss pinched her heart. She blinked away the memory. Melva wasn't Nana. She wasn't her blood. Her palms had begun sweating again, and she wiped them on her thighs. She bent at the waist, peered at Melva's hands and ears. Melva wasn't wearing her diamonds. Relief almost buckled her knees.

As Rosa Linda was straightening to leave, a faint glimmer on the side table caught her eye. She hovered her hand over the diamonds, her fingers closing in on them like one of those coin-activated claws in glass boxes. How many quarters had she lost as a kid, determined to beat the machine and capture, at long last, the plush toy of her choice? The prize had always eluded her grasp, but this bait was so easy. Surely they wouldn't have been made so available to her if they weren't meant to be hers.

Edward snored. Melva cleared phlegm from her throat.

Sugar grunted. From the hall the clocks kept time. In the distance, people came and went, unaware of her or the Kopps. Her fingers trembled. Melva was always talking about helping Rosa Linda make something of herself. Here was her chance. Even if the pawn shop only gave Rosa Linda a fraction of what they were worth, surely it would be enough to allow her to strike out on her own.

The tip of her index finger touched one ring. She had only to curl her fingers around the jewels, call for a taxi, and head for the bus depot. No, she would take a plane. No reason to pinch pennies. She could use some of her savings. She'd soon be flush with money. She'd ask about the first flights to Chicago and New York. First flight out determined her destination. Wheel of Fortune, tell me true.

Melva's mouth dropped open, and she began to snore softly. With her mouth agape she looked even older, more vulnerable. She had her soft spots, but her difficult life had built up protective callouses. So proud of buying the diamonds herself: By God, Melva Kopp had succeeded without any-damn-body's help.

"Some have family," Melva had said, "who can help them out on those hungry days, but I only had myself. So, as soon as I could save enough, I started collecting these. Investments, security." She held out her hands and shifted them so the light caught the stones. "Yessir," she said, "my hands and a strong back. If times ever get tough . . . ." She paused to wiggle her fingers, so the diamonds reflected rays of brilliance. "Would be nice, though, if I had a daughter to pass one of these on to." She had angled a sly glance at Rosa Linda.

Rosa Linda's hand twitched from keeping it in the same position for too long. She slowly withdrew her hand and let it drop limply to her side. Sugar squirmed, smacked her lips, watched her.

Would it be so bad to stay here with Melva and Edward? The Kopps would agree to her taking classes, and would probably even pay for them. Of course that would have to be negotiated. She wanted only acting classes, while Melva would insist on her enrolling in something more practical. Melva would give her anything, as long as Rosa Linda became the daughter that she'd always dreamed of having. Melva's shadow. But then there was Enon. Her mind went back and forth like the tail on the Felix clock.

When she left the room, she forgot to tiptoe, and beneath the carpet a floorboard squeaked. She almost hoped one of the Kopps would wake up, demand to know what she was up to. Maybe she'd confess the truth about what she'd almost done, see how much they liked their precious Rosie then.

In her own room, Rosa Linda pulled out the suitcase and unpacked everything but the book.

*   *   *

"Is Edward on his way out?" Melva asked Rosa Linda. Loretta would soon serve lunch, and Melva never started without Edward.

"I'll go back and see what's keeping him," Rosa Linda said. "He was right behind me."

Melva shook her head. "No," she said, "he's getting slower every day. Both his knees are shot." She held up a finger. "I hear him in the kitchen. Repeating one of his tired jokes to Loretta." She cackled. "Know what I did yesterday?" Melva asked. "Completely forgot to put up my diamonds. I could've sworn I locked them in the safe, but there they were on my side table, for chrissake. I ask you, where is my mind?"

Rosa Linda studied the old woman's face. If Melva was playing a game, she was a better actress than Rosa Linda.

"It's not like someone's going to steal them inside the apartment," Rosa Linda said. "If I'm not around to remind you tonight, you can tape a note to yourself on the bathroom mirror."

"Why aren't you going to be around?" Melva said.

"I'm just saying."

"Oh hell," Melva said, "where's our lunch?"

"Actually," Rosa Linda said, "I was going to see Donnie

Ray at Powers. I asked Geneva to throw a cheeseburger on the grill for me to go." She would say good-bye to Donnie Ray first, tell him he was right about going for her dreams. Later in the day, as she built up courage, she'd speak with Melva, give her a few days to start looking for a replacement. If Enon didn't make problems before then.

The swinging door to the dining area wheezed open, and Loretta quick-stepped in from the kitchen with Edward following behind her. Loretta sat down the specials — Swiss steak, glazed carrots, and scalloped potatoes — in front of Melva and Edward.

"Nobody told me Donnie Ray came in today," Loretta said. "But you're so smart," Loretta said to Rosa Linda, "maybe you know something we don't."

"Retta, quit riding the girl," Melva said. She jerked hard at the rolled napkin and the flatware tucked inside clattered onto the table.

"I'm just offering some information," Loretta said. "Fact is, I don't think the man came in today. But," she added, clicking her tongue, "I thought Rosie would know that, what with them two being such good friends and all."

"Listen up," Jaybird called from his bar stool. He pointed to the TV. "Some gal's got herself raped or something down to the Washington District. Over by that hoity-toity college."

"What the hell you blabbing about?" Melva said.

"Uh-oh," Jaybird said, "this isn't going to be good for business down there. Loretta, turn up the sound, won't you?"

Rosa Linda stared transfixed at the screen. The newscaster reported that the student, name withheld because of the nature of the crime, a junior at Mad River University, had been walking from her dormitory building to that of a friend late Saturday night when an unknown assailant jumped out, knife in hand. He dragged her behind some large bushes. The student was assaulted and raped. She was later treated at the nearby Riverview Hospital.

The assailant, the report continued, wore a ski mask and gloves, so the description was sketchy: male of medium height and build, with light-colored eyes. The student stated that her attacker never spoke, but kept a knife at her throat. Right after the assault, voices could be heard approaching, and the man ran off.

"Mad River University," the announcer said, "reports to Channel 2 News that security guards will escort female students who do not wish to walk across campus alone. Students are also warned against venturing into some areas in the proximity of the university."

"The Holler is what he means," Jaybird said.

"Rosie, weren't you down in the historical district?" Melva said.

"Not really." Rosa Linda held onto the back of a chair to keep her balance. Had that girl been at the Free Will over the weekend? Maybe she was one of the girls on the dance floor, silhouetted in the upstairs window, or among the circle that had surrounded her when she fell.

"I'll bet he was colored, or one of them others," Loretta said.

"Nah, they'd say if he was black or some such," Jaybird said, "so I reckon white."

"Jesus H. Christ," Melva said, "rape is rape. Everybody shut up for a blasted minute. Rosie, you've gone pale as a ghost. Retta, bring her a glass of water."

"Hold on," Jaybird said, "there's more. Appears folks are already protesting down there."

"Now what?" Rosa Linda thought and returned her gaze to the TV. A reporter was at a playground, the one down by Bottoms Up. A young woman with a face as pretty as a doll's was telling the reporter how much the playground meant to the people in the neighborhood.

"Nah, they're already talking about something else," Jaybird said. "A bunch of troublemakers whining about wanting more tax dollars."

Loretta turned down the volume and drew a glass of water. She smacked the glass down on the table in front of Rosa Linda.

"Here you go, your royal majesty."

"You know something about this, Rosie?" Melva asked. "You're acting awfully strange." She glanced at Rosa Linda's hand, clutching the edge of the table, her knuckles white.

"No, no. Just interested." She released her grasp on the table. "Maybe I'll get some fresh air, take a little walk."

"There's not a thing wrong with that girl," Loretta said, speaking as if Rosa Linda had already left the room. "She's just got to be the center of attention, that's all."

"Maybe you better lay down," Melva said. "You're downright green around the gills."

"I'm fine," Rosa Linda said evenly.

Edward coughed with purpose. Melva turned to him. "You got something to say, Edward?"

"Since Rosie said something about going out tonight . . . ." Edward's sentence trailed away.

"Spit it out, old man," Melva said.

"The weatherman's predicted rain," he said, "so I thought . . . well, mostly on account of that guy, I'm thinking . . . ." He shifted his bulk, reached in his front pants pocket.

"I'm warning you, Edward," Melva said, "shit or get off the pot."

Edward pulled out his key ring, worked off the house key. "What do you say, old girl? We don't want that maniac getting at Rosie because she can't get the door open. Maybe — "

"Why in the hell is that rapist going to be down here all of a sudden?" With the tip of one scarlet nail, Melva pecked the key that now lay in the center of the table.

"Sometimes they move around, don't they?" Edward said. "But for sure, she won't have to wait out in the rain, catching her death because she's got no key." Edward winked at Rosa Linda. Under the table, she squeezed the hand he rested on his leg.

Melva scooted the ring in a circle. "That weatherman's been predicting rain for weeks." She pecked at the key again. "We haven't had more than a sprinkling. But I don't guess it'll hurt anything."

"Well, I never," Loretta said. "A key? Why, you don't hardly know her, Melva."

"Thank you," Rosa Linda said. Standing behind Edward now, she wrapped an arm around him, pressed the side of her face to his large head. "You're too kind to me," she said. She glanced at Melva. "Both of you. I won't forget."

"Nonsense." Melva shooed Rosa Linda away with a flap of her hand. "If you're going to go soft in the head about it, I might change my mind."

"I'll be back in a little bit," Rosa Linda said.

"If she's not high-tailing it over to the Powers, I'll eat my hat," Loretta said.

"Didn't she say she would?" Melva barked. "The girl's got a right to her break, Retta."

At Powers, Rosa Linda discovered Loretta hadn't been lying. Kelly Powers was there again and explained that he'd discovered he was well enough to last the shift.

"Donnie Ray might come in to visit now and again," Kelly said, "but it's me you're gonna see in here from now on." He added that he'd welcome friendly visits from a pretty gal.

* * *

Outside Donnie Ray's bedroom window, the wind howled, blowing memories into his room. He dreamt of Shayne riding his bike against the wind, peddling as hard as he could. Donnie Ray ran alongside the bike, calling for Shayne to stop. But Shayne bent his head into the strong current and peddled on. Faster and faster, until Donnie Ray was having trouble keeping up.

"Slow down," Donnie Ray called.

Shayne peddled faster.

"Hold on," Donnie Ray shouted louder to be heard against the blasting air. There was something he had to know. "What's it like to be dead?"

Suddenly Shayne and Donnie Ray were moving in slow motion. Shayne turned and gazed at him with his blue-gray eyes. "Sometimes it's like this," Shayne said, "but mostly it's just nothing."

Shayne turned forward again, his legs a whir of motion. Donnie Ray ran faster, faster, but Shayne left Donnie Ray running against the wind. When he awoke, his legs pumped air.

Donnie Ray sat up, lit a cigarette, his gaze on the bike hanging in its place on the wall while he waited for his heartbeat to slow. Shayne had loved taking his bike out when they had to fight against the weather. On Shayne's first ride, it had been an overcast winter day. No white Christmas that year, but the bitter cold was challenging enough.

Shayne had gotten only two blocks when four punks jumped him, knocked him off the seat. Less than half an hour later Shayne returned to Donnie Ray's and burst through the door, shouting, "You shoulda been there, Donnie Ray. It was me and him, like we was brothers. We took 'em."

Shayne held up his bruised knuckles. "Check this out. I almost broke my hand on one of the punk's faces. You shoulda seen."

Shayne, who had been beaten up before, but had never gotten in any good licks himself, broke down the fight. "They were planning on taking my bike," he said, "when of a sudden — boom — here comes Rafael. Out of nowhere. Like he was The Hulk himself. So he shoves in between two of these guys so fast they don't know what's going on, grabs hold of my arm, yanks me up, says, 'Back-to-back,' and I know just what he means like I was reading his mind. So we're circling — back-to-back — like in a movie fight or something. I swear to God his fist strikes out — pow — like some kinda hammer, knocks the holy shit outta one guy. I mean the guy actually pooped his pants."

When Shayne stopped for a gulp of air. Donnie Ray asked him who his attackers had been.

"Don't matter, Donnie Ray," he said, "you don't gotta take care of nothing. Me and Rafi got it under control."

"Who now?"

"Rafael, but he says to call him Rafi. So, these guys take off, and they're yelling, 'wetback,' and 'wetback lover,' running like pussies the whole time. I was so pissed."

"Rafi looked at me, and says, 'Idiots. I'm Puerto Rican.' Me and him look at each other, and we cracked up laughing."

Shayne hadn't run into Rafi again until they met again at the gym. They were tight until the last year or so after Shayne dropped out of school, and Rafi spent more time with his sports and classmates.

Outside, the wind moaned, and between the panels of the curtain Donnie Ray could see the leaves of the maple had turned over, exposing their pale undersides, warning of an impending storm. Maybe that forecasted deluge of rain was finally going to hit.

In the living room, the phone trilled. He took his time, hoping the caller would give up before he reached it. He snatched up the receiver. "What?"

"Where are you?" Rosa Linda said. "Why didn't you tell me you weren't coming in to Powers anymore?"

"What's up?"

She asked him if he'd listened to the news. When he said he hadn't, she said, "Enon, he raped a girl and tried to kill her. Held a knife to her throat. Just like with me."

His grip on the receiver tightened. "They got him?"

"Not yet," she said, and paused. "What if he attacks more women? I can't let this happen again to another girl."

"They said it was Enon, for sure?"

"I don't . . . I guess . . . who else could it be? The assault happened down there near the university, off Washington Street. Maybe right after he tried to get me, maybe it made him mad and—"

"Your story's full of *maybes*. Let's stick to the facts." He asked her for the description of the rapist, and when she repeated what she'd heard, he said, "Could be him, could be a thousand other guys. Hell, that description fits me."

"I *know* it was him." They both fell silent, each lost in thought. "I've been thinking about leaving town," she said, rushing her words. "Now's a good time actually because I'm guessing he'll go away if I do." She took a breath. "I just don't want him following me."

"You're leaving?"

"I was thinking about what you told me about dreams—"

"You don't need to explain to me," he said.

She started to speak, and again he cut her off. "Forget your plan," he said. "Even if he let you leave, which I doubt, who's to say he won't do this to someone else here or somewhere else?"

"Enon's my problem. I don't want you getting in trouble."

"Don't worry about me," he said. "I was already on it before you told me the news. I drove to Melva's, cruised the area, came back down here and drove around the Holler. No sign of him. But if he's anywhere around here, I can flush the rat out."

"Do you have a plan?" she asked.

His voice barely audible, as if speaking to himself, he said, "I'm sure as hell not messing around the university. They'll be on alert, and no one's going to mistake me for a student or a professor. The cops'll pull my Holler ass over for being the rapist. Wednesdays are Ladies Night at the Free Will. Might attract him."

"Sounds good to me," she said. "I'll take the bus down there."

"You stay out of this. I told you, I know what I'm doing."

"Me stay out? Are you kidding? Anyway, you don't know what he looks like. I've got to point him out." Without her there, things could get out of control, she thought. Enon needed a good scare, that was all.

"I'm pretty sure I've seen the guy before," Donnie Ray said.

"But you can't be positive," she said. "You wouldn't want to make a mistake. I'll identify him for you, to make certain."

He paused. "I'll pick you up," he said.

CHAPTER FIFTEEN

Rosa Linda slid into the front seat next to Donnie Ray, and as he eased out of the lot, she glanced in the rearview mirror. Melva shaded her eyes from the sun, low in the hazy sky, and watched the car with an expression that Rosa Linda had seen Nana wear, a brave smile that didn't manage to mask the worry. Rosa Linda felt as though fishhooks had pierced her flesh. She was being reeled in and away from herself. Commitments to others detoured her dreams. This time she wasn't taking off impulsively with no thought of others nor was she flying away like a piece of debris in the wind.

"Does she know about Enon?" Donnie Ray said.

"Not that he knows me. But I'm not too worried. Just the thought of a rapist on the loose, anywhere in Mad River, and Melva's already called the security people to get down here and install an alarm system. I mean she's got every window and door wired. Good thing I've got a key." She patted her purse. "And that viejita has already said that she's not opening the door to any-damn-body she hasn't known and pretty much trusted for at least ten years."

Since Loretta's outburst on Monday, Melva had been extra nice to Rosa Linda, and tried explaining the other woman's behavior. "It's not just you, Rosie," Melva had said, "she's going through the change is my guess. And it's the getting old, too — feeling like others think you're used up and ready to be replaced by the new. You'll get old too, even if now you can't picture it. To sweeten her up, I reminded her how I already let my lawyer know she's to get one of these." She wiggled one hand. "Of course, I do have a second one." She chuckled.

Almost shyly, Melva added, "Edward's driving me out to Brandt's Orchard tomorrow for some apples. You're welcome to come. That is if you're not tired of being around us old-timers."

Rosa Linda sensed it was not so much about the company, but that Rosa Linda would make pie-baking a part of her ritual, too. Rosa Linda mumbled that she'd think about it. She could have used the moment to tell Melva that she was leaving soon, so no pies. But Melva gazed at her with such hope, she couldn't force out the words. Good-byes were difficult enough, why prolong them with a preamble?

The farther they drove from Melva's, the threads that tethered her to the old people were stretched until they almost broke.

As Donnie Ray turned into the Washington Historical District, slowly cruising while his gaze roamed the street, she said, "It's too early for this. You told me we could go to your apartment and chill."

"A quick drive through on my way to the store is all," Donnie Ray said. "Keep a lookout. That's why you said you needed to be here, remember? To i-den-ti-fy."

"Store?" she asked, and he said that he thought they might watch a movie at his apartment but needed snacks.

"I'll buy," she said, and smiled. "The Kahlo movie, the one I told you about, yes?"

"Not this time. You'll see."

The car window was open about five inches, and she rolled it all the way down. She thought of Enon, of how he'd tried to permanently take her breath away. She glanced at Donnie Ray, his jaw muscle working. She patted the ojo de venado hanging around her neck. She hoped this would end well.

"Here we are," Donnie Ray said.

He parked the car in front of a two-story brick building with a sign hanging over the door, Corner Store. "This is the last mom-and-pop operation around here," he said. "Vern and Wanda O'Neal, the owners, they live upstairs, have since forever." He told her that there was once another little store a few blocks over, but when Kroger came into the area, the small shops couldn't compete with a big chain.

"The O'Neals have two kids, but one's up in Michigan, and the other one I don't know where she got to, but she took off right after she graduated high school. When Vern and Wanda are gone, that'll be it for this place. Even if it could compete with the chains, young people don't want to take over these little businesses. The old neighborhood's dying bit by bit."

"That's kind of sad," Rosa Linda said, "but I don't blame the kids for getting out. I mean, you can't stop progress."

"I'll keep that in mind," he said, his tone sarcastic.

Inside, Donnie Ray chatted with the older couple who asked about his mother and sister before turning their attention to Rosa Linda.

"Who's this pretty girl with you?" Wanda asked.

"A friend," he said, "Rosa Linda's her name. In Spanish it means beautiful rose." He turned to walk toward the chip aisle.

"Why, that's real sweet," Wanda said. Raising her voice, she called out to Donnie Ray, now out of their view. "You hear about that new restaurant opening up on Maple Street? Course they're calling it a bistro. Good old English ain't enough for them, I reckon."

"That's so's we'll know it's not the likes of you and me they want eating in there," Vern said. He stood behind the deli counter at one end of the store. "It's more of them damn yuppies, or whatever they call theirselves."

"I'm giving my business to Willa's, same as always," Donnie Ray said, "and I don't rightly care what others do." He placed a bag of tortilla chips and a jar of salsa on the counter, telling Rosa Linda to pick out a bottle of pop. At the deli counter, he asked Vern to slice him a pound of olive loaf and a half pound of extra sharp cheddar cheese.

"Not your regular colby?" Vern said, and grinned. "Look out, Donnie Ray's getting mighty adventuresome."

"Doesn't hurt to try a little something new," Donnie Ray said, and cocked one eyebrow at Rosa Linda.

"Cheese is a good start," she said, and laughed. She dug in her purse for her wallet, but Donnie Ray pushed her hand aside.

"Ladies don't pay when they're with me," he said.

"OK," she said, "but next movie is my choice, and I buy the munchies." It wouldn't hurt to act as though there would be a next time.

"Come back here in ten years," Donnie Ray said, once they'd returned to the car, "and you probably won't even recognize this street. Damn flukie-dukes are buying us out, building by building. They want to be rid of us. Oh, they don't say as much; they just charge prices they know us riff-raff can't pay."

"Then maybe you should get out before it's all gone."

"Now I know I picked the right movie."

"Oh?" she said.

"You'll see."

"James Bond? Just joking," she said. "It's got to be a black-and-white detective movie, Bogie and McCall? *The Big Sleep*?" He shook his head, and she smacked her forehead with the heel of her palm. "Of course — a western. That's why you went all Southwestern with the snack."

"You'll see," he repeated, but she could tell by the pleased expression on his face that she had guessed.

As he drove into the lot of his apartment, she glanced in the side-view mirror and thought a brown car similar to Enon's passed by. But by the time she got out of Donnie Ray's Chevy and got a better view of the street, the other car had vanished. When she thought about it, the car might have been a burgundy shade.

* * *

"Let's see what you think of *The Wild Bunch*."

Always a sucker for westerns, she was hooked from the start with the images of the cowboys and their lived-in faces. One opening scene took her back to her own childhood in Nopal, Arizona. In the movie, the children laughed as they tormented a scorpion by dropping it onto a hill of fire ants. Ants swarmed, red and hot as embers, onto the scorpion. It thrashed wildly with its stinger. That sting, Rosa Linda understood, burned like a fire of its own (she'd never been stung but had heard stories of those who had) and in some cases could be fatal.

In the film, when the scorpion tried to escape, the kids had forced it, with sticks, back into ant hell. The boys in her Nopal neighborhood had done the same to a scorpion, also forcing it back when it tried to escape its tormentors. Other kids gathered around cheering. She had been one of those in the outer circle, neither encouraging nor enjoying the torture, but standing among those who merely observed. Finally, she turned her back and walked away from what she could not understand, and did not want to think about.

The movie camera kept its eye on the scene with close-ups of the children's smiling faces as they observed the ants' red anger, and the scorpion's blind strikes, in final desperation, turned upon itself.

"Well?" Donnie Ray said when the gunfire and mayhem finally wound down to its blood-soaked ending, and the surviving cowboys rode away into their new reality.

"I liked it," she said, thinking of the aging cowboys who no longer fit into the changing society with its technology and progress, railroads, cars, and planes pushing their way of life. She had some doubts about the Mexican officer Mapache, like maybe she'd seen that character once too often in American movies. And then there were all the whoring women. But that conversation they could have the next time they watched the movie together. She liked to think that would happen.

"It was sad, you know, that the Wild Bunch felt it was better to die than to try and . . . accept the changes. Or maybe they could've gone someplace else."

"They were leaving, but to where? Where the hell else would they go?" He lit a cigarette, exhaled. "Change is everywhere. I like it right where I am, and nobody's pushing me out."

"I didn't mean you."

"What are you trying to change about your life, Rosa Linda? You have these dreams — very vague dreams. But you just sit back and wait for the answers to fall in your lap. That could be a form of self-destruction."

"How about you?"

He held up a hand to stop her response. "Don't try to psychoanalyze me."

"Same here." She held a chip, and now she crushed it and dropped the crumbs in the bowl. "Anyway, didn't you kind of already give me this lecture?" Here would be the perfect time to tell him she was leaving. But good-byes — she hated good-byes.

After a moment, he said, "It's a movie my brother and I used to watch together. He liked to imagine us as part of the Bunch."

Donnie Ray flipped the top of the Zippo, open, shut, open. He lit a cigarette, inhaled, exhaled, his eyes shiny with a strange light she hadn't seen there before.

"Last time," he said, "when you read the newspaper article, you didn't ask a lot of questions." He took another puff. "I appreciate that."

She nodded.

"My sister Dee took him to that bastard's house." He spoke in starts and stops, as if a valve inside him was opening and shutting, and she was afraid if she interrupted him he wouldn't finish what he needed to say. He explained how Dee had been dating a married man, a lot older, and how she was impressed that such a successful businessman would be interested in her.

"The guy," Donnie Ray said, "had probably gone to the District to pick up a college girl. I hear that the place is crawling with old geezers looking for young girls who've had so much to drink they don't half know who they're going off with. Anyway, he drops into the White Castle after hours and sits next to my sister."

He reached for another cigarette, lit it without realizing the first one was still burning in the ashtray. "So, Dee's all impressed with the guy, his expensive suit, his fat wallet. One night she invites Shayne to go with her to Dunlap's house. His wife was apparently out of town at the time." He tapped the ash on the edge of the ash tray, saw the other live cigarette, stubbed it out. "Shit," he said.

One of Rosa Linda's calf muscles cramped, and she quietly slipped a hand behind her leg to rub the knot. When, after long moments, it seemed he would not speak again, she cleared her throat. She was glad now that she hadn't told him about leaving. Would he have opened up to her if she had?

"Why did she invite Shayne to go with her?" Rosa Linda spoke softly.

He grunted. "Who knows?" he said. "Maybe she wanted to show her little brother how the other half lives. Maybe it was her way of trying to motivate him to improve himself. She seemed real impressed with all the things Dunlap could buy: his big house, his Cadillac, the swimming pool, Jacuzzi. That's what everybody's working to get these days, right? It's nothing I ever wanted." He lifted his hands, a show of exasperation.

"Or maybe," he said, "she wanted Shayne to be impressed with her, how well she must be doing if she could snag such a winner." He twisted the last word.

Rosa Linda felt she should respond but didn't trust herself to find the right words. She nodded, encouraging him to go on.

"So Fred and Dee get roaring drunk," Donnie Ray continued, "and start pushing each other around. Fred slaps the hell out of her, Shayne jumps in. Big man. My brother was hardly any bigger than you." He pressed his finger and thumb to the bridge of his nose.

"The paper didn't say much about your sister."

"Dunlap knew a lot of big people in town, maybe some beholden to him," Donnie Ray said, his voice bitter, "and they sure weren't going to mention that this respectable married man had a woman on the side. Anyway, the cops give the media their story, and the media reports it as fact. If the truth ever comes —

which it did not in this case — well, by that time, the first version has already been around so long, it's accepted as the truth."

"And the truth? What was it really?"

"Well, I'm going by what my sister says," he said, "and Dee has been known to leave out details that she can't face." He shook his head. "Hell, maybe we all do, but her more than most. Thing is," he said, his voice rising slightly, "the way she told it to me, she doesn't come off looking good, so I'm thinking her version is pretty much right on."

He played with the Zippo, pulled out another cigarette, laid it on the table without lighting it. "Dunlap's slapping her around," he said, his words tumbling out now. "Shayne tells him to knock it off, tries to get in the middle. Dunlap punches him and starts choking Dee. Shayne pulls him off, throws him onto the couch. And. Turns. His. Back." His nostrils flared with a deep intake of breath.

"That's when Dunlap yanks the Japanese ceremonial sword off the wall. Shayne had turned away from Dunlap to check on Dee. Dunlap runs the sword through Shayne's lower back. Self-defense, remember. And the bastard got away with it."

"My God," Rosa Linda said.

In the kitchen, the faucet dripped, and she fought the urge to jump up, run to turn it off. Anything to distance herself from Donnie Ray's sorrow.

Donnie Ray clamped his jaw, as if preventing more words from coming out. The faucet drip-dripped. Rosa Linda wanted to place her hand over his, but he looked coiled, ready to strike.

"I don't know what to say," she said finally.

Long minutes passed, maybe fifteen. Donnie Ray stirred.

Her leg muscles cramped again, and she stretched carefully, not wanting to make any sudden movements. "Why don't we just get out of here. Now."

"Washington Street?"

"No," she said. "Pack what you want, and we go get my stuff. Poof, we take off. Chicago, New York. Or . . . anywhere."

"You're nuts, kid," he said. He stood with his back to her. "You can't just pick up and take off."

"Why not? I've been doing it all my life." She grabbed his hand, hoping her excitement would be contagious. "It's not that I don't like it here. I've had some good times, met some good people. But it's . . . I can't explain . . . there are other people, other places." She threw up her hands. "It's just time to leave. Like they said in the movie, 'Why not?'"

"What about Enon? Didn't you say you don't want him to hurt anyone else?" He glanced at his wristwatch. "In fact, we probably ought to be heading out soon."

She collapsed back onto the sofa. Enon. For a few hours it had been nice to pretend she had forgotten him. "I don't want you to get hurt."

"I'm not going to get hurt, dammit." The vein in his temples pulsed.

"But it's going to storm tonight. They're saying it's for sure this time."

"If it's hard enough, rain can keep nosey people inside. Washes away a lot of evidence too."

Evidence of what? she thought. Donnie Ray's voice was so cold and distant. She shouldn't have involved him, had to do something to stop him. They began to clean up, and she worked slowly, hoping for an idea to come to her. She could call the cops, anonymously. She would disguise her voice (just in case they ever did hear her in person during their investigation), and give them a description of Enon and his car. She would say she'd seen him lurking around the university, driving slowly, ogling the girls. They'd asked the public to call with any tips — well, she had a big one for them. She'd have to find a phone booth while they were out, make some excuse.

Donnie Ray would never go along with the plan. Blood-thirst was in his eyes.

* * *

Donnie Ray drove around the block several times waiting for a parking spot to free up. Outsiders — university students and professors, young suburbanites — crowded the sidewalks, their faces wearing the exaggerated expressions of the drunk determined to show what a good time they were having. The front windows of Donnie Ray's car were open, letting in the sound of youthful exuberance that crackled in the air, the laughter and shout-outs to one another as they claimed the space.

Look at them, Donnie Ray thought, his gaze scanning the revelers; they spilled into the street, jaywalked to the other side, confident that no car would hit one of them and no cop would pull them over for public intoxication. They owned the fucking world.

Like Fred Dunlap. Only he'd come up from the working class but, like so many, forgot where he'd come from. Money and lots of it, that was what was all that mattered anymore.

Donnie Ray felt vulnerable, half-dressed in what had once been part of his neighborhood. He didn't know the rules they played by, couldn't see beneath their sheen of entitlement. The flood of strangers eyed him with a mixture of amusement and contempt, as if he were the outsider, some stray hillbilly. How long before the Bottoms Up became a trendy bar with chrome, mirrors, and glass? Brownie's Books bought out by a chain?

"ID?" the doorman at Free Will said, and cocked one eyebrow.

As Rosa Linda dug in her purse for her wallet, a sudden flash of white light lit up the area, and she startled.

The doorman laughed. "It's only a little bit of lightning," he said. He studied her ID and then her face. "You look kind of familiar," he said.

"Never been here before," she said.

"Whew," she said to Donnie Ray when they were inside and out of the doorman's earshot. "For a minute I thought he recognized me from that little problem the other day. But I was all surfer girl then."

"Asshole," Donnie Ray said, "he's just trying out one of his pickup lines." He was shouting over the music. Let the doorman hear him. Donnie Ray's eyes scanned the room, hoping one of these flukie-dukes would make a crack or stare in his direction a second too long.

"Loosen up, will you?" Rosa Linda said, her lips close to his ear. "You look like you're out for a fight. They're just people, like us."

"Keep your eyes open," he shouted.

Rosa Linda grabbed his wrist, pulled him behind her, confident, as if she felt at home with these creeps. He wondered if Shayne, as a misfit, would one day have also felt comfortable in this crowd. Rafi would be attending Mad River University next year on a football scholarship. Maybe Shayne would have eventually joined Rafi at the university.

"Come on," Rosa Linda shouted and laughed too loudly as if she'd forgotten why they were here.

The beat of the music vibrated up through the floor and into the soles of his feet, as if angry wasps, drunk on overripe fruit, swarmed beneath the floorboards. The shit that was playing — Madonna? — was not his kind of music. The only movement it inspired in him was the desire to escape.

As they wove around bodies, making their way to the bar to order a drink, Donnie Ray told Rosa Linda to give the bartender Enon's description, so they could take care of business and move on. Being around a crowd of these people was like having his back exposed no matter which way he turned.

"A friend of ours was supposed to meet us here," she yelled to the bartender, and gave him a description.

"Take your pick," he said, gesturing to take in the bar. "Fits a lot of the guys in here." Donnie Ray gave her an "I told you so, look."

Rosa Linda started for the stairs, but Donnie Ray stopped her. "Let's check it out down here first," he said.

"How about you take one floor, and I take the other," she said.

He shook his head. "We're sticking together."

Upstairs, she pointed to the tall windows at one side of the room. "Yikes," she said, her body jerking. "Lightning. I guess I'm a little jumpy."

*   *   *

They'd had no luck at Free Will and were on their second drive through the historical district. Rosa Linda lifted her ponytail away from her moist neck and wrapped the swath of hair in a topknot secured with a pencil pulled from her purse. Tonight, the Midwestern humidity seemed heavier, more suffocating. She glanced up at the sky, the heavens low with darkening clouds.

"I'm thinking he's traveled on," she said. She hadn't had the opportunity to call the police and put her plan into motion. She'd spotted one phone booth on the street and asked Donnie Ray to pull over so she could check in with Melva. "So she won't worry," she said. The grimy phone was out of order.

"Look, I came up with a plan," she said, when she got back in the car. She feared running into Enon before she could call the cops. Better to go back to Donnie Ray's apartment and use his phone.

She paused for so long, he said, "Yeah, so?" and eased back into the traffic.

"It might take things out of our hands. That would be a good thing, yes? It's how we can give the problem to the people who get paid to do these things."

"Can you just spit it out?"

In a rush of words, she explained about the anonymous call to the police that would set them on Enon's trail.

"Before you were all fired up about this guy, explaining why something had to be done about—" He turned to look at her, and an oncoming car honked. He swerved back into his lane.

She braked her feet on the floor of the car. She wanted him to concentrate on his driving, but she couldn't stop from defending herself. "I only wanted you to talk to him. I didn't mean you had to do anything to him."

In the distance, lightning lit up a halo in the clouds.

"That's your problem. You can't make up your fucking mind, Rosa Linda. Back and forth, and hope that other people guess what you want. Things go wrong, well, it's not your fault."

"That's not fair," she sputtered, her voice dropping with each word.

His jaw muscle worked, and his hands clenched the steering wheel. "Your plan," he said in measured words, "is stupid. A description they've got, but have they pulled anybody in? A few more details from you aren't going to help. Meantime, you want another girl to get raped?"

Thunder cracked. The storm blew closer.

"I don't want to argue with you—"

"And by the way," he said, "since when have the cops become your friends?"

She unwrapped a stick of Trident, slipped it into her mouth. In the distance the neon flashed at the Bottoms Up, bottle tipping, straightening. She snapped-popped her gum.

He exhaled. "Let's take a break," he said. "We can go back out later and try again."

The parking spaces in the front of the bar were full, so he drove around to the street off the alley, squeezed into an empty spot between a pickup and an old car with fins at the back that looked like something out of an old movie.

"I've got a key," he said, "we'll go in through the back way. I need to check on an order."

"Wow," she said, waving a hand at all the parked cars, "this place is jumping, too," and ran to catch up with Donnie Ray. "Hey," she said, now only feet behind him, "let's call a truce, forget about Enon for tonight. Let's have a good time."

When he didn't answer, she said, as they turned into the alley, "I bet you're a good dancer, aren't you?"

"No complaints yet," he said.

Her smile froze on her face. She reached for his upper arm. "Hold on," she said. "That smell."

His biceps tensed, hard and round beneath her hand. He squinted into the darkness and sniffed the air. "Somebody's burning trash. They're not supposed to, but . . . ."

She peered at the dark area farther down between the wooden fence and the tree where Donnie Ray had hidden before. A shadow shifted.

"What was that?" she hissed. "Over there." She gestured with her chin.

Donnie Ray started toward the spot she pointed out, and she joined him. "That branch?" he asked.

Wind, heavy with the moisture in the air, tunneled down the alley, causing the branches of the small tree to sway again. A clanking shriek followed by the scrape of metal on metal stopped her cold.

"It's only the swings," he said, "in the playground across the street. You're bound to have seen them."

She tried to laugh with him but couldn't. Something was wrong, she could feel it. An odor, so faint she could barely detect it, floated on the breeze. A chill tingled up her spine. Old Spice. Or was it her own paranoia she smelled?

She glanced over her shoulder. The shadow dashed from around the building, charged toward Donnie Ray.

"No!" she screamed. And as if her scream had called upon a response from above, the heavens split open. A torrent of rain burst free, pelting them with slanted sheets of water. Lightning flashed and thunder bellowed.

Donnie Ray turned toward the sound of her voice just as Enon swung with the board, so that the blow, rather than hitting him square in the back of the head, bounced off the side. Donnie Ray reeled, stumbled backward, crashed back into the fence. Stunned, he slid halfway down.

Rosa Linda searched for a weapon — something to knock out Enon. She'd changed her purse for a smaller one this evening, and there hadn't been room for the rearview mirror. Nothing. Nada. The wind scattered papers and dirt through the alley. Thunder cracked with deafening resoluteness as lightning, blindingly bright, dazzled in its proximity. One burst of light revealed Enon hulked over Donnie Ray, bending to pick up a rock, swinging it up.

The lightning had struck nearby, and the lights from businesses and streetlamps beyond went black, as did those glimmers twinkling through the fence from the houses beyond. The snapshot of Enon disappeared as quickly as it had come, but it had revealed Enon bringing the rock down. And the empty quart beer bottle near his foot.

Rosa Linda slid across the space between them, swooped up the bottle, and smashed it against the back of Enon's head. She expected him to fall; instead he turned and stared, his arms stretched above him, still holding the rock. His eyes flashed in the lightning, a white-hot neon of hatred.

"Bitch," Enon whispered hoarsely, "you ain't better'n me."

Donnie Ray, palms against the fence, pushed himself upright. At the same time he told her to move it, his voice calm and cold. He grabbed Enon's arm, and Enon lost his balance, grunted. The rock flew from his hand as he crashed to the ground.

Rosa Linda sucked in her breath, taking rain into her nose. She coughed. Donnie Ray stood over Enon. He kicked him in the face, and blood spurted from his nose. He kicked him in the ribs, once, twice.

She wanted to tell Donnie Ray to kill him. She would be rid of Enon forever but in the same moment imagined Donnie Ray behind bars, caged up and far from his beloved Holler.

"Stop," she shouted, "enough, basta. Basta."

Enon gasped in pain, and Donnie Ray lifted one foot over Enon's head.

She pushed Donnie Ray's shoulder. He jerked away, whipped toward her. The rain had slowed but steady streams, mixed with blood, ran off his head and down his face.

"Stop," she repeated. "Your mom and sister, they need you."

He turned away from Enon, glared at her. My God, she thought, was he really going to kill Enon? She didn't want this.

Yards away, the back door of Bottoms Up opened, and she and Donnie Ray froze.

"What the hell's going on?" Arlie's voice sounded muffled through the steady rain.

Arlie, in silhouette, turned to someone behind him, and muttered words swallowed by the dark and rain. Another head appeared. The second man hunched over, charged toward them, a baseball bat in his right hand, held straight out like a sword. His left arm hung useless at his side.

"Git," Leland screamed.

"It's me," Donnie Ray hissed, but instead of slowing, Leland lunged forward. He tripped and stumbled, grazing past Donnie Ray. Enon, now with one palm against the fence, had dragged himself up, while his other hand reached in his pocket. The switchblade locked into place with a click. Leland rammed the bat into Enon's shoulder.

Rosa Linda skittered to one side as Enon stumbled backward. Arms windmilling, he bellowed like a raging bull, and grabbed at a branch of the small tree. The branch snapped, and he fell backward onto the wet ground. His head hit something hard and thwacked with a cracking, hollow sound. He lay still.

It happened so quickly that for a moment, Donnie Ray, Rosa Linda, and Leland stared at one another through the driving rain. Donnie Ray bent down, close to Enon's face. "Hey," he said.

When Enon didn't respond, Donnie Ray ran his hand behind Enon's head. He lifted it from the large, jagged stone, and ran his hand around the back of Enon's skull. When he pulled his hand away, Donnie Ray lowered Enon's head, and stared at the blood and gore on his hand.

Lightning zig-zagged, and the surge of electricity tingled through Rosa Linda's body. Donnie Ray stood and lifted his eyes to the chaotic sky. He inhaled a deep ragged breath.

CHAPTER SIXTEEN

"He was g-gonna c-c-cut Donnie Ray," Leland stuttered.

Enon's arm, bent at the elbow and Cisco's knife clutched in his hand, seemed to be shaking a fist at them. The rain had slowed, soft drops splattering off Enon's eyes, open and staring. His dilated pupils had been straining to let in the light when he died. Pale gray barely ringed the pools of darkness. Rosa Linda leaned over, protecting his face from the rain. She studied his features for a glimpse of the sad smile that had, for a fleeting moment, tugged at her heart when she'd first met him at the Buckeye Diner. She peered into his eyes for a hint of the dreams he must have once had.

Now she saw only a death-mask scowl, full of anger and pain. She did not see her reflection in his empty eyes. And even if she had seen a glimmer of herself inside his darkness, she would have rejected it. Her will was strong.

From the corner of Rosa Linda's eye, something flitted. She turned her head quickly, but it was only a shadow of a swaying tree branch. She reached toward Enon's fisted hand.

"Leave it," Arlie said. He grabbed her shoulder, fingers digging into the delicate space beneath her clavicle.

She shrugged free and glanced up, one hand shielding her eyes from the rain. "The knife," she said, "is mine."

"*Your* knife?" Donnie Ray whispered in her ear as she stood.

"Borrowed," she said. "Enon took it from me, and I have to return it to the owner." A question flicked through Donnie Ray's eyes. What else had she neglected to tell him?

"Can it be traced to you?" Arlie said. Before she answered, he said, "OK, let's not take that chance." He glanced at Donnie Ray, who nodded in response.

Rosa Linda folded the blade into the handle, clutched it tightly to her chest, and stood with the others in a close circle around Enon, rain pounding their bowed heads.

Leland propped the bat on the ground like a walking stick, leaning his weight on it. "I seen the knife; he was about to cut—"

"It's done," Donnie Ray said. "He ain't comin back."

"The cops'll pin this on me. I know it," Leland said. "I'm still on probation for buying those stolen tools from Snowball." His voice grew louder with panic. "They'll stick me with some kind of manslaughter. I know it, you know it."

"Keep it down," Donnie Ray whispered hoarsely. "Stop your blubbering, and let me think."

"I can't go to prison. They'll kill me, or worse." Leland's lips continued moving, but there were no words, only muttering.

"Get it together," Donnie Ray said.

"OK, Donnie, OK." Leland nodded, but began shifting from one leg to the other as if transferring his anxiety.

"Leave him," Arlie said, and gestured toward Enon with his thumb. He looked toward Donnie Ray. "Ain't that what you figure?"

*   *   *

Once Arlie locked the door of the utility room behind them, they stayed clustered in the blackness, so near their wet bodies touched, and they recycled the air they breathed. Rosa Linda shuffled backward, the first to break away. She leaned against an inner wall. Water ran in rivulets down her head and arms, dripped off her clothing, and puddled around her shoes. She shivered.

"Oh my God," she whispered into the darkness. When she'd fantasized about killing Enon, it had almost been as if she were watching a film, and she'd felt removed. Intrigued but removed. Seeing him lifeless in the mud and feeling his lifeless hand when she'd taken the knife, had made reality hit. She felt pity for him, wondered if he'd been born evil or if life had made him that way. Nothing could be done about it now, she argued with herself. And, he was bad, he was.

Arlie shushed her. Turning to Donnie Ray, he said, "Leland's probably right. That one cop's always had a hard-on for Leland, can't stand the sight of him. Hell, I heard tell of two guys got in a fight, the one fell and cracked his head open — involuntary manslaughter, they says, and sentence the puncher to four years in the pen. Fact. And you know well as me Leland won't last in prison."

Donnie Ray nodded slowly.

"OK, then," Arlie said. "Now, most everybody left during the blackout, but there's bound to be a few stragglers so polluted they haven't noticed, or don't give a shit, that the lights are out. I'll check and close up. I got some storm lanterns over on this shelf somewheres. Leland, hey, you hear me?"

Arlie handed a lamp to Leland. Within moments, Arlie lit two kerosene lamps, and they all shielded their eyes against the sudden light. The flame hissed, casting shadows on the walls. As Arlie left, Leland collapsed into a chair, his face pale. "Thank you, Jesus," he whispered.

"Hey," Donnie Ray said, and with the tip of his boot tapped one of Leland's outstretched legs, streaking blood on Leland's gray work pants.

"I ain't never been in on a killing before," Leland said, his voice shaky. "Who the hell is that guy? Seems like leastways I oughta know his name."

"Don't ask so many questions," Donnie Ray said.

Rosa Linda bent over to squeeze out some of the rain from her hair and realized she still held Cisco's knife in her hand.

Arlie slipped back into the room, and Donnie Ray turned toward him, "All clear?"

"It's only us here now," Arlie said. He nodded toward Leland and questioned Donnie Ray with his eyes.

"Shock," Donnie Ray said. "He'll be OK."

"Let's get our stories straight," Arlie said. "The way I see it, if anybody wants to know, the four of us, we were all inside, and as far as what went down in the alley, we don't know diddly. I never seen the guy and don't know shit about shit. You two stopped by, and came back here so Donnie Ray could go over some inventory. Me and Leland was out front working, but I was running back and forth, shooting the breeze with you two, when zap, out goes the lights. What were we, me and you, doing, Leland?" Arlie looked pointedly at Leland.

"Working," Leland said. "Lights went out. Other than that, I don't know a damn thing except it was so dark I couldn't see my hand in front of my face."

In the distance sirens wailed and, for a brief moment, they all listened.

"Lightning musta struck, or an accident in the rain," Donnie Ray said. He turned to Rosa Linda. "You know if Shit for Brains out there has family in Mad River?"

She shrugged. "He mentioned a brother in Chicago he hadn't seen for years. But, really, I think that was a lie. A drifter, looking for who knows what."

"If it was trouble he was looking for," Arlie said, "by God, he came to the right place."

"Did it to his damn self," Leland muttered.

"Somebody'll find his body soon enough when the weather clears," Donnie Ray said. "Maybe before. People will start drifting out to see what the sirens are about any minute. There'll be evidence he was in a fight, but, hell, the guy's head's still on the rock that killed him. And his heels gouged into the mud when he slid backward. I smelled alcohol on him."

"And even if by some slim chance there was a witness," Arlie said, "there wasn't a witness. An outsider poking around down here where he's got no business? Oh, hell, no."

A fire engine's siren shrieked. Arlie cocked his head. "In the Holler, I'd say." He pointed to Donnie Ray's chest. "Your shirt's messed up. They's some T-shirts on the shelves, and a pair of work pants. Those shoes got to go, for sure. Under that shelf is a pair of boots that oughta fit." He snatched a trash bag from a box, handed it to Donnie Ray. "Put your dirty stuff in here. I'll toss them in the river on my way home."

"How about you?" he turned to Rosa Linda.

"I've got blood on my hands," she said. She held her hands in front of her, spreading her fingers.

Arlie grabbed a pile of towels from the metal shelves along one wall and threw one to Leland. "You clean up, too," he said. He held out an open bag to Rosa Linda. "The knife. No souvenirs."

She swung her hand behind her back.

"He's right," Donnie Ray said.

"I know." She willed her fingers to open, dropped the knife in the bag.

"Let the Mad River take it all," Arlie said.

"You know," Rosa Linda said, her words questioning, "it really was an accident. And Enon attacked first. If we explained it to the police . . . ." Her words drifted. The authorities could wash away the blood by pronouncing the death as an accident.

"I told you, I don't trust cops," Donnie Ray said. "There's no telling what they'll do or say."

"I had to defend my friend," Leland mumbled.

"The four of us know the truth," said Donnie Ray, "that's all that matters."

*   *   *

Donnie Ray took the interstate, wanting to get Rosa Linda out of the Holler and away from the scene as soon as possible. He needed to be alone. His hands shook, and he held onto the steering wheel like a drowning man to a lifesaver.

He hadn't been the one to give Enon the death blow, but he'd beaten him hard enough to feel the release a fight always gave him. He'd been wanting blood, and tonight he spilled some. But a fight was one thing, death another.

"Do you believe in spirits?" Rosa Linda asked.

"You mean like ghosts?"

He glanced at his Zippo and pack of Kools on the seat between them. "Light one for me, will you?" he said.

She clicked the lighter three times before getting a strike, and her hands trembled so much, he wasn't certain she'd be able to get the cigarette going. Finally, she sucked in, coughed, and held it out to him.

"Stick it between my lips," he said. He worked it to the left side of his mouth, away from her.

"Just wondering, you know, some people believe." She clasped and unclasped her hands. "On the Greyhound, Mr. Ledbetter, his name was. Shrunken up, leathery skin, looked like a little gnome. He gets on the bus in St. Louis, and he comes straight to the seat next to me, starts talking, talking. But nice."

"When do the spirits come in?"

"I can't remember how we got on the subject, maybe I was wondering if I'd ever see my dead grandparents again. He says he doesn't believe in ghosts. He looks me straight in the eye and gets so close I smell his breath. Yuck, it smells like death itself. 'When you're dead,' he says, 'you're dead.'"

"He's probably right," Donnie Ray said. "Hmm," she answered.

Outside Melva's, they sat in silence. Donnie Ray glanced at her door. He really needed to be in the Holler, and alone. First, he had to speak to her, clear up some matters.

She covered her face with her hands. "I'm sorry," she said, her voice wobbly and broken. "This is all my fault."

"Stop it," he said so harshly she turned to stare at him.

"It's true," she said, "I bring trouble wherever I go. My mom's right. Enon wasn't your problem — I pulled you in." She was sobbing now, her wet words spraying spit.

"To hell with your mom," he said. "Don't lose control. Listen to me, Rosa Linda. Everything's cool. Remember our story and stick to it. If the cops ever question you, and I don't see that, but if they do, do not let them sweet talk you into saying something you don't want to. Believe me, they'll try to play like your friend." He lifted her chin. "Look at me. And if the cops try to tell you that one of us ratted you out or told a different tale, don't believe them. It's a trick to break our bond. Stick to the story. Stick together."

"Like the Wild Bunch," she said, and nodded. She blew her nose on a tissue she pulled from her purse, then placed a hand over her heart. "I can keep a secret."

He inhaled the air like broken glass in his throat. "Don't come around the Holler anymore."

"But I'm not going to abandon you and—"

"Don't worry about us. Things will cool down. Enon was a nobody found in a nobody place. There's not going to be a drawn-out investigation. You need to get on with your life. Your dream is to be an actress. You think because you're young you have forever. But it can all end in a second."

"But I want to be with you." As she said the words, she thought of how she had planned on saying good-bye to him, how he'd help convince her that it was time to go.

"You're just a kid, dammit. This is good-bye. Move on. For once in your life, don't take the easy way. Don't let fate make your decisions for you. You know what you need to do. And it isn't staying here."

"I love you," she said, and the words swelled her chest. She had never said them to a man before. She waited. His jaw worked. "I know you love me, too," she said. The tears dropped and ran down her cheeks.

"You love me like a friend," Donnie Ray said. "You think it's more, but it isn't. There, you see?" He touched her face. "I see what you're thinking, you realize I'm speaking the truth. You're not ready to settle down."

Her emotions boiled inside like a cauldron. So many feelings, contradicting, pulling her one way and another.

* * *

The area around Donnie Ray's apartment building was blocked off with police cars and construction horses. The rain fell softer now but still steady enough to haze his view. Police radios squawked, and knots of people grumbled and whispered in awe.

Donnie Ray stuck his head out the window and called to a huddle of sweatshirt-hooded people, "What's going on?"

A woman twisted around and shielded her eyes from his headlights. As she walked toward him, he turned them off.

She bent to see into the car. "Donnie Ray, that you? You won't be getting home tonight, doll. That tree in front of your apartment? Lightning split it in two. Half of it crashed right down on a utility pole. They say there's live wires hanging, just a-waitin' to fry a body. I think a branch or two might've broke your window."

Something deep inside Donnie Ray shifted. He wanted to yell, scream at the night, but he only gripped the steering wheel tighter. "The old maple?" he said, still in control of voice, even though he knew which tree she meant.

"Uh-huh, a downright shame," the woman said. "That pretty old tree's been there since forever. Hey, you know that better than me, living right next to it and all."

The inside of his head swarmed with the sounds around him, and he pulled back inside the car.

"They won't let you through," the woman said, as she made her way backward toward the group.

"Go on now," one of the cops yelled, "there's nothing to see here. It's a dangerous area. Go on home." He shooed at the people with his hand, and they hesitantly drifted away.

Donnie Ray reversed until he found curbside parking. He felt strange, as if he were pulling away from his body. The fight had released the tension that had been building, but now there was a hollowness in his chest. His head was spinning. He'd never been so dizzy.

Among the milling gawkers, a hot-pink umbrella appeared from a side street. Held at a tilt, it revealed the blonde curls beneath. He shifted the car into drive, but the dizziness overtook him, and he feared he would black out. Nausea waved in his stomach. He shut off the ignition, lay his head back against the seat, and closed his eyes.

The settling engine pinged, and he tried to focus on that sound rather than the bile pushing to enter his throat. The hot, acrid smell of burning filled his car, and he rolled up the window. Too late, the stink from the outside had settled inside his car. He couldn't swallow hard or fast enough to keep the bile from surging into his mouth.

He pushed open the door, vomited into the gutter, heaving until there was nothing left for him to give. Water diluted the mess, carried it away with the adrenalin of the fight. It was over. The intruder was dead. The innocent had been protected.

Now only the grief remained. Laid bare and raw like nerves from flayed skin.

He dropped to his knees, arms limp at his sides and head bowed. The rain fell softly on him. "Shayne," he whispered. Tears burned behind his eyelids, but they could not fall. The years had trained him too well.

He didn't know how long he'd stayed, kneeling, when he heard her tender voice. "Oh, babe," Tara said, "let me help you."

He turned his head, wiped the sour drivel from the corners of his mouth on his shoulder. He stared at the hand she offered. She bent her knees and linked one arm in his. "Let's get you in the car before you catch your death," she said.

He must have let her help him up because he was suddenly standing, and she had an arm around his waist, directing him. "I'll drive," she said, and he realized he was in the passenger side of his car.

"I want to be alone," he said. His lips were moving, but the words seemed to come from as far away as yesterday. "Lightning struck by your apartment," she said. "There'd a been a heck of a fire if that rain wasn't so heavy. But don't worry none, you're coming home with me." She reached across the seat and squeezed his hand. He wondered why she would paint her nails brown.

CHAPTER SEVENTEEN

"It's a beautiful drive," Melva said, still trying to convince Rosa Linda to join her and Edward on their day trip. "All that rain last night left everything looking spanking clean as a new start in life. It would do you good to breathe it in."

"Yes, I know," Rosa Linda said. "I opened my window to let in the sunshine."

"The orchard's way out in the country," Melva said. "Edward and me were thinking we might buy a little house out there if someone trustworthy took over here. Not right off, of course. I'd train her, ease her into the position."

"Not today," Rosa Linda said. Her mind wandered to the night before, in the Holler, and with Donnie Ray when he'd brought her home. Melva and Edward both watched her with anticipation, and she understood that she had to say more. "I've got things to do, laundry, other stuff. Oh," she added, as if tossing out an afterthought, "I would like to have a talk with you both when you get back."

Once Edward's Lincoln drove out of the parking lot, Rosa Linda returned to her bedroom. She'd hardly slept the night before. Sheets of rain and gusts of wind outside her window made her feel under attack. When she did drift off, she would soon hear Enon call, "Just Ophelia" and relive snapshot memories of Enon's dead and staring eyes. Enon that first day remarking on their distorted reflections in the diner window, Enon pressing his chest to hers whispering that their two hearts beat as one. Her eyes flew open; sweat soaked her pajamas. "I'm not like you," she whispered. When she closed her eyes again, the neon sign of the Free Will club flashed inside her brain.

What if the storm hadn't broken when it did, bringing Leland to the back door? And what if the clouds hadn't shifted so that the knife's presence hadn't been given away when the blade flinted in the moonlight? Would Donnie Ray be the one lying in the alley, a knife to his back? Enon had tried to rape her, had threatened to kill her. And she was certain he was the university rapist. A predator. Who would expect her to pity such a man?

The secret was hers to carry forever, like a boulder strapped to her back. But she shared it with Donnie Ray, and that made the weight endurable. She would move forward. She wasn't certain if she only loved Donnie Ray like a friend, as he'd said, but he was right about the timing being off.

She perched on the edge of the bed that had been hers, ran a hand over the silky duvet in her favorite colors of purple and lavender. As if Melva had sensed who would be coming to visit. The choice of colors was only a coincidence, of course. Melva had no way of knowing that Rosa Linda had once imagined her own early funeral in those very shades. As lifelessly peaceful as Sleeping Beauty, she rests in a white coffin lined in purple satin, upper body slightly elevated, face peeking above fragrant clouds of carnations, roses, and lilies, all in in shades of pink, lavender, and white. Prince's "Purple Rain" plays in the background while onlookers whisper about the tragedy of one so beautiful taken too soon.

All the fantasy needed was a prince to kiss her and awaken her. Donnie Ray wasn't interested in being her prince. He would tell her she didn't need a prince. And he would be correct, her brain told her. But she still felt an ache in her heart when she pictured his face, his hands. They would never forget one another. Their shared secret guaranteed that.

She lifted the ojo de venado over her head and dropped

it into a padded envelope, like the one in which Enon had returned it to her. She addressed it to Francisco Garza, and from memory, she wrote his mother's address. She flipped open a pad of paper and tapped on it with a ballpoint pen. She would make it simple.

Cisco,

I hope this finds you and yours doing fine. I'm okay, thanks to God. Here is the ojo de venado of your mother that you gave me. I'm also sending you this money order to pay back the money I borrowed. The knife I can't return because I lost it somewhere along the way. I'm sorry if I hurt you. But I always told you I was only passing through. Maybe sometimes my actions confused you, but also you did not listen. Maybe someday you'll find the one you're looking for — I'm not her.

Buena suerte,

R.L. del Río

p.s. I'm not living in the city on the postmark, only passing through. The pure truth.

She folded the note and slid it into the envelope. "Adios," she whispered, and pictured a camera on her, the close-up. She would run to the shopping center, buy the money order and drop the envelope in the mail. But first, she grabbed a fistful of change. She had to make a call before Loretta arrived for her shift.

* * *

When Melva returned, Rosa Linda helped the Kopps carry in the bushel basket of apples.

The small gesture pleased Melva so much Rosa Linda felt her own cheeks grow warm from embarrassment.

"Think we got enough for all the pies my girls are going to whip up?" Edward asked, and winked at Rosa Linda.

When Rosa Linda told them that she'd waited to have lunch with them, Melva nodded. "You want to talk. I remember," Melva said, and smiled, proud of her memory.

Rosa Linda, rather than ordering off the grill, asked for the special, Polish sausage and potatoes fried with peppers and onions. "Better be careful," Melva said, with a chuckle, "you're turning into one of us."

"That wouldn't be such a bad thing," Rosa Linda said. She thanked Loretta when she set the plate down in front of her, even smiled, but Loretta only eyed her suspiciously from the corner of her eye.

The local news came on the TV, and Jaybird told Loretta he wished he could hear, the way he always did. Rosa Linda had once asked Loretta why she didn't turn up the volume beforehand, in anticipation of his request. Both Loretta and Jaybird had given her a look that said, "Why don't you mind your own business?"

"They talking about that college rapist?" Loretta asked Jaybird.

"What about it?" Melva said. She speared a bite of sausage and a diced potato and waited.

"Nope, some dead guy," Jaybird said. "Down to the Holler."

"The sausage is local. You like it?" Melva said to Rosa Linda, raising her voice to talk over the reporter.

Because Rosa Linda knew how much Melva hated it when anyone spoke while chewing, she stuffed a huge chunk of sausage in her mouth. She tapped her cheek to show she couldn't speak yet and turned her eyes to the TV.

The story was brief: A white male, age forty, had been found expired in an alleyway behind the Bottoms Up Bar in east Mad River. Although the victim had been identified by his driver's license and car registration, his name would be withheld pending notification of family. Authorities did reveal that his auto, located nearby by police, was registered in Florida but carried plates stolen from Ohio. Bruising on the body and knuckles, the police said, suggested he had been in a recent altercation. Foul play was suspected, and an autopsy would determine the cause of death. Potential witnesses or anyone who knew the deceased were asked to call Mad River police.

"Doesn't sound like he had any business down there anyways," Jaybird said. "Anybody could've warned him not to go poking around."

"Maybe visiting family or friends, you don't know," Loretta said. The report went on to talk about last night's storm, the damage that had been caused in the area, and Jaybird's eyes shifted from the TV to Melva.

"When I woke up this morning," Jaybird said, with a chuckle, "I was worried that storm might've shut down Melva's."

"Nope," Melva said, "we caught it but not as bad as some areas."

"Good thing," Jaybird said. He rotated the stool to face the bar again. "That special's making my mouth water, Loretta. I believe I'll sign up for one."

"What in the Sam Hill are you thinking about?" Melva said to Rosa Linda. "You're a thousand miles away."

"Sorry," Rosa Linda said. She'd been holding her forkful of sausage midway between the plate and her mouth, and now she dropped it back on the plate. "I was thinking about some things I need to do."

"I hope pie-baking's part of those plans," Melva said. "I'm only doing apple this time. I don't know what I was thinking buying so many. Regular-sized pies and little fried ones. And, you know, I might make a strudel."

"We'll see," Rosa Linda said. Donnie Ray had said he didn't want her in the Holler again. But then, she was free to do what she wanted.

Rosa Linda took a deep, slow breath. "So what I want to talk about . . . ." she began, and paused to find the right words.

Edward glanced from Rosa Linda's face to Melva, and saluted with his two fingers. "Good day, ladies," he said, and picked up his empty plate to take to the kitchen.

"You should stay, Edward," Rosa Linda said.

He glanced again at the two women. "Don't believe I will."

"So?" Melva said to Rosa Linda. "Don't just sit there like

a lump. Speak up." She turned to the bar. "Turn that damn TV back up for Jaybird. And you, Loretta, don't you have something to do in the kitchen?"

Rosa Linda spoke quickly. "I'm going into acting; it's what I want to do."

"Not that again." Melva waved a hand, whisking the dream away. "Do you realize how many young people think they're going to be movie stars or singers or whatever? Be practical."

"I don't have illusions," Rosa Linda said. "I know how difficult it is. And I know there's lots of people who try for years and never make it. But, me, I don't want to be like one of those stagnant ponds that do nothing but attract mosquitos. I'm a river, just like my name, running sometimes calm, sometimes wild."

Melva lit a cigarette. She blew smoke circles and watched them break. "You calling me a stagnant pond?"

"Of course not. You went for your dreams. You achieved them. That's what I want to do."

Earlier Rosa Linda had telephoned her Aunt Bea, and she, too, had tried to dissuade Rosa Linda from her dreams. "Look, Rosa Linda," Bea said, "you were a beautiful little girl. Even complete strangers would say so, but do you think that's all it takes? Only imagine all the beautiful women that were used up and thrown away by the movie industry. Your mami's been lucky to have my brother backing her."

"I don't want to be a movie star," Rosa Linda said. "I want to be an actress, a real one, an artist. In school, my teachers told me that I came alive on stage, that I have something spe—"

"Special?" Bea finished. "What do a bunch of schoolteachers know about the real world? If they knew mierda about anything, they'd be out there *doing* instead of teaching."

Rosa Linda was preparing to thank Bea for her time when Bea said, "Sure, come on up. You're a big girl now, we'll be roommates." Bea said that she was in the process of ending a relationship and needed a couple more weeks to get him out.

"Then you take a bus or train, whatever you can afford. But this setup will only be for two, three months, tops. That'll give you time to get your own place or find a roommate your own age."

Rosa Linda had assured her that was all the time she needed. "I'll be taking classes," she said now to Melva.

"You can do that right here in Mad River," Melva said. "Or drive over to Columbus." She shoved plates to one side then the other, her fingers searching around them. "Where's a goddamn ashtray when you need one?" she said, her voice trembling. She jammed the cigarette into her pile of fried potatoes, and the butt sizzled.

Loretta placed Jaybird's order before him, and then she walked over and reached for Melva's plate. "You want something else—" Loretta began, then glanced at Melva's face. "You OK?"

"Worry about my customers, will you?" Melva said.

Rosa Linda shifted in her chair. She thanked Melva for all she and Edward had done for her. "No one has offered so many opportunities to me. But if I put off my dream, it might slip away. I'll come back to visit you. I promise. You and Edward have almost treated me like a daughter."

Melva's eyes filled with tears. "Oh, horse poop," she said. "For all the good it's done."

Back in her room, Rosa Linda inhaled, expanded her chest wide, wider. She was free.

* * *

Someone was breathing on his face. Half-asleep, Donnie Ray tried to pull his memory together. Was he awakening from a night of blackout drinking? Was he going to find some strange face on the pillow next to him? Tongue kisses warm and wet on his mouth, up his nose.

He swiped at his face, jolted awake. Spike stood on the pillow next to him, wagging his tail and yipping. The fountain of fur standing up from the top of his head vibrated with every movement. Ready to play.

With one hand, Donnie Ray rubbed his eyes, with the other he tousled the spiked fur. "Hey, boy," Donnie Ray said. "That's quite a'do you've got."

"You bad boy," Tara said, in baby talk. She strode into the room on a plume of Charlie cologne and scooped up the resisting puppy. "You weren't supposed to wake Daddy up. Go on back to sleep, Donnie Ray."

Donnie Ray looked around the room, the cream-colored walls, the curtains with a print of tiny pink rosebuds that matched the bedcover.

"Oh," he said, and remembered how he had come to be here. Enon, the letting of blood. His grief for Shayne laid bare. Nowhere to hide. For a second, he wanted to apologize for his weakness the night before, but there were times when feigning ignorance was best. He had wanted to hurt Enon, hurt him bad. All the anger had built up, pushing him forward. He hadn't killed Enon, but if Rosa Linda hadn't been there, he might have.

A second later, he bolted upright. "What time is it?" He threw off the covers. "I got work today." He remembered the fight. Saturday? "Is this Sunday?" he said.

"Honey, this is Thursday. I never seen you so muddled up. I'll call Arlie, tell him you're taking the day off—"

"I've never missed a day's work in my life. And I don't intend to start now." He'd never understood people who didn't want to work. The physicality and distraction of his work had gotten him through more than one tough spot.

"You've got time for breakfast, Donnie Ray. I'll get it on the table. You shower and, before you say anything, I washed and dried your clothes, so you don't have to worry about going over to your apartment."

He had a flash of her watching in horror as blood swirled into the wash water but remembered the change of clothes. The details were coming back to him now. He felt as if he'd been heavily sedated and was trying to push through a wall of cotton balls.

"I don't believe I ever seen you wear just a T-shirt without a shirt over it," Tara said. "Not for work. And work pants instead of Chinos. Didn't you work yesterday?"

"Don't start with the questions." He'd spoken harsher than he'd intended, so he said a little softer, "I'll change at my apartment. I need to see what the damage is anyway." He didn't mention that there was another matter he needed to take care of at the apartment.

"But your window," she began.

His expression registered his irritation, and her voice softened. "Aw, it's that tree, that's what. You loved that thing, didn't you?"

She stared into the distance, as if searching her memory. "For there is hope of a tree, if it be cut down," she said in a sing-song recitation voice, "that it will sprout again, and that the tender branch thereof will not cease. Job 14:7." Her eyes regained their focus, and she looked at him. "I learned that in Bible School when I was a kid, and I always loved it."

"You would," he said.

"I believe in looking on the bright side, if that's what you mean," she said. "Just take a look outside. Last night, folks were ready to build an ark, but this morning, why the sun is shining and the birds are singing."

How odd that he hadn't been aware of the birdsong, but, yes, they were singing their hearts out. "You look nice," he said. "Got something special going on?"

"Oh this," she said, and brushed her denim skirt with one hand. She had on a ruffled blouse and wore tan pantyhose with her high-heeled wedge sandals. "I've got a meeting." Spike's body seemed to absorb her excitement. His long, fluffy tail went crazy again, and he reached to lick beneath her chin.

"About the playground," Tara said. The jade color of her blouse brought out the green in her eyes. They sparkled as she told him about how she'd finally gotten the city's attention. "At first, they talked down to me like I was just some dumb hillbilly they was going to get rid of. They found out Tara Fugate *is* a hillbilly — darn proud of it, too — but I ain't dumb."

"Not by a long shot," Donnie Ray said. "I'm proud of you,

Tara." The words felt like clothes that didn't fit him, but they were sincere. And the happy blush it brought to her cheeks lifted some of the weight off his heart.

The emotion in the room was too much for Spike. He leaped free of Tara's arms and back onto the bed. He ran in circles from the head of the bed to the foot.

"I got all kinds of hope for this place, Donnie Ray," she said. Donnie Ray's encouragement egged her on. "Why, once we get that playground fixed up, folks around here will see the Holler's got a future."

He thought that it was more likely that the Holler was trying to hold onto the past. Or maybe just those who thought like him. He could no more hold onto the past than he could hold water in the scoop of his hands. But now he looked at Tara waving her arms, eyes shining like a lighthouse beacon, and he thought, "Why not?"

She was talking so much, his thoughts were drifting to what he needed to do at work, but a phrase caught his attention. "What's this about a memorial bench?" he asked.

"It would have a small brass plaque on the backrest with Shayne's name and his dates. I was hoping I could announce it at Shayne's memorial," she said, "but I won't say until it's for sure. They're making promises right now. I want it all on paper. I'd hate to disappoint your family."

He couldn't speak past the tightening in his throat, so he petted the dog. "You have a good heart," he said, finally, and swung his legs over the side of the bed. "I'm late."

"You are coming to the memorial, aren't you, babe?" Tara said. "Dee gave me the invitation. I'm helping plan and make the food. And we'll have music. Well, I think we can get one of these little local groups to volunteer." She nipped at his back with her words, and Spike nipped at his heels with his tiny teeth.

"I'll let you know," he said, and kept walking.

"Did you pick out your Shayne story to share?"

He continued past her into the bathroom. "Later," he managed to say, and shut the door.

After a breakfast of toast and hot wheat cereal (to soothe

his stomach, Tara said), he wanted to get away before Tara could start her chatter again. He appreciated all she had done for him. She was all about helping others. But what, he wondered, would she expect in return?

"Kiss?" she said, when he opened the door to leave.

He brushed his lips against hers.

"I know this much, Donnie Ray," she said, her voice husky, "no one will ever love you like I do."

He couldn't stop the sigh from releasing. He'd heard that from more than one woman in his life. Once, only once, he'd been tempted to say it himself.

Inside, the Bottoms Up hummed and droned. More customers than usual had made their way to the bar. They met to share what they knew about the dead body. Discovered right behind the Bottoms Up, mind you. And an outside troublemaker, to boot. They marveled how wasn't it wild that an off-duty firefighter cut through the alley and tripped over the body? Looking for a fallen tree but found a corpse, don't that beat all?

Their conversations drifted from the corpse to worry over the storm, flooded basements, no insurance to cover what had been ruined. When their problems began to overwhelm, they fell back on the novelty of the dead man. A few had heard the stranger had too much to drink. He wandered into the darkness, blinded by the rain, slipped, split his fool head like a pumpkin. No, he was the university rapist who was lying in wait for a Holler girl. Ran into some Holler boys who knew how to deal with perverts. The last theory, with its heavier dose of dramatic and heroic possibilities, proved the most popular.

When the customers tried to pull Donnie Ray into the discussion, he followed his pattern: listening, not commenting until they asked for his take. "I can't add anything. Sounds like you have it figured out," he said.

The front door of Bottoms Up opened, and two men in suits stood silhouetted by the outside light. A hush fell over the room, and they stepped inside. A few customers nodded at the older man with the lined and weary face but made a point of not acknowledging the presence of his partner. With the lead detective Tom McBain doing most of the talking, the partners began their questioning with Arlie and Donnie Ray. They stood side by side behind one end of the bar.

"Arlie, Donnie Ray," McBain said, casually as if he were only stopping by for a friendly beer and conversation. "How you guys doing?"

"Working hard," Arlie said, "just like y'all, I reckon." A good businessman, Arlie kept relationships with the police cordial, placating the cops with respect but not so chummy that the patrons, staring into their drinks as if they were oblivious to the conversation, might become suspicious of his allegiance.

McBain was a cop, and no one in the Holler ever forgot it, but over the years it came to be said that he allowed everyone, both women and men, their dignity. And that was what they needed: to be seen, to have their humanity acknowledged.

Years ago, when Donnie Ray was twenty and was hauled into the station because he didn't jump fast enough or high enough when some rookie cop demanded to know what he was doing standing on the street corner, it had been McBain who had stopped him from getting a beating. When the rookie threw Donnie Ray, handcuffed, into the elevator at the station, he'd steeled himself for the impending rain of fists. McBain had walked into the elevator behind them and, after the first punch, he said, deadpan, "Donnie Ray's got an attitude, but he's OK." And, as easily as that, the rookie pulled back.

McBain asked Arlie what he knew about the dead man in the alley. "Nothing. I mean, we know about a dead guy, and the news says it looks like he hit his head on a rock?"

"You hear any commotion back there, say, like a fight?" McBain asked.

"That night?"

"Yeah, that night," the younger detective said, scowling.

"Nah, who could hear anything over that god-awful storm?" Arlie said.

McBain flipped an enlarged driver's license photo onto the bar. "Seen this guy before?"

"Nope," Arlie said, "can't say as I recall that face, Detective. And I got a good memory."

"Uh-huh," the younger detective said. "How about you?" he said, turning to Donnie Ray. "You work that night?"

"For a little while." Donnie Ray directed his response to McBain.

"How about you?" McBain tapped the photo.

Donnie Ray shook his head. "No," he said.

"When that lightning hit, we closed," Arlie said. "I sent everybody home. I mean, the lights were out, what's the point?"

The detectives interviewed some of the patrons, but those who admitted to being there that night said they'd left before Arlie chased the others out.

As they walked out the door, the younger detective said to McBain, loud enough to be heard by all, "Funny thing about the Holler, nobody ever sees or hears shit."

An old man at the bar held two thumbs up.

CHAPTER EIGHTEEN

Rosa Linda stood behind the chain-link fence surrounding the playground. Donnie Ray sat on a swing, his back to her, his gaze directed at the ground. With his feet on the hard earth, he pushed. Five inches forward, five inches back. The chains creaked with accumulated rust.

She had taken the early morning bus to the Holler. Over two weeks had passed since that night, and Donnie Ray had not answered his home phone, and never called back when she left messages at the Bottoms Up. Enon's fifteen minutes of fame had crumbled to dust, the media no longer interested in him or his death. If the police suspected him of being the university rapist, they did not communicate their suspicions to the public. When the media was still interested in Enon's death, the police simply said the investigation was ongoing. Tomorrow morning, Rosa Linda was leaving Mad River, and she was determined to say good-bye to Donnie Ray.

After a few moments, Donnie Ray turned and glanced over his shoulder, as if sensing her presence. She waved. Something flickered across his face before he could mask it with his usual stoicism. He was happy to see her, she was certain. He turned away. She trotted to the gate and walked toward him. He stopped rocking.

"Hey," he said, and lifted his eyes.

She sat on the swing next to him. He said nothing, returned his gaze to the ground. She searched for something to fill the void.

"When I was leaving Mad River the first time," she said, "way back when I accepted that ride with Enon? I looked down from the overpass, and right away my eyes found the Holler. This playground. It was so early in the morning, that ghostly light that comes before the sunrise. And on that swing where you're sitting, this little boy was swinging. Those first rays of sun burst over the land and caught the light in his red hair. Really high he was swinging. It was kind of weird. So early and him so little and all alone."

Donnie Ray turned to her. She couldn't read his eyes, but they seemed different: the skin around them less tight, the gaze less guarded.

"What's wrong?" she said.

"Nothing," he said.

"I saw on the news," she said finally, "how they're going to give this playground a facelift. Some woman, I don't remember her name, really fought for the changes. I liked her attitude."

"Tara Fugate," he said, "businesswoman, community organizer, and all-around good Samaritan." He paused, and added, "And a damn good friend."

"Of yours?"

He went back to rocking. The swing groaned. "Why are you down here?"

"I'm flying out for Chicago tomorrow. The Kopps bought me a plane ticket. They insisted. I'm not running into nothingness this time. I got plans. I'm taking your advice."

"I advised you to not return to the Holler," he said, but grinned.

"Going for my dream," she said, "like Frida and Patsy. Only for me, acting. I made a decision, didn't take the easy way and wait for things to fall into my lap. I'm going to be with my Aunt Bea until I get a job. Maybe I'll find a roommate with one of the other acting students. A serious one."

"Good for you, kid," he said. "Now's the time." He tightened his hands around the chains.

Rosa Linda spotted a green bike pedaling up the street, the rider's head bent into the wind. Her eyes widened with recognition as it zoomed past. "It's that kid Rafi," she said, "and isn't that bike—"

"Yeah," Donnie Ray said. He shut his eyes. "Shayne's bike." He opened his eyes. They were clear and his gaze met hers. "I gave it to Rafi like Shayne would've wanted. He's on his way to work at Willa's."

He stood. "Speaking of which, I'm supposed to meet my friend Boom Boom over there. My turn to buy breakfast."

Rosa Linda wanted to invite herself, but Donnie Ray was starting to walk away, taking his leave from her. She pulled *Buffalo Soldiers* out of her purse, handed it to him.

"Sorry," she said. "I took it. A memory of you, you know."

"Yeah, I know," he said, but didn't reach for the book.

"But it's better you have it to remember me," she said. "And maybe one day, you'll go out that way."

"Keep it. I belong in the Holler," he said. "I'm not like you. I know where I want to be, and I'm not going anywhere. Whatever change comes along, I'm sticking."

"Maybe just to visit?"

"Maybe," he said.

She opened her arms and stepped toward him. He hesitated before wrapping her in his arms. She wanted to whisper in his ear that she loved him. His body stiffened as if he sensed her next words, and he began to pull away. She held onto him, and said, "Let's keep in touch."

"Yeah, sure," he said, and released her.

"I know. Everybody says that, but I mean it. The Kopps want me to come back and visit. You know they say I'm like family. Well, I know not really, but it's nice to hear. And they gave me some money to get started. They wouldn't do that if they didn't care, right?"

He turned his head away from her, said nothing.

"I'll never forget you," she said, and her voice cracked.

"Sure," he said. "Me too."

"Wouldn't it be cool if someday we met right here on this spot at a designated day and time, like in the movie?" she said, and his blue eyes clouded. "Or maybe out West," she said, "my grandparents have this little house."

"My ghosts are here," he said. "Whatever's chasing us — me, you — it won't go away. Not if we're running, not if we stand still, so you choose your position and live with your choice."

She wrapped her arms around him and hugged tightly, but he kept his arms to his sides. She wasn't sure if she was trembling or if it was Donnie Ray. Maybe both of them. When they separated, she started to say good-bye. "Don't say anything," he said, "I see it in your eyes."

As she walked away, she felt a tugging at her back. She wanted to turn around and meet Donnie Ray's eyes. He wouldn't want that. A breeze whined through the gazebo, the air breaking into whispers. She imagined she heard her name on the wind. But the whispers broke up and scattered into the Holler.

* * *

Donnie Ray didn't watch Rosa Linda walk away. He wouldn't be able to look at her without holding his breath. He wished she hadn't come down to the Holler, yet he was glad she did.

After Enon's death, he'd felt so tired and hollow. He'd thrown up, a throat-burning bile, and with it anger, chunky and bitter, poured out of him. He hadn't meant for Enon to die. One man's death would not resurrect the other. He pushed his feet, moving the swing. "Shayne," he whispered, swaying forward. "Shayne," he whispered, swaying backward. Shayne was gone, but the pain would never leave. That, he understood. But would the anger seep back into the void, if he didn't consciously push back?

Tomorrow, the workers would arrive at the playground. All the old equipment would be hauled away. Tara said it was a good thing because the old wasn't safe.

"Higher, Donnie Ray, higher," little Shayne used to shout, pumping his feet until the swing almost flipped over at its highest reach. When he rode up into the wind, his hair flattened against his head, and when he flew backward, the wind blew his hair straight up like a red halo. The swings could never fly high enough for Shayne.

Donnie Ray loosened his grip on the swing chain.

The broken window had been replaced at his apartment, the downed electrical lines repaired, and the fallen portion of the maple hauled away to clear the street for traffic. No more fingered branches scratching at his screen. Sunlight that had once dappled his room through the branches' filter now nearly blinded him. Only the scent of charred wood reminded him of the spot where Shayne had carved his initials. But he would wait for the new shoot to sprout.

Shayne's memorial was today. Donnie Ray breathed in the early morning air. Of course he would go. How had he ever thought he would not? He'd always advised Shayne to stand and fight his tormentors. Now, he would face his own inner demons. And Shayne would love having all the attention, all the shared memories of the good times. Rafi told Dee that he'd tell a story about Shayne and The Hulk.

Thirty minutes later, Donnie Ray parked beneath the locust trees across the street from the Mad River along a line of apartments and houses. He opened the trunk for an old bedspread that Dee had picked up at the Goodwill near his apartment. Dee, afraid that his car might break down during a blizzard, was convinced that the blanket would save his life. She couldn't lose the only brother she had left.

Blanket rolled under his arm, he walked up the grassy knoll, picked his way down the steep embankment to the river. Rumor had it that the city would soon create a paved path for bikers and joggers — exercise and recreation instead of blue-collar people on bicycles getting to work. People like Rafi, riding The Hulk. But what the hell, no matter why it was built, Holler folk could still use it. He half-chuckled. Tara's *bright side* was starting to rub off on him.

Donnie Ray continued along the bank until he found the familiar cottonwood and spread his blanket beneath the canopy of branches. To the right, he could spot the curve in the river that he and Shayne used to follow to a large, flat rock where they would sit in silence and fish for hours. They didn't catch much, and always set free what they did.

As a little boy, Shayne would run down the embankment. Once, when he was maybe about five or six, he'd picked up speed, stumbled over a rock at the muddy bank, lost his balance and kerplunked into the river's shallow edge. A current swirled around him, pulling him in deeper. Donnie Ray dove in and pulled him back to shore. He wouldn't tell that story: happy ending, but maybe it had also foreshadowed Shayne's early death.

He would tell them about the day Shayne became determined to catch a large bass that had stolen his bait more than once before flitting away. Two hours in, Shayne finally hooked it. He held up the line, his trophy flopping at the end. He whooped and hollered. A moment later, the corners of his mouth turned down, and he released the bass back into the river, its scales shimmering beneath the shallow water before it dove into the deep. The fish had fought so hard, Shayne said, so it wasn't fair to not allow him to live. Shayne was big on second chances. "Second chances," Donnie Ray said aloud. "Why not?"

Donnie Ray had never come to this area with anyone other than Shayne. But maybe one day he would bring Tara here. And Spike. To keep Spike from falling into the river, Tara would want to put him on a leash. Spike hated leashes — he did, too — but he understood Tara meant well and wanted to hold on to those she loved.

He pushed himself up and made his way to the river's edge. A morning mist lifted off the river. He closed his eyes, the moist cloud tickling his face. In the distance the river murmured, sh-rush, sh-rush, and he felt the emptiness inside him filling with light. He crouched and cupped the water in his hand, and watched it leak through his fingers and reenter the Mad River. When he bowed his head, light burned behind his eyes, and one small tear rolled out.

ACKNOWLEDGEMENTS

I give thanks to Jerry Holt for his moral support and for cheering me on when I fought for my health while writing this book. I appreciate his insights and his faith in my writing. There have been many other fellow writers who have offered encouragement along the way, including those at the Indiana Writing Center and the Midwest Writers Workshop, and I thank them all. A special shoutout to Barbara Shoup and Jama Kehoe Bigger. I appreciate Mouthfeel Press for giving *On the Mad River* a home. And a big thanks to editors Toni Kirkpatrick and Traci Cumbay for their intelligent feedback, helping me to write a stronger story for these characters I love.

AUTHOR'S BIOGRAPHY

Lucrecia Guerrero's short stories have appeared in numerous literary journals and have been anthologized in Fantasmas, *Best of the West*, *Not Like the Rest of Us*, *Puro Chicanx Writers of the 21st Century*, and *Indomitable / Indomables*. *Chasing Shadows*, Chronicle Books, is a collection of linked short stories. Her first novel, *Tree of Sighs*, Bilingual Press/ASU, received a Christopher Isherwood Foundation Award and the Premio Aztlán Literary Award. She grew up bilingual and bicultural on the U.S./ Mexico border but now lives in the Midwest with her husband Jerry Holt. She enjoys facilitating writing workshops for all levels of writers.